USHANKA

USHANKA
by
Paul Anthony

Published by
Paul Anthony Associates
http://paul-anthony.org/

By the same author

~

In the 'Boyd' Crime Thrillers...

The Fragile Peace

Bushfire

The Legacy of the Ninth

Bell, Book, and Candle

Threat Level One

White Eagle

The Sultan and the Crucifix

Thimbles

The Journey

Ushanka

*

In the 'Davies King' Crime Thrillers...

The Conchenta Conundrum.

Moonlight Shadows

Behead the Serpent

Breakwater

Harbour Lights

~

By the same author

~

In the Thriller and Suspense Thrillers…

Nebulous

Septimus

Sapphire

Quest

*

In Autobiography, true crime, and nonfiction…

Authorship Demystified

Strike! Strike! Strike!

Scougal

*

In Poetry and Anthologies…

Sunset

Scribbles with Chocolate

Uncuffed

Coptales

Chiari Warriors

Walking With Heroes

*

In Children's book (with Meg Johnston) …

Monsters, Gnomes and Fairies (In My Garden)

~

To Margaret - Thank you, for never doubting me.
To Paul, Barrie and Vikki - You only get one chance at life.
Live it well, live it in peace, and live it with love for one
another.
To my special friends - Thank you, you are special.

~

With thanks to Margaret Scougal, Pauline Livingstone and
Patricia Henderson for editing and advising on my works over
many years.

~

... Paul Anthony

When the power of love
overcomes the love of power,
the world will know peace...

Jimi Hendrix...

AUTHOR'S NOTE

~

Welcome to Paul Anthony's world of writing.

This is a story about power.

Power is the ability to act in a particular way to the degree that you consciously and habitually achieve prominence over others. The capability to harness that power enables you to direct, control or influence the behaviour of people, or the course of events, because of the reputation you have attained, and the authority others grant you.

But this unique tale is about more than that. It's about how power is won and lost, its use and abuse at the individual and organisational level, and how power and peace sometimes cohabit but are often at odds with each other.

It's also about winning and losing the power struggle.

You can experience notions of power either as a manager in an organisation or as an individual who is a megalomaniac within that organisation. You can also witness the by-products of power by experiencing the effects that the powerful inflict upon you.

Power is everywhere and is often visibly represented by a car such as a gold-plated Rolls Royce, a private jet, a stately home set in twenty acres of land, or just by the physical presence of a determined figure. In almost every situation, there is a status symbol on display, and it is a status symbol that most people recognize.

In this story, the status symbol is a ushanka.

A ushanka is a traditional Russian fur hat. It has ear flaps that can be tied at the chin to protect the ears and neck from the cold. In the West, it is often known as a 'shapka' which, in the Russian language, means 'hat'. 'Ushanka' is derived from the Russian word 'ushi', meaning 'ears'.

The hat is historically made from sheepskin, rabbit, or muskrat fur. Hats with ear protection have been worn in

Russia for centuries. The modern ushanka became popular during the 1918-1920 Russian Civil War. (The Bolshevik Revolution).

During the conflict, Admiral Alexander Kolchak rose to prominence and is revered as the man who popularised the ushanka across the biggest land mass on the globe: Russia. Kolchak was an admiral in the Imperial Russian Navy, a fearsome military leader, and a polar explorer. As a political leader in Siberia, Kolchak established an anti-communist government and quickly became recognized as the 'Supreme Leader and Commander in Chief' of all Russian Land and Sea Forces. Kolchak's position in life equates to that of the current Russian president.

The anti-communist regime was known as the White movement. The admiral based his government in Omsk, in southwestern Siberia, and was applauded by western politicians. During the Bolshevik Revolution, Admiral Kolchak led the White Army. His opponents were communists in the Red Army led by Vladimir Lenin.

Kolchak refused to consider autonomy for ethnic minorities and refused to cooperate with non-Bolshevik leftists. He sought foreign support for his endeavours and was always encouraged by Western political powers.

Eventually, the White Army lost to the Red Army and Lenin took over as 'Supreme Leader and Commander in Chief'. Kolchak was condemned to death and shot by a firing squad in 1920.

Admiral Kolchak, however, was remembered for the ushanka. Its popularity grew throughout the Soviet Union which was created in December 1922 and collapsed in 1991. The headgear is now part of the uniform of those in both the Russian army and the police. Indeed, the popularity of the ushanka, and its history, signifies how the importance of the headgear has been present throughout the rise of the superpower we know as Russia.

President Leonid Brezhnev began wearing a reindeer-fawn hat and introduced the mink ushanka. Vladimir Putin often wears a ushanka and many Western politicians have been photographed wearing a ushanka in the company of Russian leaders.

In the centre of the hat lies a military insignia. Those made from artificial fur usually sell at an affordable price. However, those desiring headgear of superior quality often find the ushanka in an eminent fur shop where the price will be much higher. The condition of a ushanka, therefore, often conveys the status of the person wearing it. Many Russians wear one made from artificial fur. The more powerful and influential individual will choose an expensive top-quality ushanka made from real animal fur.

In Russia, a ushanka is a true status symbol.

Essentially, this is a tale about Andrey Petrov: a powerful man of some notoriety and consequence. It is the story of a Russian gentleman who wears a hat. It is his status symbol. He is the head man of the organisation that serves the Motherland. The Motherland is Russia and its various republics that stretch across the globe.

To British Intelligence, Andrey Petrov is USHANKA.

But to understand Andrey's power base, we need to begin with the years following the Bolshevik Revolution and place its importance in the fictional story which gradually, and deliberately, takes you into today's world.

... Paul Anthony...

~

1

~

Makhachkala.
The Republic of Dagestan.
Southwestern Russia.

Following the Bolshevik Revolution, the Muslim Ottoman armies from Persia, who had fought side by side with the Bolsheviks to defeat the White Army, duly occupied Dagestan. The Bolsheviks, however, did not support the occupation of their lands by their allies and an argument over sovereignty led to more fighting. The Ottoman armies were defeated, and the Bolsheviks were victorious. As a result, the Dagestan Republic was proclaimed in 1921. It swore allegiance to the Soviet Federation centred in Moscow. The victorious Bolsheviks ultimately became the Communist Party of the Soviet Union. From a strong power base, they targeted religions based on State interests, and while most organized religions were never outlawed, religious property was confiscated, believers were harassed, and all forms of religion were ridiculed while atheism was disseminated in schools.

The capital, Makhachkala, now enjoys a population of over 600,000 and lies on the western coast of the Caspian Sea at the southernmost tip of Russia. Located between the Caspian Sea and the Black Sea, the Persians referred to the region as 'the land of the mountains.' They originated from the countries we know as Iran and Turkey and had significantly populated the area over many years before the Bolsheviks assumed control. Due to both the Turkish and Persian origins of this neck of the woods, the prominent religion in Dagestan grew to become Sunni Muslim and an estimated 90% of the population are followers of Islam.

Dagestan continues to share land borders with Azerbaijan and Georgia to the south and southwest, Chechnya and Kalmykia to the west and north, and Stavropol Krai to the northwest.

It was in the centre of Makhachkala that Jamil Volkov stood amongst the crowd gathered to welcome Colonel Oleg Novikova. The colonel had travelled in a military convoy from his headquarters on the outskirts of Moscow to meet the civic leaders of the historic Muslim-Russian city.

Disliking the man intensely, Jamil Volkov noted how the obese colonel waddled towards a grandstand that had been constructed for the occasion. The colonel was significantly overweight, red-faced, and breathing heavily. He looked more like a drunken buffoon than a senior military figure. More importantly, Jamil hated the colonel and his cronies because they supported the aims of the Russian president in the war in Ukraine. He knew Colonel Novikova was there only because the president had instructed him to attend on behalf of the Kremlin. In Jamil's eyes, Colonel Novikova was nothing more than a presidential parasite.

The war in Ukraine had not been an immediate success for the Kremlin. Conscription was the new government policy, and it was becoming widespread throughout Russia and its republics. It was time for people like Jamil to stand up for their fellow Muslims.

'Why do they recruit untrained Muslims into a conscripted army?' argued Jamil. 'The main religion is Russian Orthodox Christianity. Islam is followed by about ten per cent of the entire Russian population. Muslims may have been part of life in Russia since the seventh century, but the war in Ukraine is a great opportunity to use us as cannon fodder and reduce our numbers. Historically, the State has never supported any religion and would happily consign us to the dustbin. The State is good at subterfuge, fooling people, and offering a chalice of wine when it is contaminated with poison. It's what the State is good at – fabricating a false story to achieve the true objective. Is filling the ranks of the military with Muslim soldiers the Kremlin's way of quietly removing Islam from Russia? Did someone suggest that the State should glorify the Muslim conscripts when the real reason is to use the war in Ukraine to whittle away at a religion they hate?'

In his mid-thirties, tall, lean, with a head of long dark hair, and a beard to match, the outspoken determined Jamil, adjusted his sunglasses and checked his wristwatch.

At the heart of the proceedings, there was much handshaking and introductions between the overweight Colonel Novikova and the civic leaders of the Republic of Dagestan. A military band played music as he awkwardly mounted the steps of the grandstand and neared the podium from where he would deliver a speech. Only he could hear the creak of the wooden floorboards as his heavy build shuffled along.

Row upon row of the grandstand's audience rose and applauded the colonel. His resplendent uniform, bathed in medals, and his wide-brimmed peaked cap, seemed to dominate proceedings. Colonel Novikova stood well over six feet in height and the width of his large body was a sight to behold, but not necessarily to admire.

A handful of people knew the event had been masterminded by the Kremlin. All participants had been vetted by the authorities but only those who were one hundred per cent behind the president were allowed in the grandstand. Others of lesser importance were confined to a special area of pavement that had been cordoned off with purple velvet rope embroidered with gold thread. This 'special access' zone was bordered with barriers that prevented access to the street and the grandstand area to anyone not in possession of a printed invitation. Those who had not been formally invited to the event were, in general terms, almost entirely members of the public. It was the way of Russian leaders to gather the sheep around them so that the lions could not be heard. They bathed in self-righteousness and enjoyed it in abundance.

A mile away from the grandstand, a detachment of soldiers formed up outside their barracks. They stood to attention under the command of a drum major. Once inspected, their drums began to beat, and the unit marched to the grandstand.

A day of pomp and ceremony was anticipated since the colonel was expected to deliver a personal message from the Russian president. It was reported by the state-controlled media that victory in Ukraine was assured because of the voluntary contribution from the people of Dagestan. It was also stated that Kyiv, the first capital of Russia when Moscow was merely a village, would no longer belong to Ukraine. It would be Russian once more. Yet some doubted the truth and wisdom of such media misinformation. The dissidents and nonconformists who criticised the aspirations of the president suggested he would adore the title 'Emperor Vladimir of Kyiv'. Such an assumption was made due to the many emperors named Vladimir who had ruled over 'Kiev' in ancient times. He was, after all, often described by the dissenters as a megalomaniac: a person with an obsessive desire for power. And in the Slavic language, Vladimir translated to mean 'of great power'.

The soldiers' march progressed. The drums beat. The music played. And the history of Russia, which formed so much of present-day Russian politics, lay either forgotten, unappreciated, or unrecognized by many.

Colonel Novikova fidgeted with his tie, waved to the masses, smiled at those in the grandstand, and shook hands with yet more dignitaries as he prepared to take the salute.

Plainclothes police officers penetrated the crowd of people on the pavement close to the grandstand. Some were dressed like students, others like ordinary residents.

A small number of protestors unfurled their banners to reveal their opposition to the war in Ukraine.

As the detachment of soldiers marched towards the grandstand, a section of the crowd in the area where the public was gathered began chanting, 'No more Muslim soldiers. No more Muslim soldiers. No more Muslim soldiers.'

Acting as spotters, the plainclothes police quickly pointed out those responsible for the disorder. Radio signals transmitted to the uniform police betrayed the presence of the leaders of the protest, their location, their description, and who should be removed.

A unit of highly trained public order officers entered the crowd. Their uniforms were visible when they began wrestling with the demonstrators and seizing their banners. Forcing their way into the throng, they pushed, kicked, punched, and separated elements of the pack so that the 'snatch' teams could quickly insert and then extract prisoners from the horde of protestors.

There was a scream when a long police baton crashed down hard on the skull of the leading protestor. Blood oozed from his head and spilt onto the footpath. Bodies began to roll, began to swerve away from the falling baton, and began to duck and dive for cover as the servants of the State played out their role.

Still, the band played. Still, the drums beat, and the soldiers marched on to the cheering from the grandstand and the crowd on the footpath in the 'special access' zone. The soldiers were oblivious to the demonstration taking place.

Another scream rent the air and two policemen dragged a woman towards a waiting police van as she shouted, 'Don't take my son! My Muslim son. You can't take my Muslim son. He is mine. Not yours. Allah be praised. Allah be with me. Allah! Allah!'

'They're from Moscow!' someone shouted. 'The police! They've been brought in from Moscow. They're not ours!'

'No more Muslim soldiers! No more Muslim soldiers.'

'Don't take our children!

A wooden stick hurtled through the air towards the grandstand, fell short, and was hurriedly kicked out of the way by a policeman who bared his teeth. He scanned the crowd for the perpetrator and then realised he was looking at a sea of unknown faces that would forever shield the mystery he sought to decipher.

The chanting continued as more locals grasped that their police had been usurped by visitors from Moscow.

Another police van arrived, disgorged its Moscovian troops, and overwhelmed a section of the crowd where the chanting was coming from.

There was a push and a shove, a bloodied nose, a bruised eye, and a tumble to the ground when a score of uniformed police engaged with a handful of demonstrators. Another banner was unfurled before it was hastily removed and stamped beneath a pair of police riot boots.

The crowd grew silent, but the military still marched in awesome splendour when the first ranks approached the grandstand and the Colonel moved behind the podium.

The soldiers goose-stepped down the highway with acute precision. Awesome in their presentation, the troops gave the impression they were made of unbendable iron when, with each step, they slammed their boots in loud unison. It was an impressive line of legs that pounded onto the tarmac in magnificent ingenuity.

Colonel Novikova snapped to attention and smartly returned a salute whilst beaming from ear to ear.

Cheering and thunderous applause erupted from the civic leadership.

Colonel Novikova ignored the demonstrators, heard only the pounding boots from the goose step, and relished the power that he had been bequeathed that day as he glanced fleetingly at the important sections of the grandstand audience. His eyes glossed over the rich, the powerful, and the influential of Dagestan society that knew their way in life and supported the aspirations of the Commander in Chief. Long gone was the ideological concept of communism as portrayed in the origins of Lenin and the Bolsheviks. Now Russian politics were determined by the all-powerful Commander in Chief: The President. It was he who decreed morning and night, dark and light, life and death. Communism was long gone, and Marxism was an irrelevant concept for university students to discuss and write about. Individual power was the overriding element that drove present-day Russian politics.

Another banner unfurled from a different part of the crowd. Police rushed to the scene and muscled into the throng wielding their batons and dragging protestors away. There was more blood, screaming, and the weakened cry from one survivor who bleated, 'No more Muslim soldiers.'

Suddenly, it was all over. The protest died. The banners were no more. The last dissenting voice had been silenced by the Moscovian bullyboys brought in to teach a lesson to the local moaners and groaners.

This was Dagestan: The Islamic heartland of Russia, the place where the opposition feared to tread, would not be heard, and could not even have their argument discussed.

Jamil watched the scenes play out before him, saw the brutal consequences of a supposedly unlawful assembly, and for the briefest moment hated his homeland with every sinew in his body.

Colonel Novikova burped from a vodka too many, sniggered, and then placed both hands on the podium and waited patiently. Eventually, the troops came to a halt, stood to attention before the colonel, and positioned themselves so that they formed a barrier between the colonel and those on the footpath. The grandstand grew silent. The colonel's fingers swept across the switch at the base of the microphone. He was ready to speak.

Jamil reached into his jacket, removed a mobile phone, slid his fingers across the screen, and pressed an icon.

Colonel Novikova raised his arm. It was a last-second indication that he was about to speak. Silence was required.

The grandstand exploded. The podium disappeared in a cloud of smoky grey. The colonel was blown into the air, his cap reaching for the sky, his body torn apart by Jamil's bomb.

Woodwork climbed towards the heavens, peaked, and then collapsed showering people below with splintered wood that dismembered limbs and delivered horror to the crowd. The blast from the explosion rocketed towards the soldiers, blew a score of troops onto their backs, and simultaneously destroyed row upon row of civic dignitaries.

Crumbling, as if it were caught in slow motion, the woodwork finally collapsed into the unknown depths of a hastily manufactured structure. Here and there, the bodies of the innocent followed, clambering to escape, locked in a frightening time warp of chilling death and destruction.

There was blood, screaming, and then there was death.

Jamil manipulated his fingers, found the second phone number, pressed the green telephone icon on the mobile's screen, and turned his back on the grandstand.

A second device exploded and brought horrendous carnage to the landscape. The second bomb was an incendiary device designed to bring fire to the occasion.

Beneath the grandstand, Jamil's bomb ripped itself apart and delivered a scorching accelerant to the untouched parts of the extensive woodwork. Within seconds, it was well alight. Flames absorbed the atmosphere, stretched for more oxygen, and dispensed untold butchery to humankind.

In the horrific seconds that followed, a banner proclaiming, 'No more Muslim soldiers' wafted across the burning grandstand, caught fire, and shrivelled into insignificance next to the colonel's peaked cap that rolled casually alongside the mounting death and destruction.

Panic ensued with people running for their lives.

They tried to escape, to dodge the flames and debris that dominated the grandstand area. Crying, screaming, and fearing for their lives, they tried desperately to flee the slaughter that had befallen them and claimed so many lives.

Nonchalantly, without a care in the world, Jamil Volkov pocketed his phone and strolled away. He did not panic, did not run like those around him, and did not look back to see the dead and dying in the slaughterhouse he had created. He merely chuckled and felt happy. Pausing at a litter bin, Jamil produced his mobile phone, unclipped the sim card, and dropped the mobile in the bin.

Opening the front passenger door of a waiting car, Jamil nodded to the driver.

The engine fired and the Lada drove away at a leisurely speed with the driver turning to Jamil to say, 'All is well. Time is on our side. Sit back and relax.'

'I am always relaxed when the enemy is destroyed, Yousef. Take me to my destination and drive carefully.'

Yousef smiled, changed up a gear, and replied, 'No problem.'

Half an hour later, Jamil got out of the car, removed a travel bag from the boot, and made for the check-in at Uytash airport.

As Yousef motored calmly away, Jamil turned to watch smoke billowing into the air from the attack on the grandstand. The smoke had curled into the sky to form a dark haze above Makhachkala. It was visible for miles. The Russian Muslim bomber devoured the scene, felt no shame, harboured no remorse, and boarded the flight to Dubai.

The master of terror Jamil Volkov was gone from the Republic of Dagestan within the hour.

Yousef yawned. His day had ended without excitement. All was well when he drove south from Makhachkala to his home close to the beach near Kolichi. The journey took thirty minutes and Yousef thought they had got clean away with the attack. Parking the Lada, Yousef took a deep breath and looked out across the Caspian Sea before examining the tattoo of an exotic dancer on his forearm. He wondered if she needed a twin on the other arm but then changed his mind when a dark blue Transit van approached.

The vehicle pulled up next to Yousef's Lada. Three masked men jumped from the van. One pulled the driver's door open. A second dragged Yousef out of the vehicle and onto the ground. A third rolled him over and hit him savagely in the kidneys with his fist.

Yousef squirmed in agony.

Casually, the driver of the van eased himself out of his seat, strolled towards the fray, and looked down at Yousef.

Tall, dark, and handsome, the driver of the Transit had nothing to hide, did not wear a mask, and confidently announced, 'We meet at last, Yousef Abdul Halim.'

Crying out in pain, Yousef was hauled to his feet by the kidnappers and presented to his captor.

'Not me,' squealed Yousef. 'I wasn't there. It was nothing to do with me.'

The man laughed and said, 'Do you know who I am?'

Yousef shook his head.

'I am Pavel Nikita of the State Police, and you, Yousef Abdul Halim, are now in my custody.'

'I've done nothing wrong,' snivelled Yousef. 'It wasn't me that did it. I was just driving.'

The men laughed at the cowardly admission of guilt from one whom they expected to be more stubborn.

Yousef squealed again when another blow to his kidneys was struck, and Pavel said, 'We know all about you, Yousef. You are the friend and confidante of Jamil Volkov: master terrorist, killer, now wanted for yet another bombing.'

'Never heard of him,' gurgled Yousef.

Chuckling, Pavel replied, 'Not so long ago, you were with Jamil in the Chechen war, Yousef. We are not stupid.'

Yousef struggled to get free, but a sack was placed over his head, and he felt himself rolling backwards on his heels.

Shouting, Yousef screamed, 'No! Not me!'

The gang lifted Yousef from the ground and carried him to the Transit van. The door was opened, and he was thrown into the rear with the words, 'Yes! Oh, yes you!' ringing in his ears.

Men climbed in. Van doors slammed.

The engine fired and Pavel declared, 'As I said, Yousef, welcome to my world. We have you on CCTV in Makhachkala waiting in your taxi for a piece of scum that we are looking for. In the next few weeks, Yousef, you will tell us everything you know about Jamil Volkov and his friends.'

Yousef wriggled, thrashed, and resisted to no avail.

'You will learn to love me, Yousef,' proposed Pavel. 'You will eventually answer every question I put to you because you will soon forget how to say no. You are mine, Yousef. Mine!'

'No! Never!' shrieked Yousef.

'Time to go!' declared Pavel. 'We're done here.'

Kidnapping complete, the Transit van drove off with its prisoner bound and gagged in the rear compartment and the entourage heading south towards the Republic of Azerbaijan.

Four hours later, Jamil Volkov's aeroplane touched down at Dubai International Airport in the United Arab Emirates. Unperturbed by the events of the day, Jamil removed his bag from an overhead locker and ambled to the arrivals lounge where he produced his travel documents to the passport control officer.

The officer studied Jamil's passport, compared the photograph with the man before him, scanned the document into a digital device on his desk, and allowed Jamil to enter the country.

With no suitcase to collect, the revolutionary from Makhachkala strolled through the Customs area into the welcoming sunshine. Donning his sunglasses, Jamil stroked his beard, and casually beckoned a taxi to his location.

Within seconds, a taxi pulled up and Jamil asked to be taken to Five Jumeirah Village: a hotel situated twenty miles away.

The driver nodded and asked, 'Card or Dirham?'

'Cash!' replied Jamil. 'I will pay you in Dirham.'

'Very well,' smiled the taxi driver who then indicated that his fare should take a seat in the rear of the taxi.

Moments later, the taxi headed for Five Jumeirah Village with Jamil relaxing in the luxurious vehicle and the driver studying his passenger in the interior mirror.

In his late forties, the taxi driver recognised his passenger. He knew there was something unique about the man now pocketing his sunglasses.

'This is the man,' thought the taxi driver. 'I recognise him from the photographs.'

A vehicle horn sounded. The taxi driver altered his line and headed for the five-star hotel situated near Dubai Sports City and the Trump International Golf Club.

'One thing is for sure,' thought the taxi driver. 'No suitcase. He's travelling light and neither a holidaymaker, a golfer, nor a sportsman. I've got the right man, I'm sure.' Reaching into the breast pocket of his shirt, the driver activated a tiny camera that was fixed inside his taxi driver badge. Then he continued, 'You are on holiday, my friend?'

Jamil replied, 'Yes! Yes! Of course. But I am tired from my travels. I will sleep now.'

'We will be there soon. I'll wake you.'

The taxi driver knew Jamil was pretending to sleep. His fare sought no conversation. They drove on.

Traffic was hectic but on arriving at the hotel the taxi driver leapt from the vehicle and opened the door for Jamil who nodded, paid him with a two hundred Dirham note, and finalised the encounter with the words, 'Keep the change.'

The taxi driver nodded his thanks, turned his chest slightly but unobtrusively to capture Jamil's full-face image in his spy camera, and then bid his fare a good holiday.

Jamil was gone from the taxi with the driver climbing back into the vehicle thinking, 'The standard of living in

Dubai is very high and the crime rate very low. Dubai has around 52,000 millionaires and billionaires living and working here. Is he pretending to be one of them? Why Dubai? He lacks the charisma of a wealthy man. That said, I know he is Jamil Volkov, and he is a killer of men. There's no doubt in my mind now that I have seen him face to face. He thinks I'm just a taxi driver. Well, I am amongst other things. If all I know about him is true, then you, Mr. Jamil Volkov, will be my ticket out of here. A new life awaits, and I intend to take it. And the best thing is, I have your fingerprints all over a brand new 200 Dirham banknote.'

The taxi driver fired the engine as Jamil disappeared into the hotel never to be seen again that day.

Within a month, Jamil Volkov stood at the stern of a ship and gazed upon the wake disappearing towards the horizon far away. Resting his hands on the wooden handrail, he reflected upon his life and what might lie ahead. He felt the velvet smoothness of his hands, stretched his nimble fingers into an invisible chasm that lurked deep within his mind, and decided that he was still capable of putting the next explosive device together.

The ship lurched to the starboard side as the ocean grew in anger and threatened the stability of the vessel.

Jamil's precious fingers curled needlessly around the handrail.

Chuckling, Jamil stepped away from his view of the churning wake and strolled along the deck to his cabin.

His mind was made up. Jamil Volkov was on the prowl again.

~

2
~

Three months later.
The Russian Embassy.
Kensington Palace Gardens.
London, England.

A dark-coloured Mercedes saloon, bearing diplomatic number plates, swung into the entrance and stopped at a side door. A young man emerged from the building, opened the rear passenger door, bid good morning to the occupant, and then stood back as an older man wearing a full-length black overcoat, dark suit, and a black ushanka alighted from the vehicle and strode purposefully into the Russian embassy.

The car door slammed. The purr of the engine followed when the Mercedes drove off and parked in the staff car park.

Taking the steps two at a time, the man wearing the headgear was soon inside the heart of the building where he acknowledged others before taking the staircase to his office.

Upon entering his lair, the man removed his ushanka and overcoat, availed himself of a cup of tea that had been placed on his desk to coincide with his arrival, and then leafed through a pile of documents. Discarding the paperwork, he took his tea to the window and looked out across the city of London as he enjoyed the first liquid refreshment of the day.

A seven-foot-tall brick wall protects all four sides of the Russian embassy in London. Here and there, the barrier is further reinforced by a metal fence embedded in the masonry. Steel railings sprout from the wall and run around the entire length of the premises. In the heart of London, the protective boundary is the first physical defence against the enemy. The extensive curtilage of the embassy includes vehicular access to several car parks, a wooded garden area, and a grand entrance for those visiting the embassy on business. On arrival at the embassy, visitors undergo the scrutiny of officers from the Diplomatic Protection Unit of the Metropolitan police who act as sentinels to the site and patrol the immediate area. It is often the site of demonstrations and protest marches where people vent their anger at the Russian government. There is always a British police presence immediately outside the embassy, but never inside.

Legally, the embassy is the main office of Russia's diplomatic representatives to the United Kingdom. The organisation is headed by an ambassador.

The embassy building itself is made of thick concrete walls punctuated only by doors situated at the front, rear and side. Each main door has a two-inch thick metal casing covered by an attractive sheet of laminate that gives the impression of it being a wooden door. The windows are made of tinted glass coated with a substance that deflects attempts by the enemy to penetrate the embassy airspace to capture conversations, unguarded speech, and wireless signals from within. The enemy's target is the embassy's internet system, its wireless network, and the telephone system that lies therein. The careful placement of tinted windows, and specially fabricated metal grills, protect the embassy from cyberattack.

It was Andrey Petrov who peered from his office window as he watched the comings and goings of the Kensington people. It was he who studied the potential enemy going about their business on the streets of England's capital. Tall, good-looking, and aged in his fifties, Andrey sported dark short hair sitting above a rounded clean-shaven face that enjoyed brown eyes and smooth tanned skin. Toying with his tie, he flicked an imagined fleck of dust from his suit and sank another mouthful of Russian tea. The liquid was a mixture of warm black tea with orange and lemon juices infused with cloves and cinnamon that left a spicy taste on his tongue.

Seemingly miles away, Andrey watched the people before he was interrupted by someone coughing behind him. Andrey turned to see Ilya, his assistant, standing at the doorway.

'Illya!' remarked Andrey. 'Is it time?'

'*Da!*' replied Ilya. 'I have prepared an open line to our headquarters in Yasenevo. It is ready for your attendance, sir.'

'*Molodec,*' gestured Andrey.

'You're welcome,' voiced Ilya holding the door open for Andrey. 'Is my English improving, sir?'

'*Da, Ilya! Da!*'

'Good! I'm making slow progress,' responded Ilya.

Andrey followed Ilya to the heart of the embassy where they approached the safe room.

Entrance to the chamber was controlled by facial recognition, a digital code, and an encrypted swipe card. Each code was personalised to an individual and each card was bound to that digital code. It was impossible to enter using a code and swipe card that was not matched. Nor was it possible to subvert the facial recognition system.

The two men completed the protocol and entered.

More than just a safe place, the secret chamber was the most secure part of the Russian enclave in the United Kingdom. Protected by deflecting mirrors, ceramic tiles, a half-inch thick gold inlay lined with silicon, and a composite of various metals and substances, the structure of the safe room was unique in its design. Formed inside a cage, the safe room was big enough for a small group of operatives who could converse together with the knowledge that no one either within or without the embassy could hear them. Every bugging device known to man was denied access to the safe room. Its very being was beyond penetration. It was bulletproof, bombproof and soundproof. It was a secure place within a protected building inside a resilient stronghold. The safe room was impregnable from all forms of assault from the physical to the invisible cyber-attack. It was often said by Russia's enemies that this was the place where secrets were discussed, perhaps made, and where the important decisions concerning espionage were freely debated amongst the key players. It was also suggested that the only way to find out what had been said in the safe room was to employ a traitor who reported secret conversations to their paymasters. The safe room was built to protect the secrets spoken of within. Its only weakness was the people who were party to such conversations.

For British Intelligence, this was the beating heart of Russia: the embassy safe room.

Andrey Petrov was born in the town of Golokhvastovo a few miles south-west of Moscow. Like many in his line of work before him, he had attended the Yuri Andropov Red Banner Institute in Moscow where he had learnt the delicate yet complex skills of being a spy. Years later, he was posted to the Russian Embassy, ostensibly as a cultural attaché, but factually as Head of Station, London. In Russian parlance, he was the *'rezident'*.

A resident spy is a spy operating within a foreign country for extended periods. The base of their operations within a foreign country is known as a 'station.' Accordingly, Andrey, as the recognised 'resident', operated under official cover. Such 'residents' are often members of the embassy staff and might include, for example, a commercial, cultural, or military attaché. Due to this disclosure, and the principles relevant to the same, Andrey enjoyed diplomatic immunity from prosecution since his actual position in the embassy was that of cultural attaché. Andrey could neither be arrested nor charged if he was ever suspected of espionage. The UK government could only expel him by declaring him *persona non grata.*

Factually, there is very little written in legal terms concerning residents or heads of spy stations. Practically, in the world of espionage, intelligence services eventually work out who is the head spy from another country operating in the host country.

Andrey was of interest to British Intelligence. As Head Spy – Head of Station – and the Resident, Andrey Petrov had been assigned the codename USHANKA by the Security Service.

Once inside the safe room, Illya secured the door and gestured to his colleagues, Ivan and Luka, to take a seat opposite

Andrey. Both men were dressed in black suits, sported white shirts and ties, and were members of the SVR: The Foreign Intelligence Service of the Russian Federation. They were senior Russian spies accountable to the resident, Andrey, and they were tasked with intelligence gathering and espionage activities outside the Russian Federation. They were similar to Britain's MI6: The Secret Intelligence Service.

Andrey welcomed all present, withdrew a bottle of vodka from a desk drawer, and poured each man a slug. Raising his glass, he toasted, 'The Motherland!'

With the toast taken, Andrey asked Luka for his report.

'Ivan and I believe we have uncovered the whereabouts of a man wanted in Russia for multiple attacks on the State.'

'Interesting, Luka! Who are you talking about?'

'Jamil Volkov.'

Considering the name, Andrey replied, 'Jamil Volkov! He is the leader of a Muslim terrorist group if I am not mistaken. A man dedicated to Islam. So much so that if his actions involve the deaths of many then it is not a problem for him, provided he is striking a blow at the Motherland.'

'Collateral damage is always acceptable in the mind of a dedicated terrorist,' remarked Illya.

'It would seem so,' nodded Andrey. 'He doesn't care if he kills his people as long as he kills the target. Where is he?'

'Here in London,' voiced Luka. 'He's been watching this embassy. We have him on the CCTV system that monitors the street outside the entrance to our embassy.'

'Did you follow him?'

'No! We didn't have enough resources available to mount an operation against him that day?'

'I thought better of you than that. It would only take one man to house the subject surely?'

'Not for the likes of Jamil Volkov. He has been spotted at various events in Russia over the years but has the uncanny ability to disappear into thin air when he needs to. He is a professional of the utmost standing, and it grieves me to say that because we have been unable to catch him over the years.'

'Uncanny! Your English is good,' interrupted Ilya.

'Only because I live and breathe their way of life,' replied Luka. 'My mission is to blend into the English whenever possible.'

'Enough!' barked Andrey. 'This is not a classroom for language enthusiasts. Are you sure it is Jamil Volkov? Or is it just someone who looks like him? He has no striking identification marks that I am aware of.'

'Tall, lean, mean, with a beard which he never shaves off!' declared Ivan. 'It's only a question of time before he turns up again and we house him. Our team is on alert ready to move into action.'

'He has a description that would fit many of Arabic appearance,' remarked Ilya.

'Precisely!' agreed Andrey. 'I don't doubt your resolve, gentlemen, but convince me you have the right man before I contact Moscow. If it is who you say, then I will consider seeking authority to terminate from the Commander in Chief. I presume that is why you raised the matter for discussion.'

'Correct,' nodded Luka.

'Then assure me of the facts,' ordered Andrey. 'So far, all I hear is a tale that suggests a possibility, not a probability.'

Luka gestured in agreement replying, 'Our Federal Security Service, the FSB, is responsible for internal security and counterintelligence in Russia and the republics. Our people in Makhachkala, led by Pavel Nikita, have accessed flight details from Uytash airport on the day Colonel Novikova was killed.'

'Thank you, Luka,' replied Andrey. 'Did that report specifically and personally originate from Pavel Nikita?'

'Yes! It certainly did. He sends his kind regards and remembers you from the Red Banner Academy.'

'Spy school!' chuckled Andrey. 'A blur of vodka as I recall. Oh yes, a truly challenging but wonderful time.'

'Two bombs killed and injured over one hundred people that day in Makhachkala. Many were our soldiers. The rest were civic dignitaries from various parts of Dagestan.'

'Yes! I recall the incident,' admitted Andrey. 'How does this help prove it was Jamil Volkov?'

Luka manipulated a computer, swivelled the screen towards Andrey, and explained, 'This is a passport in the name of Jamil Volkov. It was issued in Kazan, in the Republic of Tatarstan, some years ago. It bears his photograph.'

Andrey looked and nodded in agreement saying, 'Interesting! Another Islamic connection. In the 16th century, all the mosques in Tatarstan were destroyed and it was forbidden to replace them, but in the 18th century, the Sunni Muslims were the dominant power and rebuilt the mosques. More than half the population of Tatarstan are now Muslim. If Jamil was schooled in Kazan, such knowledge would have been bestowed upon him by his religious teachers.'

'Arguably such learning has increased his hatred of the State,' suggested Luka. 'Dagestan is one of the most notorious places for terrorist attacks by Muslims on the State.'

'I know,' counselled Andrey. 'Dagestan is a hotbed of extremist activity. We need to crush resistance whenever we can and portray it to the population lest they forget who is in power. Fortunately, my friend Pavel is well-placed to serve us. He covers the Caucasus region between the Black Sea and the Caspian Sea. It mainly comprises Armenia, Azerbaijan, Georgia, and parts of Southern Russia that border with Iran.'

'Andrey,' remarked Luka. 'That's handy. It's good that you have deciphered Jamil's motive. That said, I do not know where Jamil went to school but compare these photographs.'

Andrey took a keen interest and leaned forward.

Luka pointed at the computer screen and continued, 'This is a still photograph of the subject taken at the check-in desk at Uytash airport. It is the same man that is in the CCTV footage taken outside our embassy. It is Jamil. The Uytash photograph was half an hour after the bomb attack. He took a flight to Dubai where he disappeared into the woodwork. A few weeks later he arrived in Paris before turning up in London. We believe he took either a train or a boat from France to reach England since we have no data indicating his arrival was by flight.'

Nodding, Andrey gestured for Luka to continue.

'Check these videos out.' Luka pointed to his computer screen and continued, 'These images have been hacked from the European aviation systems by Pavel. It's Jamil, that's for sure. He's wearing the same clothes in Paris as he was when he left Dagestan.'

Andrey nodded but challenged Luka with, 'You have no direct evidence that Jamil is responsible for the bombing.'

'Not yet! But he has a long history of such attacks as you know. No one else of his magnitude has been traced in Dagestan on or about the day when the colonel was killed.'

Andrey ran the video again adding, 'I recall a report from Pavel concerning a taxi driver by the name of Yousef Abdul Halim. He was the man who drove Jamil away from the bombing.'

'Yes,' replied Luka. 'I made enquiries with Pavel. Yousef is still in custody. They continue to extract information from him about Jamil and his contacts abroad. They've gone right back to the Chechen war and are gradually building up a picture of those who support Jamil. Your friend Pavel will not leave a stone unturned.'

'Then he has not changed,' proposed Andrey.

'Sir!' insisted Luka. 'The evidence may only be circumstantial, but Jamil is our best bet. The only evidence we have is when the local police conducted a search operation and recovered a mobile phone that bears Jamil's fingerprints. They are identical to the fingerprints he gave when he was arrested on a student protest march years ago. The fingerprints prove he was in the area at the time of the bombing, and this is confirmed by CCTV footage showing Yousef driving Jamil away in a taxi.'

'The evidence is improving, I agree,' replied Andrey. 'But we have nothing to show Jamil planting the bomb or detonating it. Did we recover the mobile's sim card?'

'Not present! Removed before dumping, I suggest,' interrupted Ivan. 'The whereabouts of the sim card are not known. Sorry, Luka. Continue, please.'

'There's no one else in the frame and he's on the 'Wanted for Interrogation' list for numerous atrocities from Chechnya to Georgia to Azerbaijan,' persisted Luka enthusiastically. 'As you said, he's the leader of an unnamed Muslim terrorist organisation. The faction is unnamed because we don't allow the media to report on terrorist groups. Volkov has supported every dissident anti-Moscow organisation known to our Federation. He's a rebellious Muslim who has been spouting about Muslim soldiers dying in the Ukraine war. He's the kind that the Western media would label a hero if they knew what he's been up to because he's on their side, not ours. Plus, the man is long thought to have been involved in the second Chechen war.'

'Yes! Yes! Yes!' replied Andrey. 'There's no need to get so emotional. I know you don't like Muslims, Luka, but he is a fellow Russian, and you should think about that.'

'I don't care what religion he is. I have no religion. What concerns me most is that he is a terrorist. I hate the ground on which he walks. He's an enemy of the State.'

'Absolutely,' nodded Andrey.

'He's here in London,' announced Luka. 'It's time to deal with the problem, and he's the problem.'

'You mean terminate him?' queried Andrey.

'We've never been as close. He seldom stays in one place long enough to lay down roots. He's here for a reason. Right now, we don't know what that reason is. I suspect it might be to raise support from the underground Muslim networks that exist in the UK. We can destroy him here in London.'

'What a message that would be,' remarked Andrey.

'Sir!' replied Luka. 'It would be a message to those who oppose us that there is no hiding place for enemies of the State.'

'True!' voiced Andrey 'But I must sanction this with the Commander in Chief. Such a killing may have ramifications here in the West and he needs to be aware of the situation.'

'The line is ready,' revealed Ilya. 'The Kremlin waits for you.'

Andrey seized the telephone but then paused and held it to his chest saying, 'Of course. Why do we rush?'

'What do you mean?' enquired Luka.

Thoughtfully, Andrey explained, 'What an opportunity to fool the British. This is an opportunity not to be missed.'

'An opportunity?' queried Ilya. 'I don't understand you.'

'Think about it, Ilya,' replied Andrey. 'We control the media at home. The most the West will know about Jamil Volkov is what they've picked up from the underground press and MI6. Dagestan is a long way from Moscow. Any intelligence sources there will be of questionable quality. It's an outpost in the sense of the Russian republics. Our terrorist Muslim is unknown to them. He's just a name they may have picked up but not much more than that.'

'And we have moles inside the underground press,' added Ivan. 'Watching, listening, reporting. So far, we hear nothing from them about the West expressing an interest in Jamil Volkov.'

'Good! We can feed material to the underground when we want to promote our agenda,' added Andrey.

'Precisely,' gestured Ivan. 'The British know we are behind recent assassinations of Russians who escaped our clutches and settled in England. We do not mourn the deaths of those who pilloried the Motherland. We have always denied our involvement in their deaths but have never been successful because the authorities here have always discovered the truth. But now, Andrey, we have an opportunity to paint Jamil our way. Forget his protest about Muslim soldiers fighting for us in Ukraine. We could present him as a thoroughbred Muslim terrorist with connections to Al Qaeda, ISIS, and the Taliban. With a bit of ingenuity, we can set the British up to think he was in London to mount a major attack on their way of life. I bet that's why he's here.'

'Your mind has joined me at last,' chuckled Andrey. 'Yes! It will need some planning, but I see the potential. The master stroke is that we assassinate Jamil on behalf of an incompetent British government.'

'After we have implicated him in the murder of the British Prime Minister, for example,' remarked Luka.

'Always a possibility,' smiled Andrey. 'I see the potential and it's never been done before as far as I am aware. It will be ground-breaking, my friends.'

'What an opportunity,' voiced Ilya.

'Indeed, and complicated. Consider this, Ilya,' suggested Andrey. 'The British are at war with us in Ukraine. They are also at war with Islamic terrorists on their soil. Jamil is a Muslim terrorist who kills Russian officers in the high command. They will love him and hate him in equal proportion. Don't you see, Ilya? One British voice will call for his termination because he is an Islamic terrorist. Another British voice will want to save him so that he can continue to murder our military forces. They will argue for days. We can mix the British a cocktail of problems. If nothing else, we will establish who makes the decisions and make fools of them.'

Ilya smiled and said, 'Game on!'

'*Da!*' chuckled Andrey before he engaged the Chief of the SVR in Yasenevo, Moscow, on the secure telephone. Repeating the information, he had learnt from Luka, and then outlining the opportunities discussed, Andrey concluded, 'Therefore, in compliance with the standing instructions, I request authority to terminate the subject.'

'Wait!' came the reply from Russia's capital.

Drumming his fingers on the desk, Andrey noted the demeanour of others in the safe room and then heard the words, 'Termination is authorised by the Commander in Chief. Proceed.'

'Public or private?' enquired Andrey. 'Bearing in mind the opportunities that are apparent?'

'Public!' replied Moscow. 'The man is an enemy and has been for many years. The opportunity to send a message to those of similar persuasion should not be lost. The other opportunities to use the subject as a pawn in a game over which he has no control are applauded by our Commander in Chief. He is watching you, Andrey. He wishes to express total support and admiration for your commitment to the State. Is that understood, my friend?'

'Perfectly,' responded Andrey as he closed the call and reached again for the vodka.

Ilya beat him to it, poured a slug each, and said, 'I have known you long enough to admire and respect you, Andrey. May I ask a question?'

'Of course, my friend.'

'I saw it in your eyes when we were talking earlier. Despite all that has been said, I believe you feel there is insufficient evidence against Jamil Volkov. Had it not been for the opportunities raised, you might not have sought authorisation to terminate?'

'It's not a question of insufficient evidence,' interjected Luka. 'The man is a terrorist and should be shot on sight.'

Ignoring Luka, Andrey engaged Ilya, 'I made my decision to request authority to terminate the subject based on Jamil's history of having no regard for the innocents around him. My decision relies on historical intelligence from the Chechen War to the bomb attack in Dagestan and not evidence. As we know, there is a difference between the two.'

'Be assured,' replied Luka. 'I shall personally terminate him.'

'No, you won't,' ordered Andrey. 'We shall reconvene here at the same time tomorrow and daily thereafter unless you have commitments that are logged in the diary.' Andrey gestured a leather-bound book on the table and continued, 'I have secured authority to terminate from on high and that is all we need for now. You see, Luka, Moscow just needs to know who the subject is. Our Commander in Chief has his faults.'

'Such as, sir?'

Andrey chuckled and replied, 'I relay to him that we have traced Jamil Volkov to London and that's good enough for him. For me, it is halfway. I want to know where Jamil Volkov lives. London is not enough for me.'

'Yet you asked for termination.'

'It would be expected of me in the circumstances. Now listen, my friends. Before we progress termination, you will convince me that you have housed him properly. I don't want to read about a dead body dumped in a back alley somewhere. I want the entire plan and I want it to be subtly carried out and made difficult for the investigators from the very start. Moscow has limited interest in how the execution might take place. On the other hand, I do. Is that understood?'

'Perfectly!' nodded Luka.

'I have spoken of opportunities to cause the British problems,' continued Andrey. 'With the right planning, we can use Jamil against the British before we terminate him. Jamil is what the British call the *Joker in the pack*. We shall use him wisely. The matter needs to be carefully considered. They have blamed us, correctly, for numerous killings relative to our people living in the UK: dissidents and those who escaped our clutches in the Motherland. Jamil may well give us the ability to turn the tables on the British. Is it not he that has been killing people in the UK?'

'You mean frame him as the Americans call it?' probed Illya. 'And make sure he gets the blame for something he didn't do?'

'Yes!' replied Andrey. 'We can make fools of the British if we try. We will manipulate the problem as we see fit and as it develops.'

'I like it,' remarked Ilya.

'Now then,' continued Andrey opening the leather-bound diary. 'May we move through our agenda? Ivan!'

'We think we may be close to identifying the whereabouts of another dissident who is already on the termination list approved by the Commander in Chief.' Ivan opened an envelope containing a black and white photograph. He laid it on the table and continued, 'This is the best photograph we have of the man. It was taken by our colleagues in Moscow when he was in his heyday. Do you remember him, Andrey?'

'Yuri Pavlova?' queried Andrey as he studied the photograph.

'That's the man,' smiled Ivan.

'Pavlova!' confirmed Andrey enthusiastically. 'At last. Well, I never. We've been looking for him for how long?'

'Five years,' replied Ivan. 'You will recall that Yuri Pavlova is a member of the Russian Orthodox Church. He criticised the politics of the Commander in Chief at every opportunity, verbally assaulted him on many occasions, and then tried to gather sufficient support in Moscow to try and oust the Commander in Chief from office.'

'Pavlova was lucky to get out of Moscow alive,' added Luka. 'He spoke publicly in Red Square about the various so-called needs of the people, blasphemed the Commander in Chief, and very quickly became too popular for the Kremlin.'

'Almost out of control,' mused Andrey. 'He would have been a leader of the White Army had he been alive during the Bolshevik Revolution. Tell me, gentlemen, where is he now?'

'A man of similar description with an interesting background has been referred to us as living with his wife in the Lake District.'

'The Lake District!' nodded Andrey. 'Oh yes! The north of England. How did you find him, Ivan?'

'We're not sure it is Pavlova yet, Andrey. But let me tell you the story that leads me to think it may be him.'

'Please do.'

'We still support the Communist Party of Great Britain. The organisation is no longer active in its broadest sense, but the ideology is still popular amongst some left-wing enthusiasts.'

'Fascinating!' replied Andrey. 'Do they know that Russia is no longer communist despite having an opposition left-wing political party that harbours communist beliefs? Russia is a dictatorship controlled by the President: The commander-in-chief, who gathers his oligarch friends around him. It's all about personal power. His party, United Russia, dominates both the legislative and executive arms of government. This gives him free rein to run the country. The cabinet fears him and I am at a loss to understand why some people in Britain still support an ideology that is no longer Russia.'

'Probably because they are still tied to the past and not inspired by their current government's political thinking,' suggested Ivan. 'Anyway, one of their number reported to us that a Russian was living in the area. Did we know who? Of course, we didn't. Stupid people some of these English. We told them to find out more. What seems Russian to them might be Estonian or Hungarian in reality. You know what English people are like. It's the only language they speak so anything they don't understand properly gets a label. They labelled the man Russian.'

'And is he?' probed Andrey.

'Turns out he moved to the area about four and a half years ago. That's about six months after he fell into the hands of British Intelligence. We worked out that might be the length of time they took to debrief him.'

Nodding, Andrey gestured for Ivan to continue.

'Our contact tells us that Yuri Pavlova and his wife regularly go to the local library and borrow books on Russian literature. They both fit the description we have.'

'I presume you are telling me so that I will authorise a team to confirm identity or otherwise.'

'That is correct, Andrey. We don't want to use our contact any further. He will continue to be of use to us for years to come if he remains unknown to the British authorities. I suggest there is enough suspicion to send a team north to confirm it is Pavlova or otherwise. This will allow us to shelve our English source and keep him for a rainy day.'

'I agree,' nodded Andrey. 'Once again, I insist that you are precise in your operations. Some recent photographs would be useful and perhaps a short surveillance exercise on the two subjects might lead to verification. Brief the team to try and identify them. Credit card use, library card use, anything like that.'

'They may be living under a new identity.'

'Most likely! But probably not under a new language or a new culture. Do what you can, Ivan. A team is authorised. Confirmation of identity only at this stage. Understood?'

'Thank you, Andrey. I'll see to it.'

'It will prove to be a yes or a no,' replied, Andrey. 'Good photographs will do. Proceed as authorised.' Andrey pushed the original photograph of Pavlova back towards Ivan and said, 'Update me as to your operational intentions tomorrow.'

'It's going to be a busy day,' remarked Luka.

'A verbal report of your visit to the submarine facilities at Faslane and Barrow is required now if you please, Ivan.'

'The Astute class submarine goes from strength to strength. We are monitoring events at both locations and are aware that the next type of submarine is designated the Dreadnought class. They will be named HMS Dreadnought, HMS Valiant, HMS Warspite, and HMS King George VI.'

'Good! An update on that monitoring is required tomorrow. What more have you to tell me, Ivan?'

Luka pushed away his empty glass, ostensibly listened to Ivan, and studied the resident: Andrey.

In his complex multi-dimensional mind, Luka stored the details of what had been said, how the resident had reacted, and how there had been no immediate advice or instruction on how Jamil Volkov might be executed. He also noted how Andrey had criticised the president by saying that he had faults. Life in the embassy was merely an extension of the Kremlin's global influence. It was a dormitory, a world in which Moscow's triumphant, undefeated, authority was encouraged and invigorated on behalf of the all-conquering, all-powerful Commander in Chief. There was no communist ideology in play. Such a concept died with the Soviet Union. Now it was all about keeping the top man in power, watching his wealth grow, and agreeing to his every instruction. Such was how things discussed in the safe room had changed over the years. But the killing! Would it be by shooting, knifing, a bomb, poison, or some other means? How would Jamil Volkov be used against the British? How was he to be terminated? Luka had expected discussion and instruction from Andrey, not just the authority to terminate.

The secret conversation between the four men continued. Each knew they were a key component of the undercover spying operations of the Russian Federation in the United Kingdom.

The safe room was safe, but the life of Jamil Volkov was in jeopardy. It was only a question of time before Jamil was traced and eliminated.

One thing bugged Luka as he listened to the others.

'Why was Jamil Volkov in London?'

~

3

A Country Mansion.
Oxfordshire.
Simultaneous, That day.

Five acres of parkland surrounded a detached Edwardian country mansion that lay twenty miles from the city of Oxford. The rural estate boasted a medium-sized pond filled with Japanese Koi carp and several water features that beautified the surroundings and aerated the water. A pride of stunning peacocks patrolled the extremities of the pond and a herd of deer foraged in the grassland. The distinctive building enjoyed the hallmarks of a stately home.

Indeed, a landscape photographer might label the scene an image of quintessential England. Others would assume the architecture of the building implied that the occupants would be rich, famous, extremely well-known, and of significant status. Yet the spacious surroundings denied any visible presence of a humdrum lifestyle. The discreet rural location provided solitude and privacy not experienced in central London. It was a private house, not open to the public, and off the beaten track. There were no gardeners present, no tradesmen carrying out maintenance work, just two saloon cars parked on the driveway at the front entrance.

Access to the estate was controlled from a security lodge at the side of the building. The touch of a button on a computerised system ensured an electronic gate opened and closed whenever it was necessary to facilitate the movement of guests in and out of the estate. Several cars were parked near the security lodge and the eagle-eyed visitor might acknowledge a CCTV system on the roof and at key points throughout the estate.

The building boasted two main entrances and a side entrance that led to a kitchen. Two suits manned each entrance and wore tell-tale radio earpieces that could be seen by the discerning eye.

Once inside the mansion, a sizeable vestibule welcomed visitors and spread across the lower levels of the house. A baroque staircase gradually curved upstairs and was adorned by thick carpet and an array of attractive oil paintings.

The tinkle of glasses and the murmur of conversation seeped from the library where the Head of the Secret Intelligence Service (MI6), Sir Julian Spencer, K.B.E - Knight Commander of the Most Excellent Order of the British Empire – was enjoying a small Spanish brandy. Educated at Marlborough College, Sir Julian stood six feet tall. The dark-haired gentleman wore a dark grey suit, pristine white shirt, and a dark blue-grey tie. A mahogany coffee table separated Sir Julian from Sir Phillip Nesbitt, K.B.E – also a Knight Commander of the Most Excellent Order of the British Empire – and the Director General of the Security Service (MI5). The table was garnished with a tray laden with crystal glasses and a decanter of brandy.

In the heart of Oxfordshire, the two most senior men in British Intelligence met in secrecy, away from prying eyes.

'More brandy?' enquired Sir Julian.

In his fifties, Phillip leaned into the plush leather sofa upon which he sat and gestured adversely, adding, 'Kind of you, Julian, but no thank you. I'd rather keep a clear mind. After all, I'm here at your invitation. A day in the country is fine but what is it that you want to discuss that cannot be spoken of in London? Why here and why now?'

'It's our favourite: Magnos brandy. A small top-up?'

'Perhaps an answer to my question.'

Julian sighed, returned the decanter to the tray, and sat down opposite Phillip with the words, 'Ushanka! I wondered if you shared my view that he is worthy of investment?'

'You mean turning?'

'Of course!'

'An investment in an operation to persuade Russia's head spy to jump ship and work for us is always worth discussing, Julian. The problem is Andrey Petrov is a very experienced operator with proven capability. He is akin to a Knight of the Realm wearing a suit of armour. Impregnable! His presence alone is enough to frighten people off. He has an unexplainable aura that surrounds and protects him from his enemies and bestows upon him the ability to wheedle his way into society with consummate ease. I'll tell you now, my friend. In my view, the chances of turning a man like Andrey Petrov against his Motherland is highly unlikely.'

'Do you think so?' posed Julian thoughtfully.

'You haven't dragged me into the quintessential backwaters of bucolic Oxfordshire to tell me you think we can turn Ushanka. You know that is fraught with both political and physical danger.'

'Which is more important, the political or the physical?'

'Stop playing games, Julian. What do you want?'

'Boyd!'

'Commander Boyd! What do you want him for?'

'To run a covert operation against Ushanka, front the approach, and stay on it for as long as it takes. The detective has an unbeaten track record of talking people down and winning them over. He's the best we've got, and I want him.'

'No deal!' chuckled Phillip. 'Commander Boyd is mine. Hands off! His Special Crime Unit is not for sale. The detachment is a relatively small elite band of high-quality operatives. And by the way, Julian, Boyd is a serving police officer. He is not a member of either your service or mine. It just so happens that the Special Crime Unit works primarily with my organisation and not yours. That said, his boss is the Commissioner of the Metropolitan Police. It's a rather independent and unique position that is out of the reach of our selves despite the presence of the best mix of officers from organisations throughout the country that are seconded to it.'

'Sir Henry Fielding, the Foreign Secretary, thinks otherwise. He suggests it is time he took direct control of the unit if it becomes necessary.'

'You mean if I don't agree to allow Boyd and his unit to work for M16 on this idea that Ushanka will collapse at the first shout?'

'That is one way of analysing the situation. Yes!' smiled Julian. 'Sir Henry is adamant. The Foreign Secretary is used to having his way. Boyd will be formally seconded to MI6.'

'I see,' mused Phillip. 'You don't know Boyd very well. He's not the kind of man who follows instructions that easily. Boyd doesn't take kindly to being messed around.'

'Things can change,' remarked Julian.

'I presume you have told our political masters something they want to hear. Let me guess, the Russians have mounted so many assassinations of their people on our soil that they are running out of dissidents and defectors to trace and eliminate. Yes, we've identified the killers now safely home in Russia, but we have a poor record of bringing such people to trial in this country. We know why. They travel here undercover, usually poison their target, or design and cause a so-called accident, and are back home in the Motherland before we've found the body of the person they've killed. Am I right in thinking that the Foreign Secretary and his cronies have rattled you to the extent that you feel you are at fault for not finding out that these spies were leaving Moscow to mount attacks in England?'

'I couldn't possibly answer that one.'

'That makes a change, Julian. You usually say I can neither confirm nor deny. They've got you, haven't they?'

'Well, perhaps but…'

'Don't perhaps me again, Julian. You are a man of some magnitude and a close friend of many years standing. Why on earth have you agreed to try and get Andrey Petrov on our side? Do you think we have coded him Ushanka because it matches his socks? Of course not. He's the head honcho: The head spy in the UK. He virtually lives in the safe room inside the embassy. Like the cage, he's impregnable. And you want me to take Boyd off the streets to challenge him. No! Never!'

'As it is, Phillip! You gave me the idea because you are the only intelligence officer in Europe to have met Andrey Petrov face-to-face. I recall he used diplomatic channels to request to see you about a matter concerning the exchange of spies. We had captured some of theirs following a failed espionage attempt in Scotland.'

'Oh yes! Thimbles! I remember giving Andrey the thimble that one of his spymasters had dropped on the shores of Loch Ness. He wasn't best pleased.'

'They wanted to exchange some of our officers who had been caught in Russia whilst engaged in intelligence gathering. A swop was agreed, and an exchange followed.'

'Yes! I remember it,' gestured Phillip.

'During those proceedings,' continued Julian. 'You and Andrey agreed that often people like us - Directors of intelligence organisations - hold such a position that opportunities arise whereby we can change the course of government policy by moderating our approach, failing to comply, or producing evidence of an unreliable situation. Phillip, our power base is such that we can influence the course of politics in this country.'

'And other countries,' added Phillip. 'I understand your comments. They are close to the truth. It's history that an MI5 officer helped bring peace to Northern Ireland by defying government orders. He revealed that he met IRA leaders in March 1993 despite talks being called off by the British government after IRA bombs killed two youngsters in England. What he said encouraged the IRA to declare a ceasefire and move towards what became the 1998 Good Friday Agreement. He told the IRA that the final solution was that Ireland would be as one. That was never the government's intention, and his remarks were not authorised.'

'Yes, I am aware and read it in the media recently,' admitted Julian. 'I'm rather pleased the officer was a free thinker rather than a government puppet.'

'I wonder how many lives he saved by stepping over the line?'

'Potentially thousands, I would say.'

'The point is,' argued Phillip. 'I don't subscribe to the fact that you think Ushanka will come over.'

'Yet, Andrey agreed that if you and he got together, you were a power to be reckoned with because either of you could send false messages to your political masters.'

'And thereby cause changes to political policy.'

'Precisely!'

'Idle chatter!' replied Phillip. 'Intelligence often changes and persuades a political rethink.'

'I agree,' remarked Julian. 'But I'm talking about situations whereby a false flag is raised, wrong intelligence is sent to Russia, and you and he control the balance of power rather than politicians.'

'We all have weaknesses,' suggested Phillip. 'Ours is to agree that we are all powerful but, we are not. We just think we are. That said, our political masters are always temporary, Julian. They get elected for a few years, make a mess of it, fall out with people, and lose an election. We remain unconcerned, still in post, and still doing the same old job on behalf of another body in either a suit or a dress. God help us! The way things are going in society suggests that we may well be governed one day by a non-binary penguin.'

'I rather like penguins,' remarked Julian.

'Oh no! Really! I've changed my mind. I think a very large brandy at this juncture may well assist me, Julian.'

Chuckling, Julian poured Phillip a liberal tot of brandy and continued to listen to the MI5 director.

'Prime Ministers are temporary weeds in the garden path, Julian. They get tugged out now and again and thrown away. We supervise the garden where the blooms flourish and the temporary weeds get snagged from the thorns and leave when their time is up.'

Julian chuckled before stating, 'Gardening! Phillip, I want Boyd to go to Ushanka with that very same message. I want to break the Russian stranglehold in England concerning the espionage stakes. I want Ushanka on our side.'

'And the Americans?'

'Are not involved,' replied Julian. 'I don't intend to discuss the operation with any of our allies. You should know that I have appointed Antonia Harston-Browne to mount a 24/7 surveillance operation on Ushanka. I want to know what his pulse is, what colour socks he wears, and what weaknesses he has that we can recognise and penetrate to our best advantage.'

'Antonia? I can't argue with that decision. That said, I'd like to point out that my service, MI5, has the responsibility to investigate the Russian embassy in London. Not yours. Your battleground is the rest of the world, not our homeland.'

'I know, but I envisage a joint task force comprising of both services. We have a mutual understanding and a joint desire to be successful. How say you on this, my friend?'

'Excellent!' nodded Phillip. 'I agree. I just wouldn't want us to get our roles and responsibilities mixed up. Antonia may well be the senior intelligence officer in the Special Crime Unit, but she is also one of my senior MI5 officers, and she is of the highest repute.'

'Are you both still in love with each other?'

'I can neither confirm nor deny that remark,' declared Phillip with a wry smile. 'Does Ushanka move much?'

'No! But when he does,' explained Julian, 'It is always to visit somewhere of interest like a school, or a university. He is a cultural attaché. Occasionally, you'll see him in the company of the ambassador. Ushanka uses his position to learn about our culture whilst always taking the opportunity to reveal the philosophy of his country to an audience. He promotes Russia whenever he can. Sometimes he promotes the best place in Russia to go on holiday. Other times he speaks of the architecture that dominates some of the older cities in his country.'

'It is a beautiful country, that's for sure.'

'I agree, except for Siberia,' chuckled Julian.

'Where is Ushanka now,' enquired the MI5 man.

Julian removed a device from his inside jacket pocket. The item resembled a mobile phone because of its size but when he tapped an icon a map of London appeared on the screen. He studied the data and replied, 'Ushanka has not left the embassy since his arrival there earlier today.'

'I see. Am I right in thinking your ultimate target is peace between East and West?'

'Yes,' replied Julian. 'One step at a time.'

'Why choose a senior police officer who will be known to Russian intelligence because of his public profile?'

'Accountability, Phillip! As you mentioned, Boyd is neither an M15 nor an M16 officer. If things go wrong, then the media will have a field day bashing the police whilst we remain untouched, unaware, and able to rebut any accusations. Do you see where I'm coming from?'

'Boyd would be made a scapegoat,' suggested Phillip.

'Yes! And we would be unblemished.'

'You mean the government would be unblemished.'

'Well, it ought to look that way, Phillip.'

'So now we have two scapegoats in play. Boyd and yourself. Have you not stopped to think that the Foreign Secretary is making you a scapegoat too?'

Julian stared at Phillip. It was as if the penny had dropped hitting the bottom of the pile with a clank.

'Your problem, Julian, is that you think you know Boyd and you don't,' declared Phillip. 'I do! We have a working relationship obviously, but he is a good friend. He'll have you worked out inside an hour. The man has a brain that is three moves ahead of everyone else. I suggest you leave well alone.'

'I disagree. Where is he now, Phillip?'

'I think it's team training day.'

'Team training day?' queried Julian.

'Yes! Boyd insists his team are reasonably fit and he's right. They are too often called to action and need to be on their toes if they are to respond effectively. But you should know this, Julian. I intend to remove Boyd from the battlefield for a couple of months.'

'Why?'

'He is tired, worn out and overworked. The ageing process is telling on him. His hair is greying, and his reflexes are slowing.'

'You'll be having his eyes and hearing tested next?'

'I think not,' chided Phillip. 'For the last few years, Boyd's battlefield has seen numerous operations against terrorists, spies, and the criminal megalomaniacs of society. Power-mad idiots of the highest order, I can assure you. But they are no match for Boyd. The man is a genius when it comes to detective work. The streets he polices are not where you will find community officers drinking tea and exchanging pleasantries with the locals. He is burning out and will one day make mistakes if I do not rest him. He is the best but then so am I because I can recognise the time when a man such as Boyd needs to be pulled out of the front line for a while.'

'What will you do with him?' enquired Julian.

'I'm going to send him to America for three months to study how the FBI investigate crime. I've already discussed it with my counterpart in Washington. The J. Edgar Hoover building will welcome Boyd with open arms. Did you know his reputation extends across the ocean?'

'I'm not surprised. He is a legend in some quarters and an unwanted headache in others.'

'The change will rest his mind from the pressure of life as the boss of our most elite unit. It will do him good.'

'I can offer Boyd a holiday too,' smiled Julian. 'But I'll remind you of my question, Phillip. Where is he now?'

'Epping Forest! Amongst other things, there's a firearms range there. They must keep their eye in.'

'Well,' considered the M16 Chief, 'It's been very quiet recently. Maybe they're just having a day off in the country. If I recall, there's a good Mexican restaurant in that neck of the woods. Anyway, that's by the by. Not only do I want to brief him, but I have a message for him. An old friend has asked to speak to him. I'm planning a holiday for them both.'

'The mind boggles. And the friend is… ?'

'Mine!' smiled Julian.

'I see,' replied Phillip picking up a telephone on the desk. 'I didn't know you had any other friends, Julian. A man in your position ought not to gather friends or even boast about them. What would others think of that?'

'That my life was similar to that of Ushanka?' suggested Julian with a cynical smile.

'You got me there,' chuckled the M15 boss. 'I'll have Boyd paged on your behalf. I'm sure he will decline to assist you in your endeavours.'

Julian nodded politely and sipped on his brandy wondering whereabouts in Epping Forest Boyd was situated.

~

4
~

A Post Office.
North London.
That day, simultaneously.

'**C**alling all Lima Deltas,' rippled across the airwaves as Commander William Miller Boyd drove the Special Crime Unit's armed response van through the traffic lights and slid into the offside lane. 'All Lima Deltas need to be aware that the digital map platform is down. Stand by for manual response replacement.'

'What the hell does that mean?' snapped the auburn-haired Detective Inspector Anthea Adams from the front passenger seat. 'Manual response replacement!'

Boyd chuckled, glanced at his second in command, and replied, 'The digital map on the wireless operator's screen in Scotland Yard has gone down. Probably a minor glitch. I'll guess it will be back up in no time at all.'

'So why the radio shout?' enquired Detective Sergeant Janice Burns: a feisty Scot and time-served team member of some repute. 'We're on our way to the training camp. Switch it off, Guvnor. It's our day off. We're non-operational today.'

'All Lima Deltas North London,' sprang from the wireless. 'Armed robbery in progress. Lima Deltas report positions please.'

'Typical incompetence,' snapped Anthea angrily. 'The Yard has no idea where the mobile armed response teams are. Switch off, Guvnor. It's a training day. Leave it to someone else. We had the tactical lectures this morning. Now it's time for running! Weights! Stretches! Judo! We're out of the zone, out of the equation, and I booked the Mexican for six o'clock. It's time for tacos and wine.'

'Tacos and beer,' corrected Janice.

'Where's the shout?' queried Boyd.

'Armed robbery in progress,' repeated across the airwaves followed by an address and the words, 'Hostages taken. All units in North London attend!'

'That's done it,' murmured Detective Sergeant Terry Anwhari from the rear of the van. 'The Yard has lost radio communication and the Guvnor is driving a van when he should be driving a desk. Are we anywhere near the location?'

'Take the shout,' replied Boyd as he slammed on the brakes, snatched a lower gear, and swung the van around in a tight circle narrowly missing an oncoming cyclist who mounted the footpath as he shouted an obscenity at Boyd.

'Lima Delta Zero Zero attending. E.T.A. four minutes,' radioed Anthea who then turned to Boyd and remarked, 'Watch what you're doing. I knew I should have driven. You're a bloody danger to the public when you're in one. But no! Oh no! Why did I let him drive?'

'Because you're the second driver on training day,' voiced Boyd as they took the road towards Enfield. 'Mount up! Draw weapons from the safe. Body armour. Let's do it!'

'Pray tell us the operational brief, Commander,' sarcastically requested Anthea. 'Tactical talks this morning didn't mention emergency shouts that have probably spoiled the Mexican meal I had planned for us all.'

With a smile on his face, Boyd replied, 'Briefing? Oh yeah! Arrive at scene! Contain the situation! Deal with it!'

'Is that it?'

'Yep!'

'It's that easy,' replied Anthea shaking her head. 'Gloch or Smith and Wesson?'

'Gloch!' replied Boyd powering towards Enfield. Lifting the transmitter, Boyd said, 'Lima Delta Zero Zero responding to armed robbery. Lay down a red blanket. Armed officers only at this location. Update from scene required. Over!'

'Another Gloch for me in the back,' yelled Ricky French from the rear. 'And one for Bannerman.'

'Bannerman!' ordered Anthea. 'Take a couple of stun grenades with you, just in case. You never know!'

'My pleasure,' murmured the voice of the giant that was Inspector Bannerman.

'I'll take the wee shotgun,' twisted Janice as Anthea began dishing out weapons from the safe situated between the front driver and passenger seats. 'Just in case. You never know, as Anthea says.'

As Boyd listened to the radio update whilst careering the vehicle through the traffic, Anthea remarked, 'Guvnor!'

'What?' queried Boyd.

'Try these! Pop the switch!'

'Huh!'

'You alright, Guvnor?'

'Yeah! Why?'

Anthea reached across the dashboard, flicked a switch, and declared, 'These! I knew I should have driven.'

Boyd glanced at the switch and then Anthea as he realised there was more to the vehicle than just a steering wheel, an accelerator, and a braking system.

The electronics on the new armed response vehicle burst into life. Ultra-bright headlights flashed a deep blue colour. Simultaneously, a wailing siren penetrated the streets of the capital.

'Oh yeah! Cool!' remarked Boyd. 'Which switch was it?'

Inside the post office on the outskirts of Enfield, the muzzle of the robber's pistol pressed hard against the hostage's temple when the gunman slammed the old man to the ground, glanced towards the counter, and shouted to the female assistant, 'Fill the bags with cash. Everything you've got. Everything! Or he gets it.'

'No! Not me!' squealed Isaac, the terrified old man. 'Why me? I'm collecting my pension. Why me? I didn't do anything.'

Ginger Gerry, the robber, thrust the muzzle into Isaac's mouth threatening, 'Shut it, you old codger! Head or mouth! I don't care where the bullet goes. Just shut it!'

Bernie, Ginger Gerry's accomplice, slung two kitbags over the Perspex counter screen ordering, 'Fill the bags or you'll both get it!'

The empty bags landed at the feet of Laura. The dark-haired postmistress looked down at her feet, glanced at the two bags, and then froze. Fear crept across her normally pink cheeks and changed her persona. A pale white veil replaced her usual façade. It was as if she was immobilised, captured inside a situation where her body clock had stopped.

'The money!' screeched Bernie. 'Now! Goddamn you!'

Inert, Laura tried to reply but her lips were locked. Her brain stalled with her foot firmly over the electronic floor alarm button that had generated the police response a minute ago. Only an instant nightmare of terror filled her mind.

'Why now? Why here? Why me?' she thought.

Part of the ceiling exploded when Ginger Gerry pulled one of the triggers of his double-barrelled shotgun and a fluorescent lighting tube crashed to the floor and exploded into a dozen fragments. A lump of plaster crashed to the surface causing a cloud of dust that congested the air.

The crook's finger curled around the other trigger, pulled, and set off another slug in flight.

More ceiling debris slammed into the vinyl flooring, mushroomed into the air, showered the two gunmen and the three customers who had been queuing at the counter, and then settled to the sound of approaching sirens.

Laura moved. Only an inch, but she took a step forward and bent to pick up one of the kitbags.

Bernie jumped onto the counter, realised he couldn't climb over the Perspex barrier and began hitting it with the butt of his shotgun whilst shouting, 'The money! Empty the safe! Empty the drawers! Quickly!' Then he turned towards the queue of customers now transfixed by the shock and horror of it all and screamed, 'All of them! I'll kill them all! The money! Now!'

The alarm system switched from the covert to the overt when the covert electronic alarm changed to a piercing shrill. Pandemonium erupted when the pitch reached the zenith of its operational capabilities and pierced everyone's eardrums.

Between them, the trio of customers dropped a shopping bag, a leather handbag, and a newspaper when the sound of the alarm hit a fever pitch and they could bear it no longer.

Hands clasped around ears and tried to deafen the sound, thwart the audible attack on the auricles, and caused the armed robbers to panic. Neither of them expected the alarm to explode into a cacophony of unbearable noise beyond human tolerance.

Outside, at the side window of the post office, a young policewoman panicked, dropped her radio, covered her ears with her hands, and then slid to her knees. Mustering a double dose of courage sprinkled with a few weeks of preliminary training, she grabbed the radio, pulled it closer to her, and shrieked, 'I'm shouting it again. Is anyone there? Shots fired! Shots fired! Three hostages. One female staff member. Two robbers with shotguns. Over! Is anyone getting this? What do I do? Over!'

In the control room at New Scotland Yard, the radio operator brushed a key on her computer keyboard, read the collar number of the officer concerned, turned to the duty Inspector, and said, 'Did you hear that voice on the radio? Total panic! She's lost it.'

'Who is it?'

'PC 6724X! Sonia Campbell! She was outside the post office when the covert alarm activated. Thank God she didn't go inside. She's new to the job, boss. First week outside and alone. Might even be the first crime scene she's ever attended.'

'Just what we don't need,' replied the Inspector. 'Respond! Acknowledge! Tell her we are on our way.'

The operator flicked a switch on her console and immediately replied, '6724xray all received. Armed response teams are attending. Hold your position or withdraw to a place of safety. The red blanket is down.'

A weak female voice feebly replied on the radio, 'Okay! What's a red blanket? And who is Lima Delta? I'll wait here and watch through the window if I can. If I move, they'll see me. Is that the right thing to do?'

Pausing for a moment, unsure, the radio operator eventually replied, 'Stay safe, honey. You're doing fine.'

'Which unit is nearest?' queried the duty Inspector now standing at the operator's shoulder.

'I don't know,' voiced the operator. 'Lima Delta Zero Zero was first to respond. The system is down. I can't see any mobiles on the screen. I don't know who is in the vehicles.'

'Lima Delta Zero Zero!' exclaimed the Inspector. 'Is that Boyd's mob? Interrogate the callsign system.'

Fingers danced across a keyboard before the operator replied, 'Yes! Special Crime Unit! They're shown as Training Day Epsom Forest but for some reason, they are attending.'

'Then let's not complain. Get that map back up on the screen pronto. I want the locations displayed.'

'Sorry! I'm a radio operator, not an IT expert.'

'Lima Delta Zero Zero at the scene,' radioed Boyd as they tore into the street and saw the post office ahead of them. 'Who is the ground commander?'

'None appointed!' came the reply.

'Mark me, Commander Boyd, as having ground control,' radioed Boyd.

'Noted!' replied the operator at the Yard.

'I think that's me too,' radioed Sonia, the policewoman.

'Who?' queried Boyd from the driver's seat.

'6724xray,' radioed Sonia. 'At scene. I'm back on my feet looking through the side window. Are you Lima Delta?'

Anthea nudged Boyd and pointed to the policewoman some distance away kneeling at the side of the post office.

'Got her,' nodded Boyd who swivelled his head to the rear of the van and said, 'Guys! We have one of ours locked down at the side of the building. She's uniform, unarmed, and exposed. Worst of all, I think she's fresh out of training school by the sound of what she's just said on the radio.'

There was a murmur of understanding from the rear of the van before Bannerman replied, 'They'll fall over her. Take me in close. I'll do a snatch and take her out.'

'Stand by,' replied Boyd. 'That's one taken care of, Bannerman. We have four customers and one postmistress to release too.'

'Does the postmistress have a husband or family living on the premises?' queried Bannerman. 'Or is that the full house and no more to look out for?'

'Terry?' remarked Boyd.

'I'm on it,' replied Terry Anwhari as he activated his mobile phone for an enquiry with the Post Office Investigation Branch.

'How are we going to play this?' asked Anthea.

'Not sure,' replied Boyd. 'I think we have a couple of amateurs in play, so we need to tread carefully.'

'Why do you say that?' queried Anthea. 'What makes you think they are amateurs, Guvnor?'

Boyd studied the post office before replying, 'No one plans robberies at banks or post offices anymore, Anthea. It's all cybercrime, internet scamming, fraud, or whatever. Today's criminals sit with a keyboard and steal money. These guys are not youngsters. Of course, I may be mistaken but I reckon we've got a couple of middle-aged robbers with a history of old-fashioned crime. Armed robbery, burglary, the old brigade stuff! Ask control if they have any idea of the age of these people?'

'On it,' replied Anthea hitting her mobile phone.

'Bannerman!' remarked Boyd.

'I'm listening.'

'Forget the snatch. We've no one at the rear and I don't want to use that petrified young policewoman. Slip out the back of the van and circumnavigate until you find the rear of the post office. Cover the escape route if you can.'

'Got that,' from Bannerman, as he stepped over Terry Anwhari, loosened the rear door, and began jogging away from both the armed response vehicle and the post office. Bending low, Bannerman hugged two stun grenades to his body and then changed direction towards the rear of the post office. He glanced at the building, swerved to the left, and kept himself out of line of sight as he made his approach.

'Ages not known,' remarked Anthea. 'Control agrees with your assessment and thinks they'll be well known.'

'And used to firearms,' replied Boyd. 'Shots fired already apparently and we're presuming no one is hurt.

'No family in the premises,' interjected Terry Anwhari. 'The post office tells me it's a single-unit occupation. One female postmistress with over fifteen years' experience. It's just one staff member with four customers to look out for. There is a part-time staff member who is on long-time sickness. The building also has a shop area displaying birthday cards, postcards, envelopes, and cabin flight luggage.'

'Thanks,' voiced Boyd. 'Two robbers and four customers inside plus one postmistress. One unarmed officer outside in a precarious position.'

'They're all precarious,' remarked Janice as she loaded her shotgun with slugs. The Scot then selected a Gloch pistol from the firearms safe, loaded it, and holstered the weapon at her side. Rearranging her body armour, she declared, 'I'm ready when you are, Guvnor.'

'Shields!' replied Boyd. 'Janice!'

'Aye! I'm with you!' replied the Scot.

'Guvnor!' remarked Anthea twisting a concerned look.

'What's up?' replied the Commander.

'Slow down! It's not a race. We've just arrived. There's no cordon in place. Easy does it. Is there an upper floor?'

'I got you, Anthea. You're right but we're all agreed. There are two amateurs in there. Now listen up!'

Anxious, Anthea stared into Boyd's eyeballs. She did not reply but shook her head in discontent for all to see.

'Terry! Anthea! Egress the van and fan left and right, ordered Boyd. 'Anthea snatch the policewoman if you can. Bannerman has the rear. Simultaneous assault on my command. Ricky, deploy drone coverage to cover any escape and maintain radio contact.'

'Got that,' from Ricky as he quickly opened a metal suitcase and removed a drone the size of a frying pan.

'In position,' replied Bannerman as his shoulder rested against the rear wall of the post office and he took a deep breath.

Boyd holstered his Gloch and said, 'Everyone ready?'

'No! Hold!' snapped Ricky. Ten seconds later, there was the soft buzz from the heart of a drone before Ricky chuckled, 'Ready for take-off, Guvnor. I'm launching as soon as we are out of the van. I'll have control of the skies.'

'In that case, stand by!' replied Boyd. There were several supportive replies before Boyd activated his throat microphone and radioed, 'Lima Delta Zero Zero at the scene. Instruct all units arriving at the scene to form an outer cordon. Stand-off one hundred yards. Lock down the perimeter.'

'Acknowledged,' from Control.

'We're making a direct frontal approach,' radioed Boyd. 'Trigger! Trigger! Trigger! Firearms in use. Armed officers engaging. Drone coverage is active. I have control. Stand by! Stand by! Go!'

Boyd and his team moved towards the post office.

Inside the post office, Ginger Gerry heard the siren, saw the van arrive with its headlights flashing, and then screamed, 'It's the police. What do we do?'

From the shop area of the post office, a third robber appeared wearing a mask and carrying a sawn-off shotgun. Dressed in denim jackets and jeans, a black roll-neck sweater and trainers, he slid the shotgun down his jeans trouser leg and said, 'Time to get out the back before we're surrounded. Come on. They've only just arrived. Ditch the guns and make a run for it. The car is fifty yards away. We can make it!'

'No way!' screamed Ginger Gerry. 'You clown.'

'We haven't got time to smash the Perspex barrier down. Leave it, guys. We'll find another blag soon enough. Leave this gaff alone. Move out!'

Bernie grabbed Isaac, dragged him to the open doorway, and shouted, 'Back off! Back off or he gets it!'

Ginger Gerry leapt into the centre of the post office sweeping his shotgun from left to right shouting, 'Get down on the ground. Everyone! Down on the ground!' Stepping backwards towards his accomplice, he said, 'Great idea, Bernie. Use them as a bartering chip. We can get out of here without getting locked up.'

'No one is locking me up,' snarled Bernie. 'I'm not going inside again. No way! I thought you said we'd be safe?'

'She must have set an alarm off. I don't know. Just get us out of here. Bobby! Where are you going?'

A figure dressed in denim crouched low, tightened the mask on the bridge of his nose and replied, 'Out of here. That's for sure. I'm gone.'

'One each,' growled Bernie. 'Get hold of a woman, Gerry! Use her as a shield.'

'Where's the car, Bobby?'

'To hell with the car,' snarled Bernie. 'We're taking the cop van. Come on!'

Outside, Boyd and his team closed the gap when they took shelter behind a ballistic shield and trained their firearms on the post office door.

The policewoman stood up and was immediately spotted by Bernie who yelled, 'You! Come here! Get down on the ground!'

Petrified, the policewoman held her hands up, froze for a moment, and then inched forward.'

'I got a cop!' screamed Bernie. 'Down, woman! Down! Crawl to me on your hands and knees!'

'No!' replied Sonia. 'No! No! I'm not coming to you!'

Bernie pointed his gun into the air and pulled the trigger. Scores of shotgun pellets flew above Sonia's head, and she let out a terrifying scream before slamming herself against the wall.

Ginger Gerry stood next to Bernie close to the doorway. A gap between them opened up.

'Bannerman!' radioed Boyd.

There was a blinding flash of light and a huge explosion when Bannerman pushed open the rear door of the post office and threw a stun grenade into the gap between Bernie and Gerry. The flash temporarily affected the cells in the retina of all present. Everyone was blinded for about five seconds and at the height of the detonation, the decibels reached were such that temporary deafness disturbed the fluid in the ear and caused a loss of balance to the robbers, Isaac, and all those present.

Pressure from the detonation blew the robbers off their feet.

Bannerman burst into the post office wearing ear defenders.

A figure in denim crouched low and slid behind Bannerman and into the street. Seconds later, Bobby dropped to his knees, rolled over, and felt the shock and distress of the stun grenade.

The stun grenade did not fragment. It wasn't constructed to do so, but the heat of the explosion ignited nearby inflammable objects and a pair of handbags, some birthday cards, and woollen articles for sale in the shop area suddenly caught fire. A mix of potassium nitrate inside the capsule had also escaped into the atmosphere and presented a health hazard to all present.

Flames consumed the oxygen and extended the fire.

Fresh air quickly filled Bobby's lungs when he egressed the building by the rear door. He scrambled to his feet, stood tall, shook his head, and regained his senses. Then he strolled naturally away from the post office towards a row of parked cars. Only a slight bulge in the man's outline offered a clue to the sawn-off shotgun in his possession.

'Strike!' ordered Boyd as he led the rush into the building. 'Strike! Take them out!'

The team landed on top of Ginger Gerry and used those precious five seconds the stun grenade tactic had provided to overpower the crooks. But when the handcuffs appeared, Bernie kicked out, broke loose, and reached for Ginger Gerry's shotgun.

Pointing the weapon at Boyd, Bernie lined the detective up as his finger curled around the firing mechanism.

Janice pulled the trigger of her Gloch and saw the bullet hit Bernie's torso. His body shattered with the impact, and he fell back seriously injured with blood spouting from his chest cavity like a waterfall on steroids.

'Don't move!' ordered Anthea, 'Both of you! Freeze!'

Ginger Gerry gave up, surrendered, and became lifeless as the handcuffs snapped around his wrists and he trembled slightly. His body was still in shock, still agonising from the effects of the stun grenade.

'Ricky!' radioed Boyd. 'We have control. One tango down. Both tangos are detained. Fire Service and ambulances are required at the scene. Pronto!'

'Understood!' replied Ricky who relayed to the Yard, 'Lima Delta Zero Zero reports Ground Commander has control. Fire Service and two ambulances are required.

Suggest senior command to the scene. Shots fired. We have control. Repeat, we have control.'

Janice found a fire extinguisher in the back of the shop and began dowsing the flames. She would have the fire out before the arrival of the Fire Service.

'Noted, you have control,' replied the wireless operator.

'Did you say pronto!' snapped Anthea. 'You make it sound like a Wild West show, Guvnor!'

Shocked, Boyd glanced at Anthea and replied, 'We took them out, Anthea. That's what we do. We took them out!'

'And everyone else too,' growled Anthea who gestured at the pensioner Isaac, the postmistress Laura, and the other customers saying. 'Look at them. What have you done? And that smell!'

Boyd's chin dropped when he realised that Bannerman's stun grenade had also affected the customers who were now ailing victims. Blood trickled from Isaac's ears. Laura, the postmistress, wobbled on her feet. She could not maintain her balance, and the other customers were in a state of total disarray. The stun grenade, detonated in such a confined space, had caused a degree of deafness as well as eyesight problems. Every victim except Laura was an old age pensioner. An invisible shadow of potassium nitrate was moving into a position whereby it could weaken the human body and attack the frailty of all present. The compound was not usually hazardous to human life but when mixed with an explosion and fire could potentially cause eye and skin irritation, destabilise breathing, and disrupt the supply of oxygen to the brain bringing on dizziness, headaches, and fatigue not normally expected in its presence.

Bannerman joined Boyd and Anthea. Satisfied they were in control, he glanced at the handcuffed prisoners, and then studied the old man, Isaac. Turning to his colleagues, he removed his ear defenders and said, 'When you shouted for me, I presumed it was to stun and disorientate the two robbers. I didn't realise the room was full of customers. Had I known that I'd never have thrown the grenade in. A room full of armed robbers, terrorists, or gunmen?

Then yes! But not one containing the public. Never! That's not the protocol. We try to save lives, not endanger them.'

'My fault,' replied Boyd weakly. 'Where was I? You never use stun grenades in a situation like this.'

Terry Anwhari was kneeling by Isaac, tending to the old man's injuries, when he looked up at Boyd and said, 'This man is out of it, but he's responding to my voice. I can hear him whispering. Fingers crossed. But what's that smell?'

'You think you've got problems,' remarked Janice. 'I think my tango is on the way out.'

Blood poured from Bernie's chest.

Terry laid Isaac down, removed his police anorak, and moved over to Bernie. He pressed the anorak upon the robber's chest and stemmed the flow of blood.

'Rotten eggs!' exclaimed Boyd. 'Could be a faulty stun grenade. Potassium nitrate! Out! Get everyone out just in case. Out! Evacuate!'

Outside the sound of ambulance sirens and police cars filled the atmosphere, gave credence to the bizarre unearthly situation that had encompassed the post office, and caused Boyd to drop to his knees in sheer desperation.

'What have I done?' he asked aloud. 'All these years and I stop thinking things through. What have I done?'

'You took a step too far too early, Guvnor,' suggested Janice. 'You made an error of judgement. I shot a man who is now close to death. If he dies, I'll have to learn to live with that for the rest of my life.'

'It's not the first time you've shot someone, Janice,' interjected Anthea. 'And it may not be the last. You should remember not that you wounded a man but that you saved another's life.'

Nodding, Janice handed her Gloch over to Anthea and said, 'There will be an enquiry. The Guvnor is in trouble. No disrespect is intended to anyone, but you are the senior officer commanding. I surrender my weapon to you per standing orders.'

'Guvnor!' radioed Ricky French suddenly and loudly. 'I'm double-checking the drone coverage. It shows one unidentified male crawling out of the premises by the rear door. He's dressed in denim jeans and jacket, trainers, and what looks like a black roll-neck sweater. He's on his feet. I've got him in sight.'

'A third robber?' queried Boyd. 'Or a confused customer?'

'He's not confused,' radioed Ricky who was studying the drone coverage from the rear of the police van. 'He's removed a short-barrelled rifle from his trouser leg – might be a sawn-off shotgun – can't tell from the angle displayed. Stand by. I'm moderating.' Ricky twiddled the drome controls. 'He's put it in the boot. He's driving off. Outer cordon! You got him?'

There was a quiet hush that invaded the building as the reality of life at the sharp end hit home when Boyd and his colleagues realised the outer cordon had not been established.

The wireless network remained silent.

Bobby, the mystery robber, was out of the zone, out of the immediate area, and home-free.

Boyd and the Special Crime Unit watched as other officers appeared at the crime scene. A fire engine arrived, and personnel began checking the safety of the post office. They were accompanied by a succession of ambulances along with a doctor and paramedics. And a young policewoman called Sonia wondered whether she had made the right decision to join the police.

An ambulance crew loaded Bernie into a blue light ambulance and, under police escort from two police motorcyclists, travelled at high speed to the nearest hospital trauma centre.

A Chief Superintendent from the local police station reached the scene and took over the investigation. Within five minutes he had identified Bernie as Bernard George Baxter, a well-known criminal from the north of the borough. In addition, the same officer identified Ginger Gerry as Gerald Robert Fitzpatrick of

Brixton, South London. Gerry was another well-known criminal with half a dozen convictions for robbery. Both men were in their late Fifties. The same officer surmised that the robber who had escaped might well be Robert Fitzpatrick: brother of Gerry who was currently wanted for questioning about three other armed robberies over the last twelve months. His whereabouts were unknown.

Fifteen minutes into the Chief Superintendent's enquiry, Commander Boyd, Inspector Bannerman, and Detective Sergeant Janice Burns were suspended from duty.

A call to the Commissioner of the Metropolitan Police followed and ten minutes later, Detective Inspector Anthea Adams was promoted to Chief Inspector and then Temporary Superintendent. She immediately assumed command of the Special Crime Unit, and that included not just the team she was currently part of, but all four wings of the specialised elite unit. It was a huge honour that ordinarily might have led to a weekend of celebration. Not this time.

'Sorry, Guvnor!' revealed Anthea. 'It's not the way I expected to be promoted. I didn't plan it that way.'

'I know,' replied Boyd. 'You've saved my life in the past, Anthea. I don't forget such things. I wish you success in all that you do. My problem is that I planned today's operation wrongly. I was too quick, too arrogant, and overreacted to the situation. I forgot to question myself and I forgot the basics and the basics are that the most powerful weapon at our disposal is our voice, not a Gloch 17 or a stun grenade. The voice is supervised only by a brain that analyses problems that lie ahead. I didn't use mine correctly and when I did, I thought and said the wrong things. Oh, I know how to do it. God knows I've done it countless times, but today it wasn't there, and I don't know why.'

'You've done your time, Billy,' soothed Anthea. 'Maybe all you need is rest. Get yourself home to Meg and the kids, put your feet up, uncork a bottle of red, and rest a while.'

'Yeah! I'm only ever truly home for the weekends. A stupid madcap job has turned me into an incapable workaholic. It will do us both good, Anthea.'

'You can't burn the candles at both ends for weeks on end like you do, Billy. Time to rest a while.'

'Look after the team, Anthea. You'll find none better.'

'I know. My first job will to be catch the one who got away,' declared Anthea. 'We have his image, and we have his car number. The local Chief Superintendent thinks the one that got away is the brother of one we've locked up. I expect the car will be reported stolen. We'll catch him. He's part of an attempted robbery, a conspiracy, or unlawful possession of a firearm. We'll catch him.'

'Is the drone still following?' asked Boyd.

'No! Ricky used a short-life battery drone because he didn't have enough time to set up his preferred method.'

'He should have said. I should have told him what coverage I wanted. Why didn't I think of that? Why didn't he tell me?'

'Everyone trusted you, Guvnor. They'd run through a wall for you if you asked them to. You are a powerful inspiration to so many. So, when you said go, they all went. No questions asked. They worship the ground you work on, Billy. When you say jump, they jump as high as you want them to jump.'

'Seriously?' queried Boyd.

'Today you wrongly activated a human frailty common to us all. You made a mistake,' explained Anthea. 'Ordinarily, everything would have worked out. Circumstances weren't on our side today. You lost it for the first time!'

Boyd stood and reflected on a bad day at the office. For him, it was all over. A new era in the elite squad moved into position as Boyd offered his apologies to all present and walked back to the van in a forlorn and sad condition. His mobile sounded and he answered the call.

'Are you home tonight?' queried Meg: Boyd's wife.

'Yes! For the weekend, maybe more. I'll be on the usual train arriving late at night. Might be earlier, not sure yet. Just tying up some loose ends here.'

'Good!' replied Meg. 'Get a taxi from the station. I'm working until eight. The childminder has the kids.'

'Yes! Of course! Yes!' replied Boyd wanting to explain the reasons why he was unexpectedly returning home early but unable to find the words.

Later that day, Boyd stepped from the train at Carlisle railway station. He hailed a taxi and headed to his home on the outskirts of the city.

Turning his key in the lock, Boyd took a deep breath and prepared his explanation.

Meg beat him to it, opened the door, and threw her arms around him.

'You're early,' she said as she kissed her husband and then took his hand.

'Got a few days off,' blurted an edgy Boyd as he carried his suitcase into the hall.

Meg watched him lethargically lug the suitcase down the hall. Immediately, she sensed there was something wrong. Ordinarily, her husband would be bounding towards the bedroom full of energy and renewed vigour.

'Fabulous!' erupted Meg trying to ignite proceedings. 'The childminder has gone. Our kids are sound asleep, and I have a bottle of Chablis chilling in the fridge. Get unpacked quickly. I'll pour the wine.'

'Yeah! Will do,' replied Boyd sheepishly. 'I'm just tired.'

Meg walked halfway down the corridor and then turned to face Boyd with 'Get it off your chest, Billy. What's wrong with you? What's got into you?'

'Nothing! Why the questions?'

'Because you're my husband and the father of our children. I can sense you a mile away, know you inside out, and can tell when you're not yourself. Spill it!'

'Okay! I've lost my job,' murmured Boyd. 'I made a mistake.'

'I know,' replied Meg. 'It's all over the news.'

'What?' cried Boyd in disbelief. 'You mean you know?'

'It's on the radio and the television,' remarked Meg. 'You've been suspended pending an investigation. You haven't lost your job, you idiot. You made a mistake. That's normal. Your problem is that you are a perfectionist.'

'People were hurt because I didn't think it through.'

'No one died, Billy,' snapped Meg. 'No one got hurt because you made a mistake. You'll be cleared in a week or so. Listen, Billy. Take a shower. The wine will keep for half an hour.'

'One man was killed. A few of the witnesses suffered hearing problems and...'

'And you're overthinking things again,' barked Meg. 'The robber was killed because he didn't come quietly like he should have. By the way, according to the television, the robbers had already fired into the ceiling, brought the roof down, scared a policewoman to her wit's end – she's resigned by the way - and already given the victims hearing problems before you arrived.'

'How do you know that?'

'Because I'm a nurse. A matron in case you'd forgotten. An orthopaedic one with the same qualifications as a junior doctor.'

'Oh yeah! I forgot. Three degrees!'

'Well done! That's two more than you by the way, but who am I to profess my abilities in the presence of the almighty.'

'Alright! Alright! Get off your high horse.'

'High horse! Look who's talking. I know you are so tied up in your work, Billy, that you sometimes forget who you married but I do know quite a bit about the human body. What makes it work and what makes it stop? Now get in that shower, this instance, and sort yourself out. There's no way your career is finished. You just need to relax, refresh, and renew. Take time out. You're not incompetent, just temporarily burnt out.'

There was a noise from Meg's bleeper.

'Damn it! I'm on call. Sorry, but I'll have to respond.'

Meg headed for the telephone with Boyd somewhat mesmerised that his downfall had been reported on the national news and his wife didn't seem that upset.

'Am I overreacting to events?' thought Boyd as he listened to his soulmate who was on the telephone listening intently to the voice on the other end.

The phone crashed onto its cradle when Meg cried, 'Typical! You come home. I go to work!'

'I thought you'd just finished at eight?'

'I did but like you, I'm on call twenty-four seven.'

'What's happened?'

'A multiple car accident on the motorway and the Casualty Department is about to overflow into the corridor again. I don't have enough staff. I have a shortage of triage nurses, a shortage of surgeons, a shortage of technicians and, to crown it all, there are not enough beds, and the bed manager is in Crete on holiday. I'll have to go and sort it out.'

'How will you do that?'

'I'll assess what needs to be done and act accordingly. I'm about to disturb quite a few people from their weekend off. That's the nature of my job at times. Sound familiar?'

'Oh yes,' replied Boyd still clutching his suitcase.

Meg rushed past him into the bedroom, undressed one set of clothes and emerged minutes later in full uniform still chattering at full blast with, 'I'll call in Dumfries and Newcastle if I have to. I'll be back when I'm back.'

'Understood,' nodded Boyd. 'Just so much to tell you!'

'You mean so much on your mind,' replied Meg. 'You're overloaded, Billy. I've watched you over the last few months. You're tired out. That brain and body of yours needs to switch off.' Meg paused, looked Boyd in the eye and said, 'I've got surgeons, doctors and nurses on my watch and I can tell when they've had enough. You're just like some of them. You can't keep going every hour of the day. My job is to catch them before they fall. Now I'm going to do my bit. There are no cell doors to shut tight and no high-speed chases to get involved in. You're not the only one who has decisions to make, Billy. I'm off. I'll be back when I'm back.'

'Don't make any mistakes,' suggested Boyd.

'Mistakes!' snarled Meg, and then she pulled the front door open and yelled, 'Your favourite saying in our marriage Billy. I'll be back when I'm back. Well! It works both ways.'

The door slammed tight behind Meg leaving Boyd still clutching his suitcase and staring at a framed photograph of him and his bride on the wall.

'Great day!' murmured Boyd to himself. 'Looks like my marriage could fall apart anytime soon too. What's happened to me? Where did I fall off the wagon?'

There was a cry of 'Mum! Dad!' from one of the bedrooms causing Boyd to drop his suitcase and tend to Issy and James.

'Where's Mum?' asked Issy.

'Gone to work,' replied Boyd. 'Come on, guys. Let's have some ice cream, a story, and then bedtime. Okay?'

'Ice cream at bedtime,' squealed James in delight. 'Yes please, Dad! Mum doesn't allow that to happen.'

'Because she doesn't know where it's hidden,' giggled Boyd.

Issy and James rushed to the kitchen.

Boyd jokingly served teaspoons of ice cream before changing to large dollops to the amusement of Issy and James. Then his pager sounded.

'What the hell,' he thought. 'I'm suspended.'

Checking the pager, Boyd acknowledged the message and then withdrew his mobile phone from his jacket.

'Good evening, Commander. It's Julian Spencer.'

'Yes! I apologise. I see you paged me earlier today, but the signal has just come through. Maybe I missed your first transmission. How can I help you, Julian?'

'I need your services.'

'I'm afraid that is not possible. I have been suspended from duty following an error of judgement that may have caused injury to innocent members of the public. I'm sure you know all about it. The point is, Julian, I'm inactive for the foreseeable future. I don't know how things will turn out.'

'Nine o'clock my office,' replied Julian. 'Monday morning. First thing. Don't be late.'

'Vauxhall?'

'Yes!'

'Why?'

'You're going on holiday.'

'Holiday? What the hell are you talking about? Don't you listen? I've just been suspended from duty. I issued the wrong orders. I made a mess of a firearms response operation. Yours truly almost blinded a couple of people, and one man is suffering from temporary deafness. I'm finished in this role. The media is carrying headlines that indicate the police can't be trusted to deal with serious firearms offences. My photograph will be on some of the front pages again. Don't you understand? I'm broken, Julian. Broken!'

'Temporarily, yes! I understand what you say, but what I have for you is more important than you think.'

'Like what?' demanded Boyd angrily.

'ABRAHAM!' voiced Julian emphatically.

Dumbfounded, Boyd sat down next to Issy.

'Can we have strawberries too?' asked Issy.

Boyd covered the phone's mouthpiece and replied, 'Yes, Issy, but don't tell your mother.'

Issy raided the fridge to the amusement of James who scoffed his ice cream and held his plate out for the strawberries. Issy duly obliged and the pair laughed when one of the strawberries didn't quite make the plate and fell onto the floor. Issy picked it up and popped it in her mouth.

Holding the phone close to his chest, Boyd thought about someone he had first met over twenty years ago. He shook his head and returned to the call.

'You do remember him?' continued Julian, the Chief of MI6.

'Abraham! How could I ever forget him?' replied Boyd. 'He was my first one.'

'But not the last.'

'What's going on?'

'He wants to see you.'

'What does he want?'

'My office at nine o'clock Monday morning. Enjoy the rest of the weekend with your wife and family. You may be suspended today, Commander Boyd, but by Monday morning... Well, Monday is our day, and the day I will brief you on Abraham.'

Boyd sat quietly thinking things over before enquiring, 'And if I'm still suspended?'

'You won't be,' declared Julian. 'By the way, Abraham asks that you don't forget your sun hat. What's that about? I don't recall you ever wearing a hat.'

Boyd's eyebrows shot up at the mention of a hat. He granted himself a sly smile on the phone and replied, 'He must be somewhere warm and sunny, Julian. But I'd like to know how you can be so sure I can make this mysterious holiday you mention.'

'I know people in government as you well know,' replied Julian. 'They ask me to do things. Sometimes they instruct me to do things. I often say yes or offer an alternative. When I say yes it always comes with an absolute requirement from me. Non-negotiable! No questions asked! Nine o'clock, Monday morning! Don't be late. Pack a suitcase for a week. The sun hat is optional but may not be a bad idea. A touch of sunshine and a beer or two await you. Indeed, one of us may well join you.'

The phone went dead leaving Boyd to mull things over.

'One of us may join you,' considered Boyd. 'Pack a suitcase!' He nudged his suitcase with his foot and thought, 'I've not emptied this one yet.'

Flummoxed, slightly annoyed, thinking things through, Boyd finally hit the digits on his phone and rang Antonia Harston-Browne.

Antonia was not only a Senior Intelligence Officer in MI5, she was also a close friend of Boyd and a leading member of the Special Crime Unit. Antonia was engaged to marry Sir Phillip Nesbitt: the Director General of MI5, the Security Service. Consequently, the three individuals Boyd, Antonia, and Phillip Nesbitt enjoyed a high degree of companionship.

The tall, good-looking, redhead answered the phone promptly with the words, 'Boyd! How are we today? What can I do for you?'

'What do you know about today's fiasco, Toni?'

'That you made a mess of it all and are suspended.'

'Bad news travels fast,' remarked Boyd. 'Yeah! I'm feeling down and out. Knocked out even. It's all my fault. You got to know that rather quickly.'

'Rumour and bad news travel faster than a wireless network,' suggested Antonia. 'And you seem to have forgotten that I'm manning the unit's Ticker intelligence system. I have everything from the computerised radio network and more. The Commander is now Anthea. Is that all?'

Chuckling, Boyd replied, 'I can read your mind, Toni. You know I can. I've been suspended by the police but the chief of M16 needs me. What's going on, Toni? Julian Spencer just rang me. He wants me in his office at nine sharp Monday morning. Why?'

'Because he trusts you,' replied Antonia.'

'Maybe! Maybe not! Why does he want me?'

'Now how would I know?' replied Antonia.

'But you'll find out, won't you? I want everything on the source coded ABRAHAM if you please, Antonia.'

'Antonia! You never change, do you, Billy? It's Toni, Toni, Toni but as soon as it's a favour you want then you go all formal and use Antonia.'

'Yes, well er....' blustered Boyd.

'Abraham isn't with us anymore, Billy,' softened Antonia. 'You recruited Abraham about twenty years ago, but he was traded to another agency in the progression of a joint intelligence-sharing partnership. He's been with them ever since.'

'Who?' probed Boyd.

'Mossad!' replied Antonia.

'Didn't we sign a Memorandum of Understanding with Israel a few years ago? Security and defence and a ton of other stuff!'

'November 2021,' replied Antonia. 'The Abraham transfer was many years ago and before that. The agreement still holds.'

'I see,' nodded Boyd. 'So why the clandestine meeting with a Mossad agent initially recruited by us and shared with them as part of an agreement long before the 2021 document? Israel is a good friend. Not an enemy. What's going on?'

'Mind how you go on holiday. No sand in your toes.'

'Holiday! Mossad? Sand? You know more, don't you?'

'Yes! I do,' replied Antonia in a scolding manner. 'I'm supposed to know more than anyone else. No sand in your toes!'

'I'll wear socks,' retaliated Boyd. 'Come on, Toni. What is this all about?'

'I can't say. You're suspended and so is your security clearance. Sorry, but the shop is closed.'

'Cheeky!'

'The tickets to your holiday destination will be with Julian on Monday morning. Don't be surprised to see Phillip on your holidays. It's complicated, Billy, that's all I can tell you so far. The story is slowly unravelling.'

'I see. Thank you for the so far then.'

'You're welcome. Enjoy the weekend with Meg, and Billy. Give her my love. But please remember the wine at your holiday destination is unrivalled. A bottle or two on your return would go well with our next dinner party.'

Antonia ended the phone call with Boyd still mesmerised by the complexity of the arrangements. It seemed that the tragic events of the day were of no concern to anyone he had spoken to. What was the holiday? Where to and who with? What did Abraham want? How the hell would he tell Meg that he was up and running again? Well, maybe it was just a crawl.

Boyd phoned Meg.

Meanwhile, in the operating theatre of a London trauma hospital, a skilled surgeon, a competent anaesthetist, and a team of nurses, worked away at the latest patient requiring emergency treatment. He was called Bernie and he had been shot in the chest. He had lost a lot of blood and a transfusion line was in place. Time was of the essence.

The anaesthetist voiced, 'Blood pressure falling.'

The surgeon replied, 'Noted! Nurse! Sponge, please!'

The nurse complied. The clock on the wall 'ticked' and progressed another notch around the dial.

Bernie, the post office robber, was fighting for his life.

5

~

The Following Day,
Ambleside, The Lake District,
Cumbria.

The sun-kissed waters of the lake caressed the shore, acknowledged the Cumbrian Fells, and then rolled lazily back again as a thin line of traffic navigated the narrow highway before entering the Lake District town. The traffic slid cautiously into the busy community fully aware of the winding road that bordered Windermere and penetrated the heart of the Lake District.

In a side street, just off the main through road, a campervan bearing UK registration plates was parked in front of the library. To the locals, the vehicle was just another traveller on a short stop-over while on holiday. The campervan hadn't been a problem, was just one of many passing through Ambleside, and would be gone by nightfall lest it become an unwanted eyesore to the rural population.

Inside the campervan, a man watched the comings and goings at the library. The curtains were drawn across all the windows of the vehicle except from the rear and from where he sat patiently with a highly sophisticated camera in his lap. Sat in the rear area of the campervan, he could not be seen by passers-by because a thin anti-glare tint covered the window. In any event, he was doing nothing wrong and spent his time watching the library entrance.

A post office van cruised by, followed by a supermarket delivery vehicle and then a couple of taxis. The man yawned, poured himself a coffee from a flask and then dropped it on the floor when the library doors opened and two people walked out.

Lifting the camera into position, the man began rapidly taking a succession of photographs in black and white. Then, as the man and woman he was targeting turned towards his vehicle, he set aside one camera and picked up another that was fitted with colour capability. The first camera took photographs from a distance. Now he focused for close-ups as the couple crossed the road in front of him and strolled towards a car park situated to the rear of the campervan. The woman carried a shopping bag containing a selection of library books that could be seen.

The photographer set down his camera and hit the transmit button on a walkie-talkie radio saying, 'Ivan! This is Mikhail. I have them at last. Yuri Pavlova and his wife Svetlana have just left the library and walked right past me. Multiple photographs were taken for the resident. Over!'

Parked nearby, Ivan sat in a hired car and waited for the couple to show saying, 'Got that, Mikhail. Wait one!'

The couple walked past Ivan and got into a dark grey three-litre Mercedes saloon. The woman occupied the front passenger seat and the man drove.

As the vehicle turned into the main road, Ivan transmitted, 'I confirm that, Mikhail. I am positive that is Yuri and Svetlana Pavlova. Viktor! Come through and follow them. I want to know where they live. House them!'

On a street adjoining the main road, a motorcyclist dressed in black leather and a full-face helmet kickstarted a BMW motorcycle. The machine burst into life and the rider began following the Mercedes. The rider flicked a switch on the handlebars and said, 'Viktor has them. Come through and tag on behind me. Traffic flow is light. Make ground.'

'Got that, Viktor,' replied Ivan. 'Join us, Mikhail. I want their home photographed when we house them.'

A campervan outside the library started up, joined the traffic flow, and took up a position in the convoy following a Mercedes driven by the Russian dissident Yuri Pavlova.

The Mercedes took a right at a roundabout and negotiated a steep ascent known locally as *The Struggle*. Climbing the road, the Mercedes reached Kirkstone Pass, passed the famous Kirkstone Inn, slid over the summit, and headed towards Penrith on the A592. The traffic flow was intermittent allowing Viktor to maintain a good view of the Mercedes without compromising the three-vehicle convoy.

Brothers Water and the Brotherswater Inn came into view as the glories of the Lake District were exposed for all to see.

Eventually, the Mercedes turned into a small housing estate in the village of Glenridding, on the shores of Ullswater. The vehicle stopped outside a three-bedroomed detached cottage that had been constructed in the tradition of Lakeland slate. Pavlova's unassuming home was far from Russia and nestled unobtrusively in the shadow of Helvellyn. The famous mountain stood 3,118 feet above sea level and was one of the true glories of the nation's beloved Cumbria.

A few moments later, the BMW drove by, took a right and turned into a hotel car park. The rider flicked the switch on the handlebars and radioed, 'Viktor has them. Take the second left past the shops on entering the village. It's the fourth house on the left opposite the stream that flows into the lake. Blue curtains and a couple of rose bushes in the front garden. Wait one... They are out of the vehicle and into the house... Wait one... The male is unlocking the front door with a key taken from his pocket. Confirmation! The door closes behind them. They are housed.'

'Understood,' from Ivan.

'Mikhail!' continued Viktor. 'Come to the hotel car park and select your spot. You can take photographs from the campervan and maybe walk out later for closer ones.'

'Wait there,' replied Mikhail.

'I agree,' declared Ivan. 'I'll park elsewhere in the village until you have finished. I'll do a walk past when night falls. I want the exact address and an understanding of how the land lies in the immediate area. Viktor, take a break and then scout the village. Is there a police station nearby? Pubs, cafes, parking areas. What kind of shops? I'm thinking ahead. Are you with me?'

'No! I'm ahead of you,' radioed Viktor with a discernible chuckle in his voice. 'Hey, boys. This place beats Moscow.'

'I'm taking time out,' radioed Ivan. 'I need to update Luka and the resident. Andrey will be delighted.'

In the office of the Special Crime Unit in London, Temporary Detective Superintendent Anthea Adams set the telephone on its cradle and walked into the adjoining office where the bulk of the unit was situated.

'That was the hospital,' announced Anthea.

'And?' asked Terry Anwhari eagerly. 'Bernie?'

'Bernard George Baxter died on the operating table. He was declared dead due to gunshot wounds in the upper chest.'

'Damn it!' exploded Terry. 'We needed him alive. He could have told us where Fitzpatrick was hanging out.'

'Not now,' remarked Anthea. 'I will tell senior command. There will be an internal enquiry.'

'I'll phone Janice and let her know. Do you want me to phone Boyd as well?'

'No!' rumbled Anthea. 'Whilst he remains suspended there will be no contact with either Boyd, Janice or Bannerman. That is what I have been told.'

'Pity!' frowned Terry Anwhari. 'They are our best friends, not just work colleagues. That's just not right.'

'Leave it, Terry. Someone out there is sharpening their knife and we are the target. We've lost enough as it is,' explained Anthea. 'Get to work and find Fitzpatrick: The one that got away. That's the job at hand. See to it, please.'

Terry did not reply but merely nodded.

Ricky French swivelled in his chair to face Anthea and stated, 'I'm creating a track from the post office to wherever our target might be. I'm hacking into every CCTV system from the post office to wherever until I find him. I'm concentrating on the route to Brixton, but who knows where he might be. It might be a total waste of time. We'll see.'

'Carry on,' replied Anthea. 'The sooner we get Fitzpatrick locked up the better. Boyd lost us credibility on the top landing and elsewhere. We need to get back to where we were.'

'And get Boyd back?' queried Ricky.

'Who knows?' replied Anthea. 'I'm not sharpening the knives and can't answer that. Of course, we need leaders like Boyd but when the flame in the candle goes out it usually means that the wax is finished. We all have our time. Boyd is finished. I don't even know where he is. I'm assuming he's gone to ground to get out of the limelight. He might be on holiday. I don't know. I just hope he can relax, rest, refresh, and get his mind back on track.'

There was a chorus of, 'Hear! Hear!' before Anthea raised her voice and said, 'Can we please get on with what you are all doing? We have a robber to catch. Let's do it.'

Scanning her eyes across the room from left to right, Anthea saw the gloomy faces gradually return to their workstations. Taking a deep breath, she turned on her heel and returned to her office. It had taken less than a minute to work out that the future of her leadership was not going to be an easy journey. They wanted Boyd back, but it was out of her hands and not within her sphere of operation. The priority had to be Robert Fitzpatrick and, deep inside, she knew she had to be at the forefront of his arrest.

Having spent the entire day in the Russian embassy, Andrey Petrov felt good. A recent telephone call from Ivan had updated him about the whereabouts of Yuri Pavlova and his wife Svetlana. It was confirmation that his decision to authorise operations in the Lake District had been based on the work he had been doing as the resident in the embassy. Where the current ideology of Russia was all about individual power bases granted by the president who was commander in chief, then Andrey Petrov was climbing the ladder of success and wealth. He had to ensure the operation in Glenridding ended in glory for the Motherland. Russia had to be seen to be such a power that even its dissidents, non-conformists, and revolutionists who had escaped to live abroad were fearful of the commander-in-chief. Power was embodied in every move the President of the Russian Federation made - whoever he might be - and to assist in the preservation of that power was the way forward for men like Andrey Petrov.

Andrey gathered his overcoat around him, turned up the collar, placed the black fur ushanka on his head, snug tight, and left the embassy by the side door.

Outside the embassy, on the streets of Kensington, Anthonia's team of M15 watchers suddenly burst into life after a day of idly doing next to nothing.

Andrey strolled a hundred yards or so before stepping to the edge of the footpath where he hailed a passing taxi. He leaned into the cab and said, 'Soho! Frith Street, please!'

The taxi driver nodded, unlocked the passenger door, and replied, 'No problem. Jump in, sir!'

Andrey complied and slid into the rear of the taxi as it headed towards the west end of London.

From a building nearby, a voice engaged an encrypted radio network and declared, 'This is Max. Ushanka is on the move. Mobile units make convoy on the taxi. As you will have seen, the taxi is ours. Callsign Blackjack One has the subject inside his vehicle. Destination Frith Street. Team! Make Frith Street before the subject's arrival.

An array of acknowledgements followed as Max, the surveillance controller, engaged the digits on his keyboard and updated the surveillance commander, Antonia Harston-Browne, who was in telephone contact with her team.

Meanwhile, in the taxi, the driver glanced at Andrey seated in the rear and asked, 'Busy little area is Soho, sir. Whereabouts in Frith Street do you want to be?'

'Ronnie Scott's Jazz Club,' came the reply.

The driver used his foot to squeeze a communication device built into the taxi floor and simultaneously radioed the surveillance network when he replied to Andrey, 'Ronnie Scott's Jazz Club! Frith Street, Soho! Got that! Thank you, sir.'

Andrey peered out of the window as the taxi skirted Hyde Park and sped towards the West End via Oxford Circus.

'Fifteen to twenty minutes,' voiced the taxi driver.

Seated on a sofa in her apartment, Antonia checked the time, decided it was too late to join in, and poured a glass of white wine before relaying to Max, 'Ronnie Scott's? Ushanka has no interest in jazz as far as we know. Get the team to cover Zima. It's the Russian restaurant next door to Ronnie Scott's. I bet that's where he's headed. I want to know who Ushanka meets at Zima.'

'Understood!' replied Max.

Antonia settled down on the sofa with the surveillance network engaged and a tipple of wine to comfort her.

The follow continued and in Frith Street, Soho, the taxi pulled in and Andrey got out, paid the driver, and then climbed the steps into one of the most popular Russian restaurants in England. The *'front of house'* at Zima, (meaning *'winter'* in English) welcomed Andrey and escorted him inside where he joined two men at a table.

A complimentary round of 'Russian Caravan' was offered and accepted amidst the handshakes. The popular blend of Chinese oolong and Keemun black tea went down a treat and was followed by a round of vodka that heralded the friendly chink of glasses.

The trio ordered Royal Siberian caviar and beef stroganoff followed by a dessert called medovik. The sweet was a layer cake popular in the countries of the former Soviet Union. The ingredients are honey and smetana (sour cream) or condensed milk. Medovik is well known for its lengthy preparation time because it consists of layers of sponge cake with a cream filling and lashes of honey. Accordingly, as the dessert was being prepared, the trio ordered more vodka and drank toast after toast to whomever to whatever before the course finally arrived. They spoke in both English and Russian but paid no attention to a middle-aged couple who sat in a corner of the restaurant and enjoyed chicken Kyiv. Unknown to Andrey and his friends, the couple were part of Antonia's team engaged in following him.

As the chatter of the restaurant grew in admiration of the fine food being consumed and the friendly atmosphere, Brendan, the male surveillance officer, activated his transmit button and quietly reported, 'We have USHANKA and his colleague FEDORA - (Luka) - from the embassy under observation. They are with a third person not known to us. He is speaking English and throwing in the odd word of Russian, but we're not able to confirm his accent or any name that Ushanka is addressing him by. All three are eating a meal and drinking vodka like it's going out of fashion. We're unable to deploy listening devices due to noise levels. Stand by for details of the new target designated MEDOVIK.'

A description of the unknown individual rippled gently across the airwaves and Max, the surveillance controller, replied, 'All received. Team One takes Ushanka. Team Two takes Fedora. Team Three takes the unknown party — Medovik - when they leave. House and identify Medovik.'

The night wore on. Andrey and his friends engaged in some form of celebration of which only they were aware.

Quietly listening to the surveillance network, Antonia was puzzled about what might have recently occurred that would cause such an obvious celebration. Racking her brains, she could not find an answer to the dilemma, but neither could she comprehend why Ushanka had left the embassy late at night to attend what appeared to be an important meeting in the west end of London. Yes, Ushanka was a cultural attaché, but such a position involved attending daytime conferences as a delegate, and on a formal basis. This meeting was not the usual activity associated with Ushanka.

'One of the men present speaks English,' thought Antonia. 'If English then who is he and what business has he with the Resident and the Foreign Intelligence Service of the Russian Federation.'

Midnight arrived. The wine ran out, and the surveillance teams worked until dawn before they were relieved by others.

Later that day, Max prepared a report for Antonia. The gist of the document revealed that the target MEDOVIK was indeed an Englishman. The surveillance team had housed him at a hotel in Soho where he had given his name as Alexander Lowther with an address in Windermere, Cumbria. Details of the credit card Lowther used to pay for the hotel accommodation confirmed his name and address. Lowther had no further contact with either Ushanka or Fedora once they had left Zima. Both Russians had returned to the embassy. Lowther, however, returned to his hotel but midmorning he took a taxi to Euston railway station where he caught a train north, got off at Oxenholme, and was met by a woman now identified as his wife who was called Sheena. He was housed by a surveillance officer at an address on the outskirts of Windermere. Scrutiny of intelligence data held by the service revealed Lowther to be a member of the Communist Party of Britain. Before that Lowther was a member of the Communist Party of Great Britain: a political party that lost support when the Soviet Union collapsed.

Antonia sat at her desk, read the report, and began interrogating the state-of-the-art computer system known as Ticker. The standalone desktop computer contained a million pound plus cyber package protected by an extremely expensive anti-hacking system. There was no other computer system like it in the world of espionage and intelligence gathering.

Entering the names Alexander and Sheena Lowther, Antonia gradually began to build up a picture of their lifestyle, their financial standing, associations, and the organisations they belonged to.

Later, Antonia poured herself a black coffee and read the product of her search. She created an intelligence folder and named it 'Supporters of Russia in Cumbria'. She found nothing illegal in her investigation of the Lowther family, but then years of experience in the world of counterespionage led her to believe the surveillance operation had been a success.

Antonia surmised they had uncovered at least two people in Cumbria who had worked for Russian Intelligence over the last twenty years. They were only minor contacts, or so it seemed. Eyes and ears who reported anything of interest to their handlers. They were hardly spies in the true sense since neither had access to secret information that would jeopardise the security of the nation. Financial irregularities in their bank accounts pointed to monies they had received from sources outside the UK. As far as Antonia was concerned Alexander and Sheena Lowther were best regarded as low-level access agents to the Foreign Intelligence Service working out of the Russian Embassy in London. The job of the Lowther couple was to identify and report upon those who might have access to intelligence regarding Cumbria that was of interest to the Kremlin. They did this by joining various clubs and organisations from the Freemasons to the Rotary Club to the Women's Institute to local libraries, gyms, clubs, knitting circles, yoga and Pilates clubs, and anything where people gathered. The sums of money in their bank accounts did not suggest they were wealthy or important spies unless there was a colossal amount hidden under a bed in the Lake District. Rather, the financial rewards were low but consistent indicating minimal importance to the Kremlin but an ace in the hole in Cumbria if they were ever needed.

Adding two sugars, Antonia stirred the coffee endlessly as if she were in a trance. It was no daydream. She tried to figure out why Alexander Lowther had travelled to the Zima Restaurant in Soho to celebrate with the resident and Luka.

There was something of interest going on in Cumbria, she guessed, but try as she might, Antonia could not get a handle on what that might be.

'They are of minimal interest to us,' she thought. 'They have no access to sensitive information, but I can see they are charged with finding people who do have access and passing their identities on to the SVR. I understand that. It mirrors what MI6 do overseas for us to a certain extent. That's a normal espionage stroke counter-espionage activity and, in the final analysis, every opposition politician in the country might mirror them to some degree, but the Lowther couple are not politicians or activists. They are of such interest that Alexander turns up in person in London.'

Antonia printed her work off. She gathered the papers, bundled them into a file, and marked it for the attention of the Director General.

By Hand. Eyes Only. Recommend closer examination at the soonest opportunity. Probable access agents in Cumbria were activated by SVR officer FEDORA. Evaluation advised.

'I wish Boyd was back in the camp,' thought Antonia as she closed the computer system. 'He'd know someone in Windermere that could befriend them, monitor them, and penetrate the problem for us. But right now, that's not going to happen. I wonder if the rest of the unit misses his presence as much as I do?'

~

6
~

Early doors.
Monday morning.
Brixton, South London.

Dawn was breaking when the Special Crime Unit's new commander - Anthea Adams - led the raiding party through the quiet streets of London into Brixton.

'This is all down to Ricky,' declared Anthea to the unit as they travelled to the target. 'He's worked all weekend tracking the movement of Fitzpatrick via the CCTV systems. You've been briefed. You know what to do. Let's make it a good clean lift. I think a celebration tonight is called for.'

'Absolutely! Well done, Ricky,' resounded around the minibus. 'Long overdue, Guvnor. We need a good night out.'

'Thanks, Ricky. Your time is much appreciated. Now then,' remarked Anthea. 'Engage a long-term drone to cover the operation properly. Understood?'

'Long battery life! Yes!' replied Ricky: The tech king.

'Make sure you have your body armour on, your weapons on safety, and plenty of ammunition. The red blanket is going down now from central control so there will be no uniforms in the vicinity of the armed raiding party.' Anthea paused nervously and then continued, 'And watch your arcs of fire if weapons are deployed.'

'Guvnor,' interrupted Terry meaningfully.

'What?' replied Anthea.

'You said all that in the office before we set off. Lighten up. It might be your first time but we're all with you.'

'Yeah! Of course, sorry! Yeah! Let's do it.'

The convoy trundled through the city streets, made for Brixton, and then separated into individual groups.

Anthea's unit pulled up fifty yards from Brockwell Park.

Morning broke crisp and clear. A cat squealed when the minibus stopped close to the kerb. Then a dog barked as the team emerged from the minibus and separated. They were over the fence, along the side, around the back, and down the front path of the target house with Anthea leading the way.

'All units, confirm position upon arrival,' she radioed.

Listening, Anthea heard the replies and studied the house but saw no signs of life. 'I have control, stand by!' The seconds ticked away. The curtains did not sway. 'All units! Strike! Strike! Strike!'

The 'enforcer' battering ram smashed into the front door of Fitzpatrick's last known address. The place where Ricky had housed him using CCTV analysis. The door splintered and Terry Anwhari stepped forward to shoulder-charge the door.

Robert Fitzpatrick lay asleep upstairs in his bed. The noise woke him. He leapt out of bed, peered through the window, and saw police beating the door down with the enforcer.

'Time to move,' thought Fitzpatrick. 'How did they know? Who grassed me up?'

The door surrendered. The team rushed in clearing every room in their search for Fitzpatrick.

Anthea darted upstairs but the bedroom was empty.

'The sheets,' shouted Anthea. 'They're crumpled as if he's just got out of bed.' Cautiously, she checked beneath the bed to no avail, pulled open the door of an empty wardrobe, and then yelled, 'The loft! Terry! He's in the attic!'

'Got it,' replied Hazel Scott: a dark-haired detective in the company of Detective George Fish who withdrew an extendable ladder from his kitbag shouting, 'Loft access ladder deployed.'

'Let me do it,' declared Sergeant Terry Anwhari as he popped the ladder against the wall and studied the loft area. 'He's in there. I can see cobwebs hanging from the loft cover. It's just been opened.'

'And then closed,' said George handing Terry a ballistic shield. 'Here! He might be armed. Take this with you.'

Anthea stepped forward and shouted towards the loft, 'Fitzpatrick! This is the police. We know you are in there. Come on down and no one will get hurt.'

Silence reigned.

'Show yourself,' yelled Anthea. 'We are armed and will take any necessary action to capture you. Give yourself up.'

Still no reply.

Inside the attic, Fitzpatrick listened to the words, chuckled, and crawled away from the loft towards the wall.

'Use the ballistic shield for cover but deploy tear gas before entry,' ordered Anthea. She handed Terry a tear gas canister and said, 'No mercy! Pop the lid, throw one in, and take him out. He's all yours, Terry.'

DS Anwhari nodded. He took the canister in one hand and the shield in the other and began to climb the ladder now propped against the wall giving access to the loft.

George and Hazel held the ladder. Terry climbed.

'Last chance, Fitzpatrick,' bellowed Anthea. 'Show your hands. Let's see those fingers poking down from the loft. All of them! I say again, last chance, Fitzpatrick. Come quietly and it will look good in court. Fitzpatrick! Fitzpatrick!'

But Fitzpatrick had other ideas and was in the process of removing a wooden partition that separated the house from his neighbours. Fitzpatrick knew his house was one in a long line of terraced houses that stretched over three hundred yards down that street. He could travel from one end of the terrace to the other end of the street by knocking away some of the wooden panels the occupants had fitted over the years. Some parts of the walled borders between the houses had been removed and wooden screens installed.

Fitzpatrick removed the last panel, moved along his neighbour's attic, and began forcing open the next partition.

Poking the loft cover open, Terry lobbed the tear gas canister into the space and then allowed the cover to drop back into place. Anthea handed him a gas mask.

Thirty seconds elapsed before Anthea nudged Terry, 'Go!'

As Fitzpatrick abandoned one attic and entered another, Terry donned the gas mask, poked his head into the loft, shone a torch, and saw a grey cloud of gas rushing to the opening to escape.

Anthea, Hazel and George all turned away quickly as the tear gas cloud billowed into their eyes. The weapon that had been designed to cause a burning sensation in Fitzpatrick's eyes and nose had backfired. The cloud rushed to the loft opening but parts of it billowed back into the attic and penetrated the neighbouring attic because Fitzpatrick had not closed the partition behind him.

Watery eyes and blurred vision accompanied by a bout of coughing, disorientation, and confusion followed and did more to help the fugitive than it did his potential captors.

'Fitzpatrick!' shouted Terry. There was no reply and no sign of the wanted man in the attic.

The cloud of tear gas slowly cleared giving Terry a better vision of the roof space.

Terry immediately shouted on the radio, hauled himself upright into the loft, banged his head on the roof, crashed into a lighting unit that exploded when his head hit it the second time, and then fell over the rafters when he lost his footing.

Lying on his back, Terry rolled over, saw the dividing panel, and realised what had happened. 'He's escaped,' yelled the detective.

'What was that?' queried Anthea. 'He's done what?'

'Escaped, Guvnor!' bellowed Terry. 'The wall that divides this house from the next one is fitted with a partition. He's in the neighbouring house.'

'Oh no!' replied Anthea.

'Oh yes!' replied Terry. 'He's crashed into next door. He could be in any of the terraced houses. They've all got party walls.'

Stunned, Anthea hesitated before updating the team.

Minutes later, there was an almighty crash when Fitzpatrick lowered himself from the loft in a neighbouring house, entered the bathroom to the astonishment of a naked woman taking a shower, and then hurtled through the window to the ground below.

Fitzpatrick landed badly but rubbed his eyes to try and eliminate a tingling sensation. Then he rubbed his ankle and stretched his leg. He made for the garden fence at the rear. Determined to escape, he leapt over the low-level trellis and ran into a detective listening to his radio.

Ducking at the last moment, Fitzpatrick pushed the detective to one side like a rugby player fending off a tackle and then pelted along the alleyway in his bid for freedom.

The radio network was jam-packed with mixed messages indicating where Fitzpatrick was located. A few thought he was still in the attic area of the neighbouring house. Others thought he was in one of the other terraced houses. One officer reported seeing him in the rear alley. The detectives were well and truly confused and out of position.

Whacking the next officer with the butt of his pistol, Fitzpatrick raced down the alley towards the main road.

A dog handler set his dog to work on a leash.

Another detective saw Fitzpatrick approaching and bent low to challenge the fugitive. He spread his legs, spread out his arms, and was about to lunge at Fitzpatrick when the wanted man aimed his pistol, pulled the trigger and caused the policeman to dive out of the way of the bullets.

High and wide, Fitzpatrick missed but Terry and the police dog were now involved, and the keystone cops were back in harness. Leastways, that's how it seemed to Ricky manning the drone and recording an aerial video.

Ricky broke into the Force radio network with, 'Special Crime Unit confirm Trigger! Trigger! Trigger! Location Brixton! Shots fired! Drone in operation. Armed officers are in attendance. Request borough borders are locked down. The target has escaped custody and is armed and dangerous.'

In Scotland Yard, the incident took centre stage and caused the officer in charge of the control room to reply with, 'All received. I'm calling Zulu 99 to the scene.'

A phone call was made. A police helicopter scrambled.

Anthea overtook two of her colleagues as they sprinted down the alley determined to prevent Fitzpatrick from reaching the main road and the nearby park. She was glad to be wearing jeans and a tee shirt, and a good pair of trainers that made her fleet of foot.

Try as they might, the police could not catch Fitzpatrick who, on reaching the end of the alley, crossed the road with Anthea leading the pack snarling like a foxhound.

'Take him, Rocky,' shouted the dog handler when he released the leash and watched his dog run free.

Bounding along at a ferocious speed Rocky passed everyone involved in the pursuit. With its mighty body surging through space, the dog extended its paws and leapt towards Fitzpatrick.

Two shots rang out from Fitzpatrick's gun when he shot Rocky and watched the dog tumble to the ground in mid-flight.

Wildly now, Fitzpatrick fired a succession of shots at his followers who ducked and dived as Anthea withdrew her Gloch and drew a bead on the target she was chasing. The sights of her gun bobbled up and down as she sought to run as fast as she could whilst simultaneously aiming at her target.

A double-decker bus cruised into the highway. The driver was unaware of the chase. Members of the public screamed, dropped their belongings, and sought cover from the crazed gunman.

'Too many people about,' thought Anthea holstering her Gloch. 'No more mistakes!'

Racing for the bus, Fitzpatrick pulled himself onto the boarding platform. The vehicle gradually drew away from Anthea and the chasing pack with a laughing Fitzpatrick waving goodbye.

Gulping air, Anthea filled her lungs and realised the double-decker was stopping at a red traffic light. She increased her pace, felt her legs stretching out further, and then surprised everyone by catching hold of the grab bar and heaving herself onto the boarding platform.

The detective was on the bus. So was Fitzpatrick.

Anthea drew her Gloch and moved along the deck. Cold unrivalled fear filled gnawed at her stomach.

Fitzpatrick fired.

The passengers dived for cover as a salvo of bullets passed each other in flight when Anthea returned fire. The auburn-haired detective threw herself into a vacant seat conscious that she was in grave danger. A window above her shattered when Fitzpatrick's shots flew over her head, smashed the window, and then carried on through the air to burst the front windscreen of another double-decker bus overtaking at the traffic lights.

The driver of the second bus was traumatised, lost control, careered across the highway, and mounted the footpath before colliding with a lamp post and litter bin that emptied onto the pavement adding to the carnage.

Wobbling, the lamp standard suddenly plummeted to the ground narrowly missing a woman pushing a pram.

Fitzpatrick rushed down the aisle. Passengers cowered at his presence. Reaching Anthea lying on one of the seats, Fitzpatrick aimed at the detective and pulled the trigger.

A clicking sound emitted from the firearm. The gun was empty. Fitzpatrick was out of ammunition.

Anthea propelled herself into his body forcing Fitzpatrick backwards and to the ground. The two wrestled on the grubby floor before Fitzpatrick broke free, struggled to his feet, and then launched himself at the nearest window.

The glass window fragmented into a thousand slivers of glass when the fugitive soared through the air, landed on the footpath, and glanced over his shoulder. He was home free with a dead dog in his wake, a mother screaming with a baby in her arms, and a breathless Anthea now trampling over passengers in the double-decker as she tried to get to the window.

And all Fitzpatrick had to show for it was another half dozen cuts to his face from the broken glass.

Back in the alley, a bruised and bewildered officer whom Fitzpatrick had earlier whacked with the butt of his pistol was now screaming for others in the street to take Fitzpatrick down.

Traffic came to a standstill. Drivers honked their delay at the roadblock. Others who knew what was happening sat tight for fear of getting involved in the shooting.

'Zulu 99! Update location!' screamed Anthea on the radio.

'Fuelling! Airborne soon!' came the reply.

'Solo One!' radioed Anthea as she tried to contact a surveillance officer riding a motorcycle. 'Where are you?'

'Two miles north! Attending! Estimated time of arrival three minutes. Traffic heavy but making progress!'

'You couldn't make it up,' thought Anthea. 'Not a damn thing is going according to plan.'

Fitzpatrick ran into an underground tube station with the team quickly surrounding the area and closing in.

Only Anthea was fit enough to break into a sprint and enter the tube station where Fitzpatrick was last seen. All those fitness days in Epsom Forest paid off when she hurdled the ticket barriers, dodged a guard trying to question her intentions, and then slid down the shoulder of the same escalator that was carrying Fitzpatrick into the depths of the London Underground system.

Moments later, Anthea arrived at the platform to watch a tube train pulling away on its way to central London. She looked around, scoured the two platforms available, and realised Fitzpatrick was nowhere to be seen.

On reaching the next stop at Stockwell, Fitzpatrick adopted a composed attitude and walked from the train. He jumped over the ticket barrier, strolled quickly into the fresh air, and disappeared into the heart of the capital.

Collapsing to the ground, then leaning against the black and white tiles that graced the walls of Brixton Tube station, Anthea was overwhelmed with a feeling of failure.

'Why?' she asked herself as her heartbeat approached breaking point and she gulped mouthfuls of oxygen into her lungs. 'Why today? I did everything right. I went for one man. Not an army. Ordinarily, I wouldn't have needed a helicopter, a hundred cops and a borough locked down. So why today? What did I do wrong?'

'You okay, Guvnor?' queried a breathless Terry when he arrived at Anthea's side. 'We'll get him. Don't you worry, Guvnor. We'll get him.'

'Yes!' replied Anthea hauling herself onto her feet. 'Trouble is I wanted him today not tomorrow or next week. Today! All I'll get now is questions, questions, and questions. We are at rock bottom, Terry. The unit is a laughingstock. Confidence in us will be lost. We're finished.'

'We're only finished when we get to the winning line,' replied Terry. 'Come on! We need a drink.'

'No! I think I need a holiday with my husband.'

'Ricky says Scotland Yard has a message for you.'

'Such as?'

'Reminds me of Boyd,' suggested Terry.

'Boyd! Bloody Boyd,' snapped Anthea. 'Shut up talking about bloody Boyd.'

'Where is he?' queried Terry.

'I've no idea. He's not with us anymore. We need to get better, improve, use the brain as well as the body. I should have locked the area down, tripled the raiding party, and arranged total closure for an armed suspect. I underestimated the enemy.'

'Message from control, Guvnor,' reported Terry. 'The Commissioner wants to see you. Sounds like a Boyd thing. I wonder where he is?'

~

7

Solitude Beach
Cabeco da Ponto, The Island of Porto Santo
Madeira Archipelago, Portugal
Simultaneously: The same day.

The never-ending waves of the Atlantic Ocean crashed onto the isolated beach where the golden sand was soft and unbroken by the presence of man. The tide ran its course, paused when the shore began to rise upwards more severely, and then returned only to surge forth again when the next wave followed in constant succession.

At six miles long and bordering the coast of the island of Porto Santo, the deserted coastline was complimented by the occasional seabird swooping unchallenged from the dunes to the beach and then onward towards the ocean where it bobbed up and down relentlessly, danced on the crest of the waves, and then soared once more into the heavens above.

Today, three strangers visited the place of pure solitude.

The trio parked their car on the roadway adjacent to the beach and sat for a while watching the surroundings. They were alone and unseen. Only the forever plunging seabirds witnessed their arrival but could not betray their presence.

One of the men exited the rear passenger compartment of the vehicle and strolled for a short distance along the highway in both directions. It was as if he was looking for something. On returning to the car, he nodded and waited for his colleagues to join him on the roadside.

They shook hands and bid farewell.

The man stood six foot tall, was cleanshaven, sported dark hair and a proportionate body, and was casually dressed in Chino trousers, a short-sleeved shirt, and a wide-brimmed straw beach hat. Carrying a holdall, he crossed the road and made for the dunes. He valued his privacy, wanted to reflect on his past, and waited for one man to appear on the beach and join him.

His two colleagues drove off and adopted a new position where they parked up and used binoculars to monitor proceedings.

'How long?' wondered the man in the dunes. Only his breathing could be heard as he waited for his liberator.

Boyd stowed the flight travel magazine and attached his seat belt as they approached Porto Santo Airport.

Located in Vila Baleira, the capital of Porto Santo Island, Madeira, the discreet private flight had taken off from RAF Brize Norton in Oxfordshire and was shortly to arrive at the military air base in Porto Santo. The base was operated by the Portuguese Air Force who shared its facilities with Porto Santo Airport.

Nudging his fellow passenger, Sir Phillip Nesbitt; Director General of M15, Boyd remarked, 'Phillip! We're almost there. We're on the glide path.'

Phillip, yawned, stretched, and replied, 'Nearly there? Oh! Where were we? What was I saying?'

'You were telling me about the reason for my holiday,' replied Boyd. 'That was over the Bay of Biscay. You fell asleep. I think it's you who needs the holiday, not me.'

'Correct,' chuckled Phillip. 'What do you make of it so far?'

'I've worked out why MI6 want me, and where you fit in. It all started with me and MI5. Years later both organisations have an interest and neither of them wants to upset the other. I can see why you have a concern. I'd call it organisational power sharing. If it goes wrong, then you'll need to label it something else.'

'Good! Glad you worked that one out. There are two reasons,' continued Phillip. 'One is to meet Abraham at his request, and the other is to lead the recruitment of Ushanka when we return to London. I understand Julian has mentioned Ushanka to you.'

'Leaving Ushanka to one side for a moment,' remarked Boyd. 'There's more to what you say than that. It's because you don't want to be connected to either operation currently underway. Today, you want me to assess Abraham and him back to your fold, his warts and all. If anything goes wrong, what better for you than to be able to point the finger at a police officer who is currently suspended from duty because he's lost his sharpness? He's stressed out, overworked, underpaid, and losing his self-confidence. In addition, one more mistake will make him a laughingstock.'

'You're talking about yourself again,' scolded Phillip with a twisted smile.

'I'm ideal for you and MI6,' replied Boyd. 'Tell me, I'm wrong in that assessment.'

Squirming in his seat, the Director General tightened his seatbelt in response to a cabin announcement, and replied, 'I respect your deliberations, Boyd, but some might say that you started this operation years ago in Carlisle when you were a young detective and you identified him to us as an Arab Jew that we might be interested in. You ought not to be complaining now. You started it all.'

'I was wet behind the ears then. I never understood what that meant,' replied Boyd. 'Arab Jew?'

'It's a term attributed to Jews living in or originating from the Arab world. The term is politically challenged, usually by people who believe in the development and protection of Israel.'

'Zionists?' queried Boyd.

'Correct! Many Arab Jews prefer to be called Mizrahi Jews because it reveals they are from the Middle East or North Africa and can trace their Jewish religious beliefs back to biblical times.'

'Interesting.'

'Many left or were expelled from Arab countries in the decades following the founding of Israel in 1948. They took up residence in Israel, Western Europe, the United States and

Latin America,' explained Phillip. 'It's estimated, for example, that when the State of Israel was created in 1948, approximately 150,000 Jews lived in Iraq. Many of them left and began new lives elsewhere. Some were expelled. Some gradually embraced Islam.'

'What, all of them followed Allah?' probed Boyd.

'Not all. An unknown number,' replied Phillip. 'The use of the term 'Arab Jew' is controversial since most Jews, with origins in mainstream Arab countries, do not identify as Arabs, and those Jews who live amongst Arabs do not call themselves Arab Jews, or view themselves as such.'

'So now I know what an Arab Jew is,' ventured Boyd. 'It's complicated, Phillip.'

'For us, it's simple, Boyd. Occasionally, Jewish people living in Arab countries may change their religion from Judaism to Islam in much the same way that a Church of England follower in the UK might change to Catholicism. For me, I see them as people with a potential to put a foot in both camps.'

'One way of looking at it, I suppose.'

'You first recruited Abraham from a doctor's surgery in Cumbria twenty years ago when you identified him as having a brother in Iraq's Republican Guard. That's the equivalent of our Special Forces and it was useful when the war in Iraq started. Abraham didn't get on with his brother, if you recall, did not share his aspirations, and was a member of the opposition Dawa party in Iraq. He gave you information regarding the local Iraqi population in Cumbria and, when you'd drained him, we took him over and handed him to MI6 who are responsible for intelligence-gathering operations in the Middle East. Remember that?'

'Oh yes, one of my first operations with British Intelligence,' replied Boyd. 'But he's not with MI6 now, is he?'

'No,' replied Phillip. 'He's with Mossad. We procured an intelligence-sharing arrangement with Mossad and traded Abraham to them because of his Arab Jew label. He blends into both arenas.'

'A foot in both camps, like you said. What did we get in return?' questioned Boyd.

'Intelligence on Hezbollah: A Lebanese Shia Islamist political party and militant group.'

'Yes, I know of them,' nodded Boyd as he peered out of the window and watched the ground coming into view as the plane descended. 'They are a proscribed terrorist organisation in the UK. They tell me Hezbollah is a state within a state, it is so powerful.'

'True, and not for the good. It is also designated a terrorist organisation in the European Union and most of the Arab league. Notably, Boyd, Hezbollah is one of Lebanon's most influential political parties. Did you know that Russia does not view Hezbollah as a 'terrorist organisation' but considers it to be a 'legitimate socio-political force.'

'That Russia supports,' chuckled Boyd finishing the sentence. 'Are you telling me Abraham is a major player?'

'Yes! He's one of Mossad's top agents but he's running out of steam. He's been in the desert, in Lebanon, in Iraq, just about everywhere. Even Dubai where he drove a taxi for a few years and penetrated big business, and anyone connected to Hezbollah and a dozen other such terrorist organisations. You know what Dubai is like. It's the world's biggest crossroads because everyone wants to holiday there, work there, set up a business there, whatever. Dubai was built on oil between 1960 and 1990. Oil gave them power. Power made money. Money is power and Dubai is where it's all at.'

'A good place for a spy, you might argue.'

'Exactly!'

'Hey! I might get a pay rise out of this?' chuckled Boyd.

'I doubt it,' replied Phillip. 'Abraham is on the verge of making mistakes and needs extracting from the game.'

'Who does he remind you of?' remarked Boyd. '

'You!' declared Phillip. 'Worn-out batteries lose their power. They need to be recharged when that happens.'

'I'm powerless to respond,' grinned Boyd.

'You're currently plugged in,' winked Phillip. 'I'll get you back online. Just bear with me.'

'So,' suggested Boyd with a wry smile, 'You want a worn-out unusable soul like me to stroll along a beach, meet an exhausted tramp of a taxi driver, and see what's on offer?'

'Yes! I trust you, Boyd. You, your wife Meg, Toni, and I, have been friends for a few years. Do you know that only you and I are allowed to call Antonia Toni?'

'I wondered if that was correct, yes,' smiled Boyd.

'Trust is a funny thing, Boyd. I trust you because I know you if you come back on your own it's a no sale and if you bring him back it's a sale.'

'I see,' replied Boyd. 'What do you think of Abraham?'

'Abraham thinks he is in danger of losing his life if Russia, or any of his enemies, know what he is doing. He's given the best part of his life to the cause of peace. I think he's had enough.'

'Why here?' queried Boyd.

'You introduced Abraham to us in a park on the banks of the River Eden in Carlisle. We took him and you never saw him again. This is where we handed him over to Mossad,' revealed Phillip. 'Far from the preying eyes of the masses. A place of true solitude.'

'Is it?' remarked Boyd. 'I've never been here before.'

'He asked to see you here in Porto Santo.'

'Why me?'

'I don't know because I've not spoken to him. I guess he wants to draw a line in the sand. It's over for him. He wants out and he wants those who started him off to finish him off. Mossad has had the best of him. My experience in handling such assets is that it's an emotional state that he finds himself in. It's like retiring and not wanting to go but you know that you should. He has a life of freedom before him and will find himself financially secure for the rest of his life if the sale is on and proves workable.'

'I'd like to apply for his job,' proposed Boyd. 'But I'm not an Arab Jew so I'll fail at the first interview question.'

'You will,' acknowledged an expressionless Phillip. 'His emotional state must be recognised, Boyd. There's a lot to play for and we've decided the situation ought not to be dealt with by a committee, a government department, or the Security and Intelligence Committee.'

'You're taking a chance on that,' responded Boyd. 'That committee is the be-all and end-all of the State's response to national security and the intelligence game. You're taking a chance, Phillip. They might bring you down if it all goes wrong. They could destroy you.'

'It's all about power, Boyd. They'll sit and debate the matter for a couple of days before deciding. Abraham wants out now. Not tomorrow or next week. He's a worried man, that much I do know. The Foreign Office oversee MI6. There's an argument that suggests we oversee the government.'

'Makes you wonder who is in power,' quipped Boyd.

'We trust you to make the right decision. See what Abraham has to offer and decide out there on your own.'

'On my own! Suspended! Unwanted! A media target back home! And you want me to make a crucial decision that is ordinarily made at government level. Have you ever considered that Mossad is double-crossing British Intelligence? Think about it, Phillip. What a way to fool you. Sometimes your closest friends will sell you down the river if it suits them, and that includes Mossad.'

'Mossad is trading intelligence and the source of that intelligence is an Arab Jew who is a taxi driver in Dubai. They want our ongoing support against Hezbollah and middle eastern terrorist organisations, and Russia. Some of whom are traced to associates in the UK, USA and elsewhere. We have high-value intelligence sources in play at the technological level. They have the physical assets on the ground. It's a perfect combination to improve the quality and quantity of intelligence gathering in the Middle East.'

'On the ground human sources and various listening posts across the globe,' nodded Boyd in silent reflection.

'Mossad want controlled access in exchange for Abraham's information that he will impart to you today. That's how they work. It's an enigmatic globe of ingenuity that proves their capabilities. They are the best intelligence agency in the world.'

'And us!

'We'll agree if shared intelligence continues. Mossad is using Abraham as a tool and he's happy to be used because he wants out.'

'The complexity of power,' replied Boyd. 'Its importance, its use, its misuse, and how the holder of power can use it to the best of his advantage when he chooses.'

'Are you in a one, Boyd? One step ahead of the game as usual. Reel it in. I haven't finished yet.'

'Sorry! You were saying.'

'Abraham wants to come back to us and allow us to repatriate him to the UK. He's in danger. He knows it and so does Mossad.'

'Then I'd recommend somewhere far away from the British Isles,' replied Boyd. 'But that's not my decision.'

The plane touched down, taxied to the stand, and was met by MI6 officers. Essentially, the two organisations – MI5 and MI6 – were working together as British Intelligence.

Sir Julian's men transported them to Solitude Beach.

Barefooted, wearing a tee shirt, shorts, and a straw beach hat, Boyd gestured farewell to the MI6 cluster and set off towards a man called Abraham. He turned and asked, 'How far before I meet him?'

'He'll join you when he's ready,' replied Phillip. 'I imagine he'll make sure you are alone. He'll be in the dunes, I suspect.'

Boyd nodded and strolled along the shoreline for what seemed like an eternity. Checking the horizon, he peered out to sea but couldn't see a ship anywhere in the far Atlantic. The Cumbrian felt the warmth of the sun on his skin, watched the seabirds cavorting along the coastline, and eventually became aware of a man walking parallel to him in the dunes.

Recalling Phillip's advice about Abraham's emotional state, Boyd slowly removed his hat and then his tee shirt. He made a show of shaking the tee shirt in the thin breeze and hoped Abraham would understand that he was unarmed and there were no wires connected to his body.

The man turned from the dunes and approached his potential liberator.

'Abraham!' voiced Boyd. 'Masada shall not fall again.'

'Tell Shamir, tell Rabin; we are the sons of Saladin.'

Boyd had deliberately opened the conversation mentioning an ancient fortification in the Negev Desert, Israel. It was known as Masada and was built by Herod the Great, the King of Judea, between 37 and 31 BC. It is where the Jewish people defended themselves from the Roman Legions that had sacked Jerusalem and to which many had travelled to make their last stand in the face of an overwhelming enemy. Masada is a place now synonymous with power, courage, and respect in the Jewish world.

Masada is also where a solemn oath is taken by all members of the Israeli Defence Forces.

Abraham's reply was a rhythmic announcement chanted by Palestinian protesters at demonstrations and was considered anti-Jewish, and anti-Israel.

When Boyd cited the oath, 'Masada shall not fall again,' Abraham knew there was only one reply Boyd would make.

'Tell Shamir, tell Rabin; we are the sons of Saladin,' repeated Boyd. 'That will get you into trouble, Abraham.'

'Perhaps, but only if I was of true Arab descent and hated Jews with every breath I draw.'

'You've not changed then,' voiced Boyd. 'You were never afraid to step out of line when you needed to.'

'I know you, Mr Boyd. It's the only response you would expect me to give in the circumstances. You were testing me.'

'Was I?' challenged Boyd. 'Why would I do such a thing?'

'Because you need to know whether my time with Israel, Mossad, and the intelligence war is over. Using the extreme beliefs of the Palestinians in response to the Jews seemed the quickest way to get it over to you.'

'You succeeded,' acknowledged Boyd with a wry smile.

'You know I am with Mossad. I'm here because I want out.'

'Then let's see if that is possible,' replied Boyd.

'Do you remember me?' asked Abraham.

'Yes,' replied Boyd. 'How could I ever forget you?'

The formalities over, the two men clasped each other's hands and then embraced like long-lost brothers. It was as if an unbroken bond existed between them. An aged relationship based on a connection between a young detective and a young informant that had stood the test of time.

'It's been twenty years since the River Eden,' remarked Boyd.

'Too long. Will you walk with me?' queried Abraham.

'Of course.'

The pair turned and walked by the sea. They stood gazing across the ocean as the tide ended its journey and drizzled across their toes in the final act before disappearing into the sand.

'Do you remember those days so long ago? I mean when I worked for you and then you passed me on?'

'I do,' replied Boyd anxiously. 'Why? What troubles you?'

Abraham chuckled and said, 'You told me when it was time to get out that I should insist on seeing you. I remembered.'

'Good!' smiled Boyd. 'It was our secret. But I never thought you would remember those words. Do you regret what I said?'

'No! I was special to you, and you were special to me. You traded me. I have no regrets. I agreed to move to where I would be more useful. Such is the way of the world, and our world is one of spying and finding out who betrays us, who we can trust, and who are our enemies.'

'That's one way of looking at it,' nodded Boyd.

'I hope I can still trust you, Mr Boyd,' said Abraham.

'I brought my hat,' replied Boyd. 'Is that not enough?'

'Perhaps,' smiled Abraham doffing his headgear in deference to the detective. 'It's something you taught me years ago. I was testing you.'

'I presumed you were. Shall we walk a little more and enjoy the sunshine and the seabirds?'

'Yes!' answered Abraham. 'They are the only witnesses to our conversation and that is what I wanted to achieve. That's why I picked a place of solitude.'

'It's a beautiful beach and I'm listening to you,' clarified Boyd. 'You asked about trust so let me tell you I believed in you years ago. Never doubted you. We've both moved on, but I can see it in your eyes.'

'What do you see?' asked Abraham quizzically.

'The same old colour, the same old nervous flash, the same old sudden movement of the eyes when you talk. Now tell me what you have to offer, my friend. That's why I'm here. Now take a deep breath and don't be nervous.'

'It's something I alone discovered and passed to my handler. I helped put two and two together otherwise Mossad would never have had the full picture.'

'I'm intrigued. Carry on,' ventured Boyd.

Abraham declared, 'I'm aware from my sources in Mossad that Yousef Abdul Halim dropped a person called Jamil Volkov off at an airport in Dagestan. The Russians abducted Yousef. He's never been seen since. Mossad presumes he has been tortured and murdered by the FSB.'

'Why was this man Yousef abducted?' queried Boyd.

'The FSB kidnapped him because they wanted to know everything about him. Leastways, that's how Mossad analysed it. But the Russians also wanted to know about Jamil Volkov whom Yousef had dropped off at the local airport. The men are best described as persons of interest.'

'Persons of interest!' mused Boyd. 'Keep it simple, Abraham. How would that put you in danger?'

Abraham paused, looked Boyd in the eye, and replied, 'I worked undercover as a taxi driver at an airport in Dubai. All I did was pick up fares and take them to their hotel, the airport, or wherever they needed to be. But part of that work involved identifying persons of interest to whom I gave lifts. I carried Americans, Canadians, Australians, Europeans, Japanese and Chinese. I carried Jews, Arabs, Christians, Muslims, and Hindus by taxi. It didn't take long to work out who was on holiday and who was on business. I soon got the hang of who was who in Dubai. For some, it's a meeting place: A stopover where money exchanges hands and ideas are discussed and either progressed or abandoned.'

'Sounds like Lisbon in the Second World War.'

'I wouldn't know about Lisbon, Mr Boyd. Mossad showed me photographs of the main people I should focus on.'

'And you have a photographic memory, if I recall correctly.'

'Precisely,' nodded Abraham. 'And it still works, Mr Boyd. Slower now as I get older, but my brain still holds what I tell it to.'

Boyd returned an endearing smile as the pair continued walking south along the beach and said, 'No taxis here, Abraham. Not even a dune buggy.'

Chuckling for a moment, Abraham replied, 'One day I picked up a fare from the airport in Dubai. It's a long story, but Yousef was a getaway driver for Jamil Volkov. He drove Jamil away from a bombing in Makhachkala to the local airport. Jamil was the bomber. I picked Jamil up at the Dubai airport and reported the matter to

Mossad. As a result, they were able to do some more work before they eventually confirmed that Jamil had flown from Makhachkala.'

'Lucky?' quizzed Boyd.

'No! I was doing my job.'

'Never heard of either of them,' replied Boyd with a quizzical look on his face.

'I didn't think you would have heard of them. The Russians still control the media and if you think the Iron Curtain is a thing from the past, then I'd say no, not entirely.'

'I'm with you,' replied Boyd. 'Go on.'

'I'm telling you the truth, Mr Boyd. Yousef was Jamil's getaway driver. That's all Yousef ever did. He was the lookout for Jamil. End of story. Jamil Volkov never operated in your neck of the woods. He was in my taxi. I secretly took his photograph, and I showed it to my Mossad handler in Dubai. It turns out Jamil was involved in a bomb attack in Makhachkala, Dagestan. Jamil detonated two bombs at a public event attended by a high-ranking colonel from Moscow called Oleg Novikova.'

Boyd committed the name to his memory.

'The colonel was killed by the bomb and hundreds were injured,' continued Abraham. 'Quite a few locals were also killed. That's the way of Jamil. If it means taking a few of his own so that he can kill a top man and make a point, then that's Jamil through and through. He's a violent man, Mr Boyd, and he'll show no mercy.'

Boyd nodded and stored Abraham's information in various segments of his brain. It was new intelligence, not heard before by Western intelligence agencies.

'The bombing was pure devastation,' continued Abraham. 'Jamil Volkov is now wanted in various parts of Russia for bomb attacks on their government. He's been a one-man army for years. By the way, he's a Muslim and he set these bombs off because Moscow is recruiting Muslims.'

'Why is Moscow doing that?'

'To send them to the war in Ukraine. They're supplementing the Russian army there. Jamil thinks it's a deliberate policy of getting rid of Muslims because they're getting a pounding from Ukraine's army. Moscow is happy to get rid of Muslims but not their people who tend to be mainly members of the Russian Orthodox Church.'

'Okay! Understood,' voiced Boyd.

'You see, Mr Boyd, Islam has never been truly welcomed in Russia. I'd say it has been allowed to evolve as opposed to having been encouraged to evolve. The Russian State has managed its presence over the years. The war in Ukraine is a way of getting rid of unwanted people. It's common knowledge that some of the conscripts Russia are using are criminals released from prison so that they can fight in Ukraine. You just call them heroes and then send them to the front line knowing they may never come back.'

'You don't mince words, Abraham.'

'It's the way it is. I've learnt over the years to question why those in power make decisions relevant to the lives of others. You put me there, Mr Boyd. What did you expect of me?'

'I capitulate,' gestured Boyd. 'It's my fault, Abraham. I never meant to cause you such problems. That said, some would say Jamil is on our side. Particularly when his target is a hostile enemy like Russia. Tell me, how sure are you that it was... err. James... Jam...'

'Volkov!' corrected Abraham. 'Jamil Volkov.'

'Thank you.'

'Oh, it's him alright,' explained Abraham. 'He gave me a two hundred Dirham banknote in payment for the taxi ride. I passed it on to my handler who later confirmed that the fingerprints on it belong to Jamil Volkov who was convicted of an offence when he was engaged in student protests.'

'Good! I understand. I'm still listening.'

'He's in England,' stated Abraham to Boyd's surprise. 'Probably London.'

Boyd rubbed his chin in puzzlement and eventually replied, 'A Russian Muslim is wanted by the Russians for killing senior Russian military officers! That's a bit of a problem, Abraham. Some politicians in London might just want to turn a blind eye and a deaf ear to that one. Jamil might kill the Russian president.'

'He's capable,' suggested Abraham.

'Do you know why he's in London?'

'I think so.'

'Tell me who told you this, Abraham?'

'I'm not just a pretty face, Mr Boyd. I'm not just a taxi driver for Mossad either. I'm an intelligence analyst too.'

'Who taught you that?'

'You! You taught me the basics in Carlisle. I improved when I went on holiday with MI6 and then Mossad.'

Boyd held his breath for a while, wondered how much Abraham's abilities had changed over the years, and then challenged the Arab Jew with, 'Those Muslims you mentioned are Russian by birth, Abraham. I'm not convinced your intelligence assessment is correct. For one thing, a significant part of the Russian army in Ukraine are mercenaries not under the control of the Kremlin. Mercenaries are famous for following the money and not the politics. I need more detail before making a final analysis.'

'I'll bear that in mind,' replied Abraham.

'Russia surely wants to win the war, not risk it by using Muslim conscripts with little expertise?'

'Then we'll agree to differ,' replied Abraham.

'Okay! We'll move on. You mentioned London,' remarked Boyd. 'Do you have anyone particular in mind that you think Jamil Volkov might try to assassinate?'

'There's no current intelligence but if you want my assessment, I'd say he intends to kill the ambassador from the embassy in Kensington. He's the top Russian in England.'

Boyd nodded casually in agreement.

'Then there's a couple of celebrity ballet dancers currently touring the UK. They are pro-Russia and support the Russian president. I made a list of possibles for you. Here it is. They've all got family connections in Russia.' Abraham handed it to Boyd saying, 'You have a former prime minister who claims his great-great-grandmother was a Circassian slave from southern Russia, near the Black Sea. She was sold to his great-great-grandfather. Then you have a former senior politician who is related on his father's side of the family to a Russian baroness of German, Polish and Ukrainian descent. He's also related to an attorney general of the Imperial Russian Senate. If Jamil knows who amongst them are supporters of the Russian State as it is at present, then his targets may be on that list.'

Boyd nodded his understanding and took stock of the man he had recruited twenty years ago as a spy for the West. He marvelled at the knowledge Abraham had accrued as he browsed the list and heard the Arab Jew say, 'Also on the list are dozens of actors and actresses who all have Russian family connections. You'll find some of them on Google if you care to search. With so many, Mr Boyd, I'm sure some of them support Russia in various ways.'

'There's always been a lot of British people with strong family connections in Russia,' replied Boyd. 'During the war, Russia were our allies. They lost millions of people and fought with us against the Nazis. If Russia hadn't joined us in the war against the Nazis Europe might look a whole lot different today. Russia could boast a thousand heroes who fought and died to deny Hitler his desire to rule Europe. You see, that's the problem with powerhouses and the media. People who have never met a Russian judge them because of what they watch on the television or what they read in a newspaper. Most of that material has to do with the President and his foreign policy. It seldom reflects the genuine Russian personality which is more akin to normal people than you might imagine.'

'You've been to Russia then, Mr Boyd.'

The detective did not reply. He glanced elsewhere.

'So that's a yes,' voiced Abraham. 'You just can't talk about it. My problem is that I don't know how those individuals on the list feel about Russia anymore. My mind overflows with puzzles to work out. But you asked for targets. You have the list.'

'Put yourself in my position for a moment, Abraham. An Arab Jew working for Mossad – part of the Israel Defence Forces that serve the Jewish nation – approaches me with a story that a Muslim terrorist is in London and is intent on killing Christians of Russian origin. But I know that some of those proposed targets are Christian-born English people with historic family backgrounds that trace to Russia. That's not at all unusual given the history of our two countries. Is the Muslim terrorist the dilemma or is the Arab Jew the problem? I know the two countries are mates via that Memorandum of Agreement but are you acting on behalf of Mossad trying to feed British Intelligence with a story that will result in us destroying Jamil Volkov and provoking his Arab friends in the Middle East? If so, Israel would not be held responsible for the killings. We would carry the can and the rest of the world would point a finger at us. A clever move by Mossad that might cause other nations to blame the British. On the global stage, Israel walks free from criticism whilst the UK must find answers to awkward questions. Are you more Jewish than Arab? I'm entitled to ask.'

'You weren't sent to help me,' derided Abraham. 'You came to assess me. I can't trust you anymore. You might even be in the pay of the Russians if you've been to Russia.'

'Trust is a two-way street,' challenged Boyd. 'Are Mossad trying to use British Intelligence like a proxy bomb?'

'What do you mean by that – Proxy bomb?'

'Ahh! Come on, Abraham. You know what a proxy bomb is. Except this isn't Northern Ireland and no one is holding your wife captive and promising to release her once you've delivered the bomb to the target.'

'I'm not married.'

'I'm losing patience with you. A proxy bomb is when you lie to someone who then goes off and kills the target because of the lie that they have chosen to believe. For example, a false story is presented and results in the British being fooled into doing Mossad's work. Assassination by deception, I call it.'

Abraham looked overwhelmed for a moment.

'Assessment? No reply! You're not doing very well. Let me test your analytical skills further,' challenged Boyd. 'Why did the war in Ukraine break out and how does the West win it?'

Abraham shook his head in annoyance and replied, 'That's the problem with you guys. You don't understand the past and how it frames the future.'

'What do you mean by that?'

'Russia once had a president called Gorbachev. He was an anti-communist, a supporter of the Israel-Palestine peace process, and wanted to cosy up to the West to make the world a safer place. He gave lots of Russian republics their freedom and ended the Soviet Union. The republics became nations governing themselves. He planned for all those republics to form a geo-political buffer zone between NATO and Russia. No one was allowed to create a military base in any of those former republics. How did NATO respond? I'll tell you, Mr Boyd. They moved into the zone before it had even been created, crept closer militarily to Russia, and ignored the hand of peace offered by Gorbachev.'

Boyd nodded his understanding and knew he had to keep Abraham talking politics for a while. Boyd recognised he had to decide where Abraham stood politically because it was part of the process that might decide whether he was part of a Mossad operation to fool the British. Had Abraham been briefed to raise specific items for discussion? Or was this just Abraham articulating?

'Instead of searching for peace,' continued Abraham. 'NATO stepped into those former republics and set up military bases. Russia analysed that as an aggressive movement towards them and it all fell through when the Russian Establishment removed Gorbachev in favour of Boris Yeltsin. Since then, Russian leaders have been trying to regain the lost republics.'

Boyd acquiesced and turned around to face the direction they had walked. He set off strolling towards the airport and noticed that Abraham immediately fell into step alongside him.

'Ukraine, Mr Boyd! Why does Russia want Ukraine back? I'll tell you one analysis and you won't like it because you've told me that you no longer trust me.'

'I didn't put it like that,' argued Boyd.

'Kyiv was the first capital of Russia, not Moscow which was once an irrelevant Slavic village. Vladimir the Great was the first real leader of Kyiv. He was a Christian. There have been at least three other emperors or leaders of Kyiv called Vladimir. The name Vladimir is of Slavic origin. It means to rule with greatness, with power, with world dominance. What's the first name of the Russian president?'

'Vladimir!' declared Boyd.

'Correct!'

'He could be replaced at any time,' suggested Boyd. 'It just needs one rival to successfully challenge his authority and his reputation will suffer. When that happens, it's only a question of time before a coup occurs and he's removed.'

'You're right, Mr Boyd. Historically, power at the top in Russia has always taken some holding onto once it has been acquired. But let me take you back to Boris Yeltsin because what I will tell you is fact, not fiction. And if the current president went tomorrow, his successor, or future successors, may well refer to the past to argue their intentions regarding Ukraine or any other former republic.'

'I'm all ears,' replied Boyd.

'Yeltsin bent over backwards to ensure his favourite replaced him. Now Russia is run by a power-hungry megalomaniac who believes that Ukraine has always been Russian.'

'His successors might follow suit,' proposed Boyd.

'But in a different manner,' argued Abraham. 'Anyway, the Russian president is a man with an insatiable appetite for power and wealth. Some Russians love him because he wants back what is rightfully Russian, not Ukrainian. And NATO's view of stopping the war is to win it. There's never been a search for peace regarding the war in Ukraine. Surely there's enough scope to talk about peace instead of war? How do we stop the war in Ukraine? Talk peace, not war! History is never mentioned by your media. Recent history yes, maybe. Ancient history that is important to the Motherland? I suggest no! You decide, Mr Boyd!'

'Fascinating,' replied Boyd. 'But then I've never had much time for the media back home myself. I've watched the media destroy public figures and often thought it was as state controlled as it is in Russia. I'm conscious that the media could destroy anyone's reputation if it wanted to. And that's before I get anywhere near to talking about social media.'

'Including you, Mr Boyd? Could it destroy you?'

'Probably, Abraham. It's just a different methodology in play to the one the so-called Motherland adopted.'

Boyd wondered if the media back home was still running stories about his failure in Brixton. Was this another slippery slope that would see him fall to the bottom of the pile?

Laughing now, Abraham professed, 'Wow! We finally agreed on something. Look, Mr. Boyd, Jamil Volkov is not just a man you need to trace and eliminate before he kills someone. He could be a vital tool in the search for peace in the war. Jamil is fighting his own battle to stop the war in Ukraine. Don't you see that if the Russian embassy got hold of him before you, they could do a dozen things in England and blame it on Jamil? They could make you guys look like fools, antagonise you in a score of different ways, and then assassinate him on British soil because you can't find him. They could blame him for everything and manipulate it into another reason why the war in Ukraine must be won. If you find him first and prove his point about Muslims being used in the war, then that might make everyone closer to talking about peace instead of planning war. What do you think?'

'I think the West see the enemy as a power-hungry megalomaniac with an insatiable desire for complete supremacy. Give him an inch and he'll take a mile, and then another one until he's got back every republic Gorbachev liberated. I understand your argument, Abraham. They are sound. The truth is that the so-called Commander in Chief isn't interested in peace.'

'I'm sorry you don't share my view.'

'Don't be,' replied Boyd. 'I think you are trying to tell me that Jamil Volkov might hold a key to peace in the Middle East and if that turns out to be the case then I'll try to turn that key to the best of my ability.'

Nodding, allowing a weak grin to crawl across his face, Abraham replied, 'That's what I wanted to hear. There are many keys to turn but if we can turn one, then it's a start.'

'Good!'

'But you are just one irrelevant man.'

'If you join me, we are two and have just doubled the club membership.'

'Maybe one day,' replied Abraham. 'We have got a long way to go.'

'Is that why you joined the spying game?'

'To enable the peace process? Yes! I suppose it is.'

'What else is for sale, Abraham?'

'Just my hat! I'm standing on Solitude Beach on an island in the middle of the Atlantic with not a friend in sight and nowhere to go. I know the two men from Mossad who brought me here withdrew and have probably been watching us for a while. Do you think they are still watching?'

'I doubt it,' replied Boyd. 'We're a fair distance from where we first began walking and I'm sure my colleagues have disrupted their activity. What have you got for me, Abraham?'

'If I turn back, I'm finished. I know it's only a question of time before I'm a body in a gutter with a hole in the head. The Russians are after me. I feel it in my bones. Maybe even Hezbollah too. After today, even Mossad might decide to terminate me. If they knew what I was about to tell you then they probably wouldn't let me walk off this beach.'

Curious, Boyd looked Abraham in the eye perplexed by the remark the Arab Jew had made.

'Can I walk a bit further with you? Give me a chance, Mr Boyd. Old time's sake!'

Another seabird swooped low over the incoming tide, squawked at a bird by its side, and then raced into the sky and headed for the dunes.

'You have my undivided attention,' replied Boyd as the pair enjoyed the sun beating down on their bodies and the waves of the Atlantic trickling over their feet as they paddled in the ocean.

Abraham removed his straw hat, used it as a fan, and then handed it to Boyd saying, 'You do remember, don't you?'

'Yes! I taught you all kinds of tricks. I see the hat has a band around it. Am I right in what I'm thinking?'

'When you examine the band around my hat you will find a microfiche hidden beneath it. You will give me your hat in exchange. That's why I asked you to bring a hat. I walked onto the beach wearing my hat. I'll walk off the beach wearing your hat.'

'Microfiche!' remarked Boyd. 'Microphotographs of what?'

'It identifies the members of Shamash operating in London.'

'Shamash? I've no idea what you are talking about, Abraham.'

'Do you know what a Menorah is, Mr Boyd?'

'It's a seven or nine-branched candelabra used in Hannukah.'

'And Hannukah is?'

'A festival that reaffirms the ideals of Judaism and commemorates the rededication of the Second Temple of Jerusalem by the lighting of candles on each day of the festival. It's derived from the Maccabean Jews who regained control of Jerusalem. It's a major part of the Jewish religion as well you know, Abraham.'

'And Shamash?'

'I've no idea,' admitted Boyd.

'You're right in what you say. A menorah is used in Hannukah, Mr Boyd. Take a nine-branched candelabra, for example. There are nine lights in a row with a special lamp in the middle. It is separated from the other eight and is called a Shamash. It stands higher than the others. This is the first candle lit in the ceremony and it is used to light the other eight candles. Shamash means servant and the Shamash candle serves and lights the other eight candles.'

'Fascinating! Are we finished? What the hell has a candle got to do with everything, Abraham?'

'Shamash is a secret organisation based in London and its function is to purge the Jewish community.'

'But you've just told me that Shamash is Jewish.'

'True! But you need to know that Shamash is a secret society that has been set up by the enemies of Israel. It is a fraud, Mr Boyd. It purports to be Jewish to attract the Jewish community. Its real purpose is to gather monies from the Jews and use it in the Sixth pillar of Islam.'

'The Sixth Pillar is Jihad?' replied Boyd. 'The Afghan Mujahideen, the Taliban, and Al Queda have all used that term in fighting wars.'

'You're forgetting the Muslims in Kashmir, Chechnya, Dagestan, the southern Philippines, Bosnia and Kosovo. Oh I could go on, Mr Boyd. Essentially, 'Jihad' means struggle and it's used to describe the war against the enemies of Islam. Shamash is a secret society with a Jewish name run by Arab warriors intent on diverting Jewish funds to the Arab war machine.'

'Whilst simultaneously identifying the Jewish community,' muttered a stunned Boyd.

'Al Queda are alive and well in London,' proposed Abraham. 'And that's where we will find Jamil Volkov. The Shamash Secret Society! It's all on the microfiche.'

Silence reigned. Boyd did not respond for a while until he finally said, 'I thought Jamil Volkov was a Muslim, not a Jew.'

'You're right. He is a Muslim and his target in Dagestan was the Colonel and the Russian State. When he left me in Dubai, he was escaping the Russians. Once in England, he needed support, finance, arms, ammunition, and maybe even explosives. He's going to get them from the Jihadists. Shamash is where he'll find support.'

'That makes sense, Abraham. He wouldn't be able to enter the country carrying an arsenal.'

'Check the microfiche when you are back in the office.'

'You're telling me that Al Qaeda is running a fundraising campaign in the UK by pretending to be Jews.'

'Yes! And with some Arab Jews at the forefront! When Al Qaeda discovered Arab Jews, they decided to recruit those who were more aligned with the Arab culture than the Jewish religion. You see, not all those Arab Jews left the State of Israel when it was born. Indeed, Al Qaeda didn't find many, but they only needed a handful to make Shamash work. Shamash will know where Jamil is because he is one of them, in their eyes, even though he's more interested in attacking the Russian government than anything else.'

Stunned, Boyd reflected on how British Intelligence had recruited an Arab Jew to penetrate the warring parts of the Arab culture only to realise on this day the enemy was up to the same trick. Right on his doorstep, and he didn't know anything about it.

'Why haven't Mossad told us this before?' queried Boyd.

'Because when I found out about Shamash, I decided not to tell my handler. I kept it to myself. I want out, Mr Boyd. My ticket is in the headband, and I call it Shamash. You were the first I worked for. You are the first I've spoken to about Shamash.'

'How did you find out about Shamash?'

'By putting together names of Jihadists meeting at the same place time and time again.'

Boyd exchanged hats and looked out to sea. He reflected on a decision to be made.

'You've gone quiet, Mr Boyd,' voiced Abraham. 'Did you hear me? What more is there to say?'

Standing, allowing the final race of the tide to tickle his toes and die in the sand, Boyd studied the horizon, a cloudless blue sky, and a dozen seabirds in haphazard flight. His eyes admired the beauty of it all as his mind wrestled.

'I'm on holiday,' remarked Boyd eventually as if he was talking to himself.

'What?' laughed Abraham. Sincerely, he offered, 'On holiday! Are you okay, Mr Boyd? Have you gone crazy? Has the sun got to you or is the sea too cold?'

'Yes! A holiday! That's why they sent me.'

'Oh!' replied a puzzled Abraham. 'I thought it was to assess me and what I had to offer.'

'No! A holiday! That's how it all started. Come on! We deserve ice cream and a long cold beer. By the way, you'll need this. Memorise the phone number and eat the card.' Boyd produced a business card bearing details of his work mobile and the Commercial Desk. 'My mobile for urgent matters. The desk is for less important stuff. It will be set up when I get back to London and not before.'

Abraham followed Boyd's instructions and replied, 'Don't like the taste of cardboard but I'll only use your direct number. I'm a stickler for personal safety. Sorry!'

'Good! Follow me,' ordered Boyd.' The two men strolled towards the airport as the detective suggested, 'We're in the same boat, my friend. No one wants us and everyone has used us and is still using us. The same people don't understand the journey we've been on, the desires we have, and the journey we are about to embark on. Come and join me in England. We will work it out there. Now that's a plan. Not a good one, but a start.'

Only a pair of footprints and a handful of seabirds witnessed the conversation. The words said and the decisions made were made in isolation. No one else heard them, not even the seabirds and the hidden crabs, not even the earthworms that lived beneath the surface of the sand.

Boyd and Abraham were united. In solitude!

Abraham gestured acceptance, casually fell in line with Boyd, and matched the detective stride for stride as they walked north towards Porto Santo and a flight to safety.

Sir Phillip nodded acceptance, knew Boyd had done the job required of him, and agreed that the story would be better told in

London. It would be some time before Boyd put pen to paper. In the quiet confines of rural England, Boyd wanted to go over Abraham's tale piece by piece before telling Phillip.

The flight took off without mishap, headed north for Brize Norton, and flew over the Bay of Biscay at thirty-five thousand feet.

~

8

The Command Centre,
The Special Crime Unit,
London, the same day.

The duty detective manned the 'commercial desk' that carried a dozen different coloured telephones in an area that was part of the unit's command centre. Situated next to the Ticker computerised intelligence office, the bank of telephones was a crucial part of the unit's work. Little was known of the 'commercial desk' outside of the unit and only those with high-grade security clearance were allowed to enter the room. The room was controlled by digital access and classified as 'Restricted' to most officers. Each phone was a different colour and purported to represent a business. But each business did not exist, was fictitious by nature, and took only incoming calls made by agents and informers in the pay of the unit.

A red telephone rang inspiring the duty detective to wheel his swivel desk chair to the location and check that the telephone was connected to part of the Ticker system. He pushed a button on the keyboard, read the associated computer screen, and reminded himself of who was calling and what his initial opening should be.

On the sixth ring, the detective answered the call with, 'Morning! Brady's Trade Centre! How can I help you today?'

'I want to book an electrician,' came the reply.

'Any particular one?' ventured the detective.

'Charlie Brady,' voiced the informant on the other end of the phone. 'Is the ten per cent discount still on offer?'

'I think you are out of date on that offer.'

'I was wrong It's fifteen per cent I think.'

'Yes, that's right. Charlie is just outside at the moment. Can you wait a few minutes?'

With an agreed protocol consisting of the previous sentences completed, the informant replied, 'I'm free to speak. The phone is good and no problems at this end.'

'What you got for us?' queried the duty detective.

'Message for Boyd from *Ground Sparrow*. Smudger, Budgie and Theo are planning a robbery on a security van. I know they are three-handed, but it's a seven-figure swoop so there might be four or five involved. I don't know for sure. Twice a day, the van collects money from businesses in South London and deposits it at the Central Bank in Dulwich. They are going to hit the security van at a department store on the High Street in Peckham close to the Legless Sailor pub. The van is constantly full of cash because it delivers to some and collects from others. Any time is a good time.'

'Got that,' replied the detective as he engaged a keyboard to map the area under discussion. 'When is it going down?'

'In an hour.'

'You involved?'

'No! I'm clean!'

'How do you know about the job?'

'A while back they pinched two chainsaws from a builder's yard in Lewisham. They rented a garage where the stuff was hidden. That's all you need to know. Tell Boyd I'll be at the usual place for a wedge. It's a good earner and I need the cash.'

The phone went dead leaving the detective tickling the keyboard to widen the map to include Dulwich, Lewisham, and other boroughs. He entered the analytical process and displayed recent crimes over the last month on the screen.

'Theft of chainsaws! Here we are,' noted the detective as he brought up the crime report and pressed a button on the underside of the desk.

A red glow emanated from a light at the entrance to the room, attracted the attention of all present, and was followed by the detective's voice on the loudspeaker system announcing, 'Listen up! The location is Peckham High Street. Target is a high-value security van containing cash. Possibly a seven-figure heist in progress! The weapons may include two chainsaws. The time of the attack is one hour. Printing off details of three suspects. Might be more. The source is recorded as Ten-Ten reliable. Guvnor! Full details to you.'

Anthea ripped the details from the printer, read the content, and acknowledged with, 'Got that!'. She shouted, 'Response teams Four, Five and Six. Mount up! Firearms are authorised! Ricky! Arrange a red blanket down on the approach. Standard Operating Procedure! Surround, contain, watch, and prepare to respond. Trigger incident is called.'

'Good luck!' shouted the detective who'd taken the call.

'Terry has command in my absence,' replied Anthea. 'By the way, cancel my appointment with the Commissioner, please. I'll touch base with his office upon my return.'

'Yeah! You sure, Guvnor?'

'Oh yes!' replied Anthea as she hit the buttons on a wall safe. 'This is what I'm paid to do and I'm going to fight to keep on doing it otherwise I'll end up sitting on my backside counting how many paperclips we use every week.'

'Okay! Right then!' came the reply. 'Are you sure?'

'Make the call!'

'Will do, Guvnor!'

A well-oiled procedure kicked into action as three response teams responded to *Ground Sparrow's* phone call. A wall safe was opened and handguns, holsters and ammunition were removed. A cabinet was unlocked, and rifles were taken. Body armour was dragged from individual wardrobes and quickly slid on. Hands reached out for ignition keys, removed them from the hook, and were pocketed. The office door was flung open. Anxious feet raced to the elevator. Buttons were pressed and the lift shaft surrendered as the soft murmur of the electronic winch whispered in the ear.

In record time, the armed response convoy of unliveried saloon cars and one command van swept out of the garage, climbed the incline, and burst out of its underground lair into the capital.

Fingers rattled across an electronic device and multiple sets of traffic lights stretching for over a mile suddenly changed to green.

The adrenaline was flowing when the Special Crime Unit answered the call, adopted the middle of the highway, and raced to Peckham scattering the oncoming traffic in the process. Headlights flashed and side windows were lowered when eager hands placed temporary magnetic blue lights on the vehicle roofs. A cacophony pounded the eardrums as the convoy thundered down the street to the sign of rhyming sirens.

A surge of adrenalin penetrated the souls involved. Heartbeats increased. Lungs breathed more efficiently. Blood vessels sent more blood to the brain and muscles. Brains became more alert and sugar levels in the blood pumped more energy into the system. There was no stronger bodily power than adrenalin.

Anthea engaged the central radio system, updated New Scotland Yard, and then radioed her team with, 'Kill all lights and sirens one mile from scene unless we are too late. Team Four straight through. Team Five plots to the near side. Team Six plot to the offside. The command van takes radio control of the operation with central command at NSY. Deploy drone surveillance – long-life battery. Trigger! Trigger! Trigger! All units respond!'

In team order, as was the custom, they responded to a voice of leadership, a determined leader, and a final message saying, 'This one is ours. No mistakes. Let's do it, guys.'

Pedestrianisation had not yet arrived in Peckham High Street where vehicles drove in both directions along the single carriageway. Only the traffic lights controlled the movement of cars when the security van drew into the kerb and parked outside a three-story department store close to the Legless Sailor.

The driver remained in the cash-in-transit van, but his front passenger slid onto the pavement carrying an empty cash deposit box. He entered the store fully aware that a third guard remained inside the rear of the van along with approximately one million pounds in cash parts of which were either being delivered to, or collected from, the various clients situated across the capital.

Inside the store, the security guard entered the administration area, opened his cash box, watched the store's finance manager fill it with banknotes, and then locked and secured the box. Using a long chain, he handcuffed the cash box to his wrist, bid thank you and farewell and, with his safety helmet firmly fixed on his head, quickly left the store.

He returned to the van parked on double yellow lines.

In a jeweller's shop opposite the department store, Anthea engaged her throat mic and radioed, 'This is the Boss. The security van is on the plot. Looks like we made it before the perpetrators. I have control. Stand by all units. The pitch is clean. We've either been sold a dummy or it's about to go down. Mobiles prepare to lock down the street. Officers on foot watch all movements! All teams to full alert.'

The security guard was at the rear of the vehicle about to push the cash box into the chute that delivered the money inside when a black Jaguar swung out of a side street and screeched to a standstill at the side of the van. One man who wore trainers, jeans, a tee shirt and gloves, leapt from the Jaguar and launched himself at the guard who capitulated with the sheer force of the attack. The masked robber overpowered him and stopped the cash box from sliding down the chute.

Simultaneously, another Jaguar hurtled into the arena, skidded to a standstill, and discharged its passengers. Two more men wearing similar attire, and full-face balaclavas, emerged from the Jaguar each armed with a chainsaw.

'Guvnor!' rattled over the radio.

'Wait!' replied Anthea. 'We need unbeatable evidence! Wait! All units wait. My decision! I have control!'

'Command vehicle confirms drone surveillance in place. Video recording, Guvnor.'

'I have that! Stand by!'

A starter handle was pulled. A chainsaw burst into life. The robber bore down on the guard who began screaming when he realised the grinding teeth were above him descending to his body.

Terrified, the guard tried to wrestle free but whilst one robber pinned him to the ground, the other mastered the chainsaw and began cutting into the chain connecting his wrist to the cash box.

'Guvnor! It's going down!' over the radio.

'Wait! I have control!' from Anthea. 'All units! Wait!'

The second robber ignored the guard on the floor and attacked the side of the van with his chainsaw.

Grinding teeth rotated at an astonishing speed whilst the decibels rose, and the noise became unbearable. The side of the van was ripped apart as the chainsaw sliced through the metal. Sparks flew in every direction as the relentless gyrating fangs tore one side of the van to smithereens as if it were a piece of paper.

Two more men carrying holdalls appeared from the second Jaguar. They dragged the remaining shards of metal away, reached inside the van, and began filling the bags with deposit boxes.

Taking a deep breath inside the jewellers, Anthea knew she had strong evidence, a great video, the whole shebang. She radioed, 'All Units! I have control. Stand by! Stand by! Stand by! ..... And Strike! Strike! Strike!'

The detective raced out of the jeweller's shop at the same time as a team emerged from the Legless Sailor shouting, 'Armed Police! Stand still! Drop your weapons!'

The two sides merged when the detectives rushed forward and the men holding the chainsaws diverted their attention to the oncoming police.

The last link in the handcuff chain snapped. Greedy hands snatched a deposit box. It was thrown to the Jaguar and shoved onto the back seat. Simultaneously, insatiable crooks delved into the open side of the van and snatched more cash deposits that were hurled to the waiting Jaguars.

The chainsaw went to work again ripping the side of the van to pieces. Its power resembled a hand tearing a piece of paper into shreds. And the noise was ear-splitting.

'Mobiles!' screamed Anthea on the radio.

Glancing in both directions, Anthea realised her teams had locked down the scene by slewing their cars across the highway and closing the street. Roadblocks were in place.

In the sky, a drone twitched, changed its angle by one degree, and captured the whole street in awesome splendour.

A Jaguar set off with its tyres squealing on the dry tarmac. The driver lost control. He crashed headlong into one of the unit's squad cars. The impact caused the squad car to spin around but it locked horns with the Jaguar bumper to bumper and took the Jaguar with it. The Jaguar was held fast.

Anthea's team bounded from their hiding place in the Jeweller's shop, pulled open the Jaguar doors, and dragged the thieves out of the vehicle onto the tarmac. Facedown with arms across their backs, they applied temporary plastic handcuffs.

The first robber armed with a chainsaw shouted, 'Spin the car around. Straight through the roadblock.'

Anthea ran, withdrew her Gloch, dropped to one knee, and ordered, 'Armed police! Throw down the chainsaws or I'll shoot.'

Relentless metal teeth crushed the air between the robbers and Anthea as the two sides closed with each other.

One robber carrying a holdall was taken to the ground by three detectives whilst two others overpowered more of the crooks and held them at bay,

A handcuff appeared. A body was spun over. The snap of the cuff on the wrist confirmed another arrest had been made.

'Armed police!' repeated Anthea. 'Put your weapons down!'

But two chainsaw-wielding crooks were determined to escape and lowered their nosy spinning chainsaws to Anthea's level. They gained speed, saw the gap behind her, realised there was a way to escape, and gobbled up the space at an incredible speed. The crooks charged the detective with the noise unbearable and the deadly lethal metal teeth getting closer to Anthea's face every second.

Calmly, the detective rolled over to escape the brutal onslaught of a chainsaw used in anger. She raised her gun, took a bead, and shot the robber dead.

Less than a second later, Anthea had rolled again, avoided the deadly teeth of another chainsaw that bit into the ground, and pulled the trigger in a lethal double tap.

Both bullets entered the robber's skull killing him instantly.

Anthea screamed and wriggled away from a hapless chainsaw that had abandoned its master. The chainsaw was free, galloping along the tarmac gobbling up everything in its path. Anthea heard the horrendous sound, imagined the Father of Time with his scythe slung across his shoulder and a smile on his face, and narrowly avoided the monster's teeth as it careered along the pavement like a demented panther looking for its next kill.

Black fragments of tarmac were plucked from the highway by a chainsaw with a mind of its own. The teeth gouged, bucked, bit again, and spat out shards of tarmac on its wild hysterical journey.

A detective's foot stamped on the handle. Fingers killed the power button. The chainsaw died along with its two handlers and the dreams of a criminal empire.

Rolling over onto her belly, Anthea trained her gun on the stationary Jaguar and radioed, 'Contact! Contact! Shots fired! Two targets down! All units, report status.'

'Taking prisoners! Trigger down,' voiced across the airwaves. 'Tigger down. Strike completed.'

Anthea rolled away from the dangers that would haunt her mind in the years ahead. She rolled again onto her back, panted, breathed out heavily as her body relaxed, studied the sky above, and stood up. With her handgun outstretched, she nudged two bodies with her foot, saw that life was no more, and replied, 'Control! Secure the evidence. Remove the red blanket procedure! Keep the street closed. Ambulance and doctor to the scene! Call Borough Command. Officer reports shooting two targets. Awaiting confirmation of death.'

The traffic was at a standstill. The street was laced with panic-stricken members of the public screaming and running for cover. A drone captured it all, and Anthea Adams holstered her Gloch and leaned against the wall of the jeweller's shop with sweat soaking her neck and the first glimpse of a tear escaping her eyes.

'All units prepare to stand down,' she radioed as she wiped her eyes and rolled her neck from side to side as she sought to relax her body. 'I have control but will relinquish to Borough Command when they attend.'

The radio was silent, manned only by an exhausted adrenaline-pumping bunch of detectives who had been tested to extremity.

Anthea sat on her haunches, heard the sirens growing louder, and studied the two bodies she had dispatched to heaven that day. 'I'd like to say I'm sorry,' she whispered. 'But I don't know who you are and I'm not sorry.'

For the Special Crime Unit, the incident was closed when the Borough Commander arrived and examined the scene of destruction and total mayhem.

As the local police chief approached Anthea, she placed her Gloch in the holster, unzipped the belt, and handed it to the officer. She pointed to two bodies and informed the senior officer, 'I shot these two men in self-defence having told them I was an armed officer and requesting them to relinquish their weapons. They were carrying out a robbery on a cash-in-transit security van and they were armed with chainsaws. They attacked me with the chainsaws. I responded by shooting them with the Gloch I have just presented you with. Take a look, sir.' She pointed at the bodies and continued, 'You seen a dead body before? Of course, you have. A doctor will confirm death. The officer in the Command-and-Control vehicle has been instructed to hand you the original video recording taken by our drone. He's been instructed by me to deliver a copy of that video to my legal representative for use in any criminal proceedings that may follow. I have nothing further to say at this time.'

The Borough Commander did not reply. He just looked at the scene of desolation around him and then threw an almost annoying glance at the leader of the Special Crime Unit before saying, 'I need to interview you under caution. Two men are dead, and you have admitted responsibility for their deaths.'

Anthea paused, took a breath, and continued, 'Make an appointment with my legal team. Command and Control have the details. I will attend that interview.'

Taking a few steps away, Anthea turned and said, 'I got it right this time as the facts and the evidence will show. Now if you'll excuse me, sir, I have an appointment with the Commissioner of the Metropolitan Police.'

Anthea brushed past the Borough Commander as she slotted into the nearest squad car and instructed the driver, 'New Scotland Yard! No rush! Take your time!'

Seven miles away, Andrey Petrov meandered through the garden of the Russian embassy before unfastening an iron gate that emerged onto the streets of the capital.

'Ushanka is moving,' rattled across the surveillance network as the controller Max alerted the MI5 team.

Max phoned Antonia Harston-Browne, the surveillance commander, who immediately left her office to join the fray.

Strolling casually down a side street wearing a dark overcoat and his ushanka, Andrey looked both ways as he crossed the road, then glanced over his shoulder. He unlocked a second-hand Ford Fiesta bearing a UK plate.

Andrey set off into Central London followed by the MI5 surveillance team strung out in his rearview mirror.

'Hang back,' ordered Max. 'Give him space.'

The radio network complied as Antonia fired the engine of her Porsche, caught up with the team, and moved into the *'Tail-End Charlie'* position of the surveillance convoy and ordered, 'Move to box formation.'

The convoy complied. Andrey unknowingly found himself in the middle of a moving box with followers ahead of him, behind hm, and on streets parallel to his journey.

Crossing the Thames, Andrey entered South London, drove through Brixton, Bexleyheath, and Dartford, and took the A2 to Gravesend. The journey took about ninety minutes.

The traffic was heavy because the route was one of the main arteries to Europe from London. Nevertheless, Antonia held her position as the rear marker.

Confident that Andrey was unaware of their presence, the surveillance team watched Andrey manoeuvre his car into a parking bay near Gravesend Promenade. He locked the Ford and walked through the picturesque gardens onto the promenade. Smoothing the line of his overcoat, Andrey settled the black fur-skinned ushanka squarely on his head. He strolled along the pathway and headed eastwards towards Gravesend Sailing Club. The ushanka stood out prominently in comparison with other modes of headgear worn by people in the area.

Stopping suddenly, Andrey checked his bearings and diverted his route away from the tarmac to the riverside where he paused again and watched the Thames as it ambled out to the Channel and the North Sea. Removing a short monocular telescope from the inside pocket of his overcoat, Andrey brought the instrument up to his left eye and studied the opposing bank of the river. He turned ninety degrees and studied people on the Promenade pathway.

At least, that's what Antonia saw from her position in the gardens about a hundred yards from where Andrey stood. The team had given Andrey plenty of room but now Antonia wondered if she should instruct Max to take closer order given that Andrey appeared to be looking for something, or was it someone? It was a difficult decision to make because the wrong decision might have alerted Andrey that he was being followed. Even the right decision might have proved wrong. She was damned if she was right and damned if she was wrong. Such was the work of a decision-maker. That said, Antonia presumed that a man like Andrey, who was the *rezident*, would expect to be followed everywhere anyway.

Antonia noted how quite a few people in the area were using binoculars to view the opposing bank and the various vessels that plied the Thames. Yet deep inside, she knew that Andrey had never been sighted in this neck of the woods before. She was unaware of any interest he might have had in Gravesend or the nearby sailing club. Antonia thought his presence at this location to be a mystery.

'Spread out and use the gardens and any building cover that may be useful,' radioed Antonia. 'He's up to something, but I don't know what. He's either checking the pathway out or looking for a vessel on the river. Mingle! Watch! Give him plenty of space.'

An ocean-going vessel abandoned its anchorage upriver and gradually cruised past at a speed of about five knots.

Andrey watched the ship move towards the English Channel before returning to the tarmac pathway where he glanced around, saw nothing that alerted him to danger of any kind, and continued his stroll along the prom.

'What on earth is going on?' thought Antonia. 'Why is he in Gravesend? What's the attraction here?'

The plot remained quiet. Nothing happened. Andrey took a seat in an open-air café, ordered a black coffee, and removed his ushanka. He placed it on the table and sat alone drinking his coffee and studying the people around him. Andrey Petrov was a people watcher and that was no surprise to any of those watching him.

Some of the passersby on the Promenade giggled when they realised that the black furry object on Andrey's table was not a cat. It was just an ordinary piece of headgear.

'He's not wearing his hat,' radioed Max. 'I'm three tables away from him and he's behind me. I was here before him. Nothing further to report.'

'Is he talking to anyone? Has he spoken to anyone?'

With his back to the Russian, Max donned a pair of spectacles so that he might keep an eye on Andrey. The glasses were manufactured with rear-view mirror technology that allowed Max to constantly know what was happening behind him. He replied, 'No! Only the waitress who took his order. I've got her covered. Nothing undue to report.'

'I have that,' voiced Antonia.

Tourists and locals alike walked the Promenade, visited the café, had a drink, and a bite to eat, and then continued their day whilst Andrey sat people watching. He ordered another coffee, checked the path again with his monocular, and suddenly placed the ushanka on his head.

Andrey remained seated with the collar of his overcoat turned up and his ushanka prominent for all to see.

'Max has the eyeball. Whatever is going down is going down very soon,' he radioed. 'He's put his ushanka back on but he's not going anywhere. It might be a signal of some kind. Stand by for a meeting everyone!'

'I have that,' acknowledged Antonia.

The comings and goings in the café continued but a short time later a foreign-looking gentleman walked into the café, ignored Andrey, but then deliberately chose a seat at a table opposite him.

Presenting a menu, the waitress took an order from the foreign-looking chap who revealed he only wanted a coffee.

Max buried his face in a newspaper as he snaffled another sandwich from his plate. Casually, he sat back, yawned, and acted as though he was engrossed in the news.

Quietly, Max engaged his hidden microphone and radioed, 'I have eye contact between Ushanka and a male. He's thirty to thirty-five years of age, slim build, clean shaven, blue denim jeans, blue denim jacket, black and white scarf, and a black tee shirt. Nike trainers, six feet tall. Designated *The Visitor*. Ends.'

'What do you mean by eye contact?' queried Antonia.

'It's almost as if The Visitor is using his eyes to say I'm here. He's looking directly at Ushanka.'

'You have control,' replied Antonia.

The Visitor acknowledged the waitress when the beverage arrived, paid in cash, and then looked around the café. He zeroed in on Max who casually finished his sandwich, folded his newspaper, and walked to the counter to pay his bill.

Simultaneously, a hitchhiker carrying a rucksack over his shoulder arrived, occupied the table Max had just vacated and plugged a cable into his ear. His name was Lance, and he was a member of the surveillance team who had replaced Max.

Music emanated from a radio in Lance's hand. He reduced the volume and tapped the table with his hand in time to the music.

Different to Max, Lance openly displayed his presence and showed no interest at all in Andrey and the visitor.

The Visitor swivelled his head to view the path along the promenade he had just walked. His eyes dissected every person who approached the café. He watched them walk by satisfied they had no interest in him.

Max stood at the counter, gestured he would like a bar of chocolate to take with him, fumbled for his wallet to pay, and used the time to watch the Visitor and Andrey.

The Visitor stood up, removed a doll from his inside pocket, and placed it on the table in front of him. He paused a second and stared at Andrey.

Simultaneously, in a move that had been choreographed, Andrey also stood up and walked towards the visitor. The Visitor walked towards Andrey. Both men walked past each other and left the café by different exits. The Visitor headed towards the sailing club. Andrey walked to his car.

Max paid for his meal, spun on his heel, and noticed that the wooden doll was missing from the table.

'Brush contact!' radioed Max as he casually left the café by the rear exit. 'The Visitor has delivered a doll to Ushanka. They've parted. Follow and house The Visitor. Out!'

Max loitered at the rear of the café not wanting to be seen. Meanwhile, Antonia split the team into two and confirmed Max's instructions to follow and house the Visitor.

'Max!' radioed Antonia. 'Can you confirm my thinking? The Visitor is a courier sent to deliver a package to Ushanka. The delivery occurred via a brush contact. Ushanka is now in possession of the package and the courier is finished.'

'Confirmed!' from Max. 'My thoughts precisely.'

'Permission!' radioed Janet from the surveillance team.

'Go ahead,' replied Antonia.

'I have an eyeball on The Visitor. I identify him as Dmitry Badak of the Belarus embassy. He arrived in the UK via Heathrow yesterday. See my report re recent arrivals. He's listed as a kitchen operative at the embassy.'

'I have that,' voiced Antonia. 'Excellent! Thank you! Stay with him and confirm his return to the Belarus embassy.'

'Will do! Out!'

'We're onto something here,' thought Antonia. 'The Belarus embassy is a five-minute walk from the Russian embassy. Yet Andrey drives to Gravesend to meet someone he could have met halfway between the two embassies. Why drive to Gravesend to hand over an innocent-looking doll? Babushka or Matryoshka?'

'Max! Describe the doll!' instructed Antonia.

'I had it sighted for a few seconds. I'd say it wasn't a babushka. They're made of cloth. The Visitor handed over a matryoshka. Wooden and heavily lacquered in various colours.'

'I have that,' replied Antonia who then thought, 'Matryoshka! The best-known and most popular Russian souvenir. It's a set of painted wooden dolls of decreasing sizes one hidden inside another. The number of nested figures usually varies from three to ten, but it can be more. What's inside the doll?'

Two hours later, Antonia moved into the backup position. She wanted to be close enough to take a proper look at Dmitry, The Visitor. She felt that she could engrain a personal view of the subject into her brain.

Dmitry approached the Belarus embassy near Kensington Court, lingered at the pedestrian crossing, and waited to cross. The traffic reduced speed, came to a stop, and allowed Dmitry, and others, to cross the road in complete safety and at a casual pace.

A black taxi hurtled past all the standing traffic, accelerated at full speed, and wiped Dmitry Badak clean off his feet when it collided with the so-called courier on the crossing. The taxi carried Dmitry's body a hundred yards or more before the driver braked, watched the body roll from the bonnet of the taxi, and land unceremoniously on the highway.

The taxi driver then drove over Dmitry's body.

Only the crunch of bone, the explosion of blood from Dmitry's skull, and the petrifying image of it all were witnessed by pedestrians and tourists on the footpath.

The lone driver abandoned the taxi and ran down the pavement where he jumped into a waiting Vauxhall saloon sitting with its passenger door open ready for a quick getaway.

Within moments, the hit-and-run driver was gone from the scene leaving his taxi behind.

'Max has an eyeball on the scene. Man down! The Visitor is down one hundred yards from the Belarus embassy knocked over by a black taxi. I'm in pursuit of the driver who is now a passenger in a grey Vauxhall. I'm losing sight of the vehicle due to high-speed reckless driving. Recommend alert police to apprehend the suspect in the Vauxhall.'

Antonia was quick to respond with, 'Negative! Abort! I repeat. Abort! That wasn't an accident. It was a deliberate hit-and-run and we can guess who carried it out. No! Abort the operation! If we give chase, we'll unwittingly inform the Russians we have The Visitor under observation. If they analyse that they'll work out that we have Ushanka under observation too. They will know the two men were in Gravesend together. No! I have control! I say again, abort!'

'You sure, boss?' challenged Max. 'We can catch the hit and run man if we pull out all the stops.'

'And tell the world what we are doing! No, Max! Abort! All units stand down to the garage for debriefing.'

Later that day, in the safe room at the Russian embassy, Andrey switched on the highly encrypted person-to-person standalone computer that was a vital part of the security network operating within his domain.

Andrey first engaged the Head of the SVR stationed in the Yasenevo district of Moscow. The Head of the SVR enjoyed direct access to the Defence Secretary at the Kremlin Andrey emailed the words, '*Receipt of package confirmed this date. The courier has been terminated. Operation Vengeance is now active.*'

'*Proceed with caution,*' came the reply.

Tapping the black and whites, Andrey then read a message from Pavel Nikita: the chief of the FSB in Southern Russia. Pavel held responsibility for FSB matters in Dagestan and its neighbours.

Andrey read the message and replied, '*Understood! Keep Yousef in custody. Continue questioning. Contacts in England known by Jamil Volkov are to be extricated from your prisoner. Ends.*'

At his base in Southern Russia, Pavel shook his head in disgust but acknowledged Andrey before ringing the Defence Secretary in Moscow and explaining the situation.

'There's nothing else this man Yousef can tell us. He's down and finished. There's no more to discover.'

'Are you sure, Pavel?'

'It's my job to extract information from the enemy. I tell you, sir. Yousef is drained to satisfaction, but the Head of Station in London still wants more. There is no more. I've repeatedly told him over the last few weeks that Yousef is drained. My problem is London no longer listens to me.'

'Our friend in London has much on his mind and an important operation underway, Pavel. You must learn not to criticise those in power above you. Andrey is a favourite of the Commander in Chief and serves the Motherland in a capacity well above your remit and understanding. I caution you as to your intentions, Pavel.'

'Then I apologise, sir. I am just frustrated, and, with respect, our prisoner has been shredded of every piece of knowledge he has ever held in his mind. He has been reduced to a blithering idiot who has lost all understanding of time and normal living. He's finished. Perhaps others, no disrespect intended to either Moscow or London, do not appreciate the depth of our interviewing skills.'

The Defence Secretary paused, sipped cinnamon tea at his desk in the Kremlin, and replied, 'Pavel! Send a message to the people. You know what to do, my friend. A ghost cannot speak. Do it for the Motherland! Terminate!'

'Da!' responded Pavel and then added, 'It will be an honour to do your bidding, sir.'

The call ended and Pavel summonsed aides to his side.

Meanwhile, in the office of the Special Crime Unit, in London, Antonia was on the phone with the Director General of the Security Services. She explained to Phillip what had happened in both Gravesend and Kensington.

Phillip replied, 'Intriguing, Toni, and very disturbing in more ways than one. Spies and murderers all in one pot by the sound of it. From what you say, which includes Janet's report regarding recent arrivals, I suggest a courier from Belarus met Ushanka by appointment in a café on the Promenade at Gravesend and handed over an article that was so sensitive that it was too important to send in the diplomatic pouch. He was then deliberately run over and killed by the very people who arranged the delivery of whatever that article was.'

'My analysis also, Phillip,' replied Antonia. 'Andrey wore his ushanka deliberately when he saw the courier coming. I'd say the courier was briefed to look for a man wearing a ushanka, do a brush contact in a busy place, and then hightail it back to the embassy. Job done!'

'Belarus is Russia's main economic and political partner,' declared Phillip. 'A conspiracy of nations or just a convenient delivery driver doing the rounds?'

'I'd say it was the Russians using a low-level contact that they flew into the UK on a flight from Moscow. He delivered the goods and was terminated by the very people who had arranged his visit to the UK. In so doing they removed a potential witness to whatever is going on. Silenced forever in the fields of law and the political power process. They are planning something important for sure.'

'I agree with you,' nodded Phillip. 'But what was in the matryoshka doll? That is the question.'

'Could be microfiche but given digital advancements that's probably unlikely,' suggested Antonia. 'Special instructions? But then they have an all-singing all-dancing safe room in the embassy to communicate with each other. I remain open-minded because I can't answer that question.'

'We must fear the worst,' voiced Phillip. 'It might be a weapon of some kind. Perhaps part of a highly sophisticated device that we have no experience of. I'm going to arrange for the national threat level to be raised as a precaution. Better safe than sorry and such a step will lead to increased security and readiness at key points throughout the UK. The Russians have got us over a barrel because they're ahead of us and we don't know what they are doing.'

'We need Boyd back and the Special Crime Unit devoted to this mystery. They may be getting bad press but let's not allow the media to cloud our judgement.'

'We have other extremely proficient investigators, Toni.'

'But none of them think like Boyd and his crew,' replied Antonia. 'The man thinks outside of the box when he needs to, and his people are all for him. He'll shine some light on the problem.'

'Even with his greying hair and the ageing process?'

'I thought he was a good friend of yours, Phillip,' challenged Antonia. 'Good friends don't usually criticise each other from afar. Perhaps your days are numbered too.'

'You're right. I'm sorry. But that reminds me, Toni,' ventured Phillip. 'The enquiry into his mishandling of the armed robbery in Brixton has been concluded. He has been cleared of any wrongdoing. The enquiry found that the customers and postmistress in the post office underwent the first attack on their hearing capabilities when the robbers fired their shotguns into the ceiling. It is held that their injuries were not a result of mistakes made by Boyd. The stun grenade used was found to be faulty and emitted potassium nitrate into an atmosphere that might have caused either an explosion or more bodily problems such as damage to the eyes and skin. Investigators discovered that Boyd ordered the evacuation of the post office. In so doing he saved lives rather than damaged them. Accordingly, the enquiry waved all complaints made.'

'He still made tactical mistakes.'

'And he has been exonerated due to his ability to read a possible health hazard and deal with it correctly.'

'Convenient?'

'I understand the Commissioner of Police intends to discuss the matter in person with him. He may circuitously offer some kind of advice to improve his skills.'

'Good! How did the holiday in Madeira go?'

Phillip smiled and replied, 'Come, come, Toni. You know what Boyd was involved in at Porto Santo. He's back in England now. At home, I believe.'

'And Abraham?'

'Housed in a nearby hotel. In essence, Boyd is debriefing him about his life with Mossad.'

'On our behalf?'

'Correct!' confirmed Phillip. 'We've taken Boyd out of the limelight for a while. It will do him good. Once he has finished with Abraham, he will be working for Julian in M16.'

'Anything else I should know?' probed Antonia.

'Yes! Ushanka has asked to meet me tomorrow.'

'What about? Tell me he's going to spill the beans about what they are up to.'

'I doubt it,' chuckled Phillip. 'But I have agreed to meet him. Please ensure we have plenty of room when we encounter each other. I would not wish our conversation to be interrupted by your surveillance team. That said, I intend to meet him at the Tate Modern. You know where that is.'

'Yes! The same place as last time,' nodded Antonia.

'Indeed! The location was his suggestion. I agreed to it. Arrange for the seat opposite to be covered by our technical team. I want a recording of our conversation and I want only you to handle the tape. Is that understood?'

'It is,' replied Antonia. 'I'll also see to it that my surveillance team does not spoil things for you. Only Max will be in the building, no one else. I'll brief him personally.'

'Please do,' agreed Phillip.

'That said,' continued Antonia. 'I'd be surprised Andrey Petrov doesn't live in the expectation of being under surveillance.'

'I'd say you are correct,' voiced Phillip. 'But the man is a genius in many ways and a formidable opponent. You were lucky to sneak a view of the brush contact in Gravesend. I presume a man in his position expects to be followed but is so highly trained that such an occurrence is of no consequence to him.'

'The Tate Modern and Orpheus,' said Antonia. 'Good luck.'

~

9

The Tate Modern Art Gallery.

Bankside, London.

The following morning.

Arriving first, Phillip took a seat in the gallery opposite a piece of sculpture that he genuinely admired.

A minute later Andrey Petrov turned up, removed his ushanka, and sat next to Phillip saying, 'Good morning, my friend. Thank you for agreeing to our meeting.'

The two spymasters shook hands.

'Good morning, Andrey,' replied Phillip. 'I trust you are well and in good health.'

'Of course,' chuckled Andrey. 'But you knew that before I sat down, didn't you?'

'Of course,' replied Phillip with a wry smile. 'I'm the Director General of the Security Service I'm supposed to know everything about everyone.'

'Most of the time,' voiced Andrey returning a slight grin. 'I see you are sitting in front of your favourite piece.'

'The sculpture called Orpheus,' admitted Phillip. 'But you knew that before I sat down, didn't you?'

'You've stolen my words.'

'But nothing else,' declared Phillip.

Andrey held an expression on his face that suggested he masterminded everything around him. The spymaster had the uncanny knack of dominating proceedings by his mere presence such was the aura that accompanied him. Here sat a man with a hat: a symbol of his authority. Yet deep inside, those who knew and feared him were aware that Andrey Petrov needed no such headgear to validate his status.

'Orpheus by a sculptor named Hepworth if I recall correctly,' offered Andrey.

'Yes! Your memory is good. You will also recall that Orpheus features three things, Andrey. Hepworth, a female sculpture of some renown, started to use sheet metal and string, as well as wood,' explained Phillip. 'She called this one Orpheus after the ancient Greek musician and poet of the same name. The sculpture brings together ideas of harmony between modern technology, musical composition, and Greek myth. They are represented by the components of the sculpture namely copper alloy, cotton string, and a wooden base.'

'Harmony?' queried Andrey. 'Peace?'

'Not quite!' replied Phillip. 'The Greek musician would have told you that it's a combination of simultaneously sounding musical notes that produce a pleasing effect.'

'I see,' acknowledged Andrey. 'So, to achieve harmony, the notes have to function together to make things work correctly?'

'You know that to be true from our last meeting here,' voiced Phillip. 'You do remember that don't you?'

'I do. You gave me a thimble as I recall.'

'Correct! One of your spies had dropped it on the shores of Loch Ness. I merely handed it back to you.'

Andrey looked away for a moment and said, 'But not the spy.'

'The Loch Ness incident is closed,' declared Phillip. 'All because of a thimble. Let it ride, my friend. We must move on.'

'I agree,' gestured the Russian despairing with his hands.

'When last we met, Andrey, we talked of how spymasters could frame the politics of a government because they so often acquired useful information long before a government did. You agreed and decided how easily people like us could change the course of government policy. Do you remember?'

'Yes! I do and that is the reason I wanted to meet you here today. I have something useful for you. I wanted to speak to you personally about the situation I find myself in.'

'Oh, my goodness, Andrey,' ventured Phillip in a deliberate attempt to woo Andrey. 'Pray proceed, my friend. I am all ears.'

The spymaster returned a well-framed polite scowl, then lightened his face with a smile, and replied, 'What I have to tell you has not yet reached the Kremlin. To speak of such things to you is to breach my position in the organisation in which I serve. I believe you call it treason or something similar when an individual contravenes your Official Secrets Act. Well, my friend, what I am about to tell you is exactly that. A secret that if it were known of in the Kremlin would stay in the Kremlin and you would not be part of it.'

'Are you at risk if you divulge that secret to me?'

'Yes! Significant risk.'

'Then I shall thank you kindly and ensure there is no connection to you should the matter need attention from my service. What have you got that causes me to meet you in an art gallery in the middle of London?'

'You have a Muslim terrorist living in London.'

'We get them all the time,' replied Phillip shaking his head. 'They come; they go. Some are homebred. Others from afar. What is it about this one that makes you single him out?'

'I know your country suffers from the unwelcome presence of terrorism, but this terrorist is a fellow Russian. He is wanted for multiple bombings and murdering hundreds of people all over our country. I doubt you will know of him since he seldom sets foot outside the Motherland.'

'Which makes him special? Is that what you are saying?'

'I'm telling you that he is a Muslim who was initially a member of the Taleban. He was trained by Al Qaeda and then joined ISIS, or Daesh as we call it.'

'Islamic State, the Taleban and Al Qaeda,' remarked Phillip. 'Why three organisations and not just one?'

'There is little between them,' suggested Andrey.

'They would tell you otherwise,' argued Phillip.

'Perhaps,' responded Andrey.

'Is he alone?'

'Yes, as far as I know.'

'How did he enter the country?

'By ship from France. He was a fare-paying passenger.'

'What is his name and why is he here?' queried Phillip.

'Jamil Volkov intends to kill your prime minister.'

The Director General gawked at Andrey, leaned across to the spymaster, and said, 'Say that again. A Muslim Russian terrorist here in London is going to kill....?'

'Your prime minister!' confirmed Andrey.

'Are you sure?'

'Yes!'

'How do you know this to be true?'

'You will need to take my word, Phillip. I decline to tell you the source of my information. Now before you take me to task, I remind you that, as the head of MI5, you have both technical and human intelligence sources from which you obtain information. You would never tell me of such sources, so I ask you to respect our profession. My friend, you know that I cannot answer that question. I refuse to declare my source.'

'Why did you tell me?'

'In the hope that you will find Jamil Volkov and deal with him before it becomes known in the Kremlin that he is in London. The man is wanted all over Russia. He is a mass murderer. Moscow will order me to assassinate him irrespective of whether he is on British soil. You see, Phillip, it is as you suggest. When we spymasters withhold such information from our governments they are weakened, and we are empowered. Moscow will want Jamil Volkov killed by a Russian hand on British soil. I see that as adding to the conflict between our countries. Your government will not want us to kill people in your backyard. It will only aggravate relations between us. Having told you the facts as I see them, I hope you will find him quickly and take action that prevents us from carrying out any orders from Moscow. Between us, we will have inserted a little bit of peace into the war in Ukraine. You know as well as I do that the war is now Russia versus NATO. Perhaps, we can reduce aggravation between the two. You mentioned Orpheus and harmony. I offer harmony to you.'

Silent for what seemed an eternity, Phillip clasped the hand of Andrey and replied, 'Thank you, Andrey. I fully understand your position. I cannot thank you enough for this secretive information. I owe you one, Andrey. I owe you.'

'My pleasure to help,' replied Andrey.

'I suggest we part now lest we become a fixture for passersby to gawp at,' proposed Phillip. 'Unless of course, you have anything else to say.'

'Harmony, Phillip! Harmony!'

Phillip smiled as he watched Andrey stand, don his ushanka, and step away. Yet before taking another step, Andrey turned and said, 'And give my blessings to Antonia.'

Andrey Petrov was gone from the meeting.

Suddenly shaken, Phillip watched him go and thought to himself, 'Blessings to Antonia! How the hell does Andrey Petrov know about Antonia?' The Director General vacated the seat and left the Tate Modern by a different exit thinking, 'This is going to get too hot to handle on every possible front. Both private and public. Not many outsiders know Toni and I are in love. Does Andrey? He mentioned her, not me. He must know we are betrothed to be married. Is Toni in danger? I want Toni safe, and I don't want MI5 looking after her. The entire organisation will crawl all over our lifestyles if I ask them to safeguard Toni. Do we have a mole or do the Russians know everything about us? It's not the harmony I want right now. It's Boyd! I want Boyd back.'

In the ensuing hours, Antonia's surveillance team followed Ushanka to a barber where he undertook his usual trim. Then they followed him to a college where, as a guest of the local education authority, he was present at a graduation ceremony for students who were awarded a degree in Russian language, history, and culture. That night, again as part of his duties as cultural attaché, he attended a ballet at a west-end theatre. By nightfall, he returned to the embassy until the next day.

By midnight, that same night, Sir Phillip Nesbitt had spoken to the Prime Minister, the Home Secretary, the Foreign Secretary, the Metropolitan Police Commissioner, and the Chief of MI6. The question was straightforward, and the answer was immediate. Boyd was back in town. The former Head of the Special Crime Unit was reinstated. Ostensibly, his private briefing from the bosses of MI5 and MI6 was to recruit Ushanka into the fold.

But that was only one reason Phillip wanted Boyd back in the camp. Phillip knew that to protect his love, Antonia, Boyd would find a way. He was the key to harmony.

~

10

~

Nabran.

Azerbaijan.

The same day. Simultaneous.

Elsewhere, in a place of unique harmony, the incoming tide was in cahoots with the devil.

Nabran is a village in the northeastern part of Azerbaijan. Close to the Russia-Azerbaijan border, the surrounding villages form a municipality which boasts a population of 300,000. Located on the Caspian seashore, Nabran features a subtropical forestland that creeps directly onto the beach. It is unique because few places feature a subtropical forest and a seashore meeting in perfect harmony.

Kirill and Irina strolled hand in hand along the beach. He in shorts and a tee shirt; she in similar attire. Their home was a short walk from the Caspian Sea, and they ventured out because of vehicle lights they had seen from their home the previous night. It was well after midnight when Kirill noticed the lights. It was unusual for vehicles to be seen on the beach, and it was against the laws of the municipality, of which they were a part, to drive on the seashore at night.

Wondering what had happened, they decided to explore the area and see how many vehicles had been involved. Irina counted the tyre tracks but wondered if they were too late. Had the tide hit the beach during the night and washed away all the evidence? They did not know.

Within a short time, they found a body midway between the seaboard and the forest. Only a pair of dark trousers graced the lower part of the body from the waist down.

Kirill noticed the trousers were not secured by a belt.

Devastated, Kirill cuddled Irina who sobbed at the shock of it all. It was not what she expected to discover. Indeed, they had expected to find abandoned beer cans following a late-night party by teenagers who should have known better.

Kirill examined the body, noticed the bruised face, and then looked at the hands and feet. They bore scuffs and scrapes that suggested the man had been bound and gagged. Irina also noted the bruises on the body. They were extensive.

Had this man been bound and gagged, tortured, beaten to death, and then dumped on the beach for someone to find? And the car tracks close to the body, had someone used a vehicle to transport the body to the beach and then offload it in the expectation that those living near the shore would find the body and report it?

'Interesting,' remarked Kirill. 'If the sea has washed this man ashore then that is a miracle.'

'Why?' asked Irina as she wiped away tears from her eyes.

'Because the tide doesn't come up this far,' replied Kirill. 'I'll phone the police.'

Five minutes later a solitary police officer arrived in a four-wheel drive Land Rover. He alighted from the vehicle, hitched up his pants in a slovenly manner, and nodded to Kirill and Irina before lighting a cigarette. With only a few introductory questions asked, the officer dragged on his cigarette before kneeling by the body and allowing his eyes to gaze upon the scene before him.

'Dead!' announced the policeman suddenly flicking the cigarette towards the forest. 'Drowned at sea.'

'I don't think so, officer,' challenged Kirill. 'He's got bruises all over, and his wrists and ankles are a lighter colour than the rest of his body in places. Do you know why?'

The policeman did not respond.

'I'll tell you!' ventured Kirill. 'Those marks are caused by ligatures that have been applied to his feet and hands. He's been tied up and dumped on the beach. He didn't drown.'

'How would you know that?'

'I'm a doctor.'

The officer stepped over the body, and said, 'Wrong! The bruises will have been caused when the sea deposited the body on the beach, but I'll ring for a second opinion.'

'I've just given you a second opinion,' replied Kirill. 'But it's not one you want to hear, is it?'

A crowd began to gather as word of the police on the beach, two locals, and a body, gently filtered through the community. The policeman stepped away, made a call on his mobile phone, and then gestured for the crowd to step back. A ripple from the incoming tide broke on the beach about twenty yards away when he knelt and searched the corpse.

Finding a driving licence in the rear trouser pocket of the body, the policeman held it for all to see and announced, 'Yousef Abdul Halim.' He turned the carcass over, compared the face with the driving licence and continued, 'I remember him. He's a taxi driver from Dagestan.'

Kirill asked, 'How well did you know him?'

Ignoring the question, the policemen stood up as a black Mercedes drew up and a man smartly dressed in a suit slid from the passenger door whilst two other suited men joined the fray.

'I think it's the police chief!' it was mumbled.

'It's the top man,' was whispered.

'State Police,' uttered another. 'Not local.'

'Pavel Nikita! He's the chief of the FSB,' was finally mouthed in awesome fear, expectation, and anxiety from the locals who grew in number as the community responded to unfolding events. The buzz grew as it swept through the gathering bringing an air of trepidation and uncertainty.

The newcomer, Pavel Nikita, wore sunglasses and looked more like a man from the mafia rather than a public service employee devoted to law enforcement and protecting the public. He strode into the group, checked the driving licence, and then casually gazed at the body.

'The doctor here,' gestured the scruffy policeman. 'Thinks the body has been bound and gagged and then dumped on the beach.'

'Does he?' replied Pavel pushing his sunglasses on the bridge of his nose. 'Well, we'll see about that.' Pointing to the body now surrounded by residents, he asked, 'Anyone know this man?'

No one replied.

Kirill looked at the mystery man, his two smart-suited colleagues, and the slovenly untidy cop who had been first on the scene. Then a dawning reality began to form in his brain.

'Was this a set-up?'

'Yousef Abdul Halim!' stated Pavel loudly. 'A well-known terrorist from Dagestan. Looks like he's drowned out there in the sea. I don't know why, and I don't much care to ask. I'd say he's had an argument with his murdering friends, and they've thrown him overboard from a yacht.'

'He has ligature marks on his hands and feet,' declared Kirill.

'And I've got a carbuncle on my arse, a flea in my ear, and a stone in my shoe,' smiled the police chief who turned to the crowd and loudly announced, 'I am Pavel Nikita! Chief of Police, Head of the local FSB, friend of the Kremlin, and defender of the Motherland! This is the body of Yousef Abdul Halim. This is what happens to enemies of the State. Be warned, ladies and gentlemen. He's been washed up on these shores and we will bury him with the rest of the garbage we find. Yousef Abdul Halim! Remember the name and remember that he died because he was a terrorist who was an enemy of the State.'

The crowd withdrew from a murmur to a fidget and then silence. It was as if no one wanted to challenge the stage play taking place before them.

The police chief moved close to Kirill and held his gaze for what seemed an eternity. Pavel stared into his face, and said, 'Death by drowning!'

Kirill nodded, reluctantly at first, but vigorously when he realised the central character in the scene was not the dead body or the scruffily dressed cop. It was the enigmatic police chief making it clear to everyone that Yousef Abdul Halim was a name to be remembered and this is what happened to those who were enemies of the State. It was a public display of death carefully orchestrated by the State for the public to see.

Pavel smiled, turned to the uniformed officer, and said, 'File your report. You know what to say. These people need to know who is in charge and what happens to those who step out of line. And they need to be aware that they are powerless to intervene to good effect. Mission accomplished! Message delivered!' Then, turning to his colleagues, he ordered, 'Get the body van down here and load this piece of scum into it. Take him away. Get him off the beach. You know what to do with the body.'

The removal work began.

Kirill stepped away, knew it was a set piece presented to the residents as a reminder of the power of the State, and why he would never speak of the matter ever again. Taking Irina's hand, Kirill nodded farewell to the police and set off towards his home nearby. Only the seagulls and a weak incoming tide that bore no malice and no roar were witnesses to the true feelings of the doctor and his wife. The crowd dispersed.

Pavel said, 'We're done here. I'll see you back at the office. I need to ring Moscow.'

The Head of the State Police, who seemed to rule everything in the area, drove the Mercedes away as the recovery vehicle drew to a halt by the body of a taxi driver now portrayed in death as an enemy of the State.

~

11

The Office of the Director General.
The Security Service, London.
Later that week.

Waiting patiently in the anteroom of Sir Phillip's office, Boyd yawned, rubbed his fingers into his cheeks to stimulate himself, and felt glad to be back in the mix. Uneasy, he wondered why his first port of call was a meeting with the Director General.

A light above the main office door began to flash and Boyd stood up, gestured his understanding to Phillip's secretary who was seated at a desk nearby, and entered the Director General's domain.

The detective was met by a huge handshake, a gratuitous smile, and Phillip's words, 'Welcome back, Boyd – or should I revert to Commander once more?'

'Whichever! I don't mind. Do you know you have an office system like a doctor's surgery? Red light for stay, green light for enter. I thought such things disappeared at the turn of the century.'

'I've never bothered to change the system,' chuckled Phillip. 'It pleases me, Boyd, and it works. Anyway, down to business. I told you things would work out well for you. I'm so pleased you are back in charge of the unit.'

'In charge, am I?' queried Boyd. 'Do you know I've only recently been told of my reappointment following the result of the internal enquiry and I've yet to visit my own office at the Special Crime Unit? The commissioner told me to present myself to you at the earliest opportunity. As far as I am aware, Anthea is in charge not me. Now tell me I've got that wrong, Phillip.'

Smiling, Phillip gestured Boyd to take a seat and replied, 'I think you will find that Anthea will retain the rank of superintendent but will revert to your deputy as it was before.' Phillip poured coffee from a cafetiere and continued, 'I'm delighted for her, Boyd. Over the years, she has risen through your command and is now granted much more authority in the unit and within my organisation. You'll find that Inspector Bannerman and Sergeant Burns were also exonerated from the enquiry. They're due back today as well. Anthea is delighted you are all back but that's not why I asked you to come to see me.'

'What's so important that this is my first port of call?' replied Boyd savouring his first hot drink of the day.

'Andrey Petrov, codename USHANKA, is the Head of Station at the Russian embassy. He is the Resident and Head spy in the UK. Do you know what I mean by that?'

'Absolutely,' nodded Boyd. 'More interest to you than me because he's in the espionage game and I'm in the serious crime game but I'm listening.'

'Ushanka, I want you to refer to him by that codename, asked me to meet him in the Tate Gallery recently. I accepted his invitation. Ushanka told me he had vital information that he wished to impart to me and then pointed out that his life would be in danger if others in his organisation knew he was telling me about a matter that not even the Kremlin were aware of.'

'Interesting! Earth-shattering and impressive,' remarked Boyd. 'Have you been trying to recruit him to work for us?'

'No! It was entirely voluntary on his part. We want you to recruit Ushanka onto our side. Julian and I want Ushanka to desert Russian Intelligence and work for us as a double agent. To that end, you'll be working directly with Julian, the MI6 chief, as well as myself.'

Boyd nodded acceptance and added, 'So that's why I'm back. Because you pulled a few strings and got me reinstated. Well, I have a lot on at the moment, Phillip so you can tell Julian that if I ever bump into Andrey Petrov, I will bear your request in mind. That's all I'm promising at this stage. Now then, go on, Phillip. What did Ushanka have to offer?'

Phillip offered a tray of chocolate biscuits to Boyd who declined. Selecting one for himself, he took a bite, and then said, 'We had an interesting conversation which culminated in him informing me that the Russian terrorist Jamil Volkov has arrived in England. Jamil wants to kill the Prime Minister.'

'And you believed him?'

'Why should I not?'

'Who have you told so far?' probed the detective.

'As you might expect,' revealed Phillip. 'I've informed the Foreign Secretary: Sir Henry Fielding, Maude Black: the Home Secretary, the Chief of MI6, the Metropolitan Police Commissioner, and the Prime Minister. I thought that was sufficient in the circumstances. I'm sure they will get back to me once they've assessed the problem, carried out a risk assessment, addressed the intended movements of the Prime Minister in the coming days, and decided what action should be taken. I'm expecting an internet conversation with them all later today.'

'Which do you want me to do? Try to recruit Ushanka or arrest Jamil Volkov?'

'Both!' replied Phillip. 'The attempted assassination of the prime minister takes centre stage for now. Recruiting Ushanka is important but preserving the life of our prime minister is obvious.'

'That's just what Ushanka wanted you to do,' declared Boyd. 'You fell right into his trap, didn't you?'

'What do you mean, Boyd? Fell into Ushanka's trap!'

'When I was with Abraham on Solitude Beach in Porto Santo, he told me a completely different story.'

'I don't understand.'

'Ushanka told you one thing. Abraham told me otherwise.'

Somewhat agitated and potentially quarrelsome, Phillip replied, 'I've yet to see your report regarding the debriefing of

Abraham. You seem to have taken your time in its preparation. It could have been on my desk some days ago.'

Annoyed, Boyd shook his head and replied disparagingly, 'That's because you took me on a so-called holiday to Madeira and we happened to visit Porto Santo. I wasn't officially working for you or anyone else at the time, was I, Phillip? Deniability and all that. I only got to know yesterday that I've been reinstated. I'd thank you for treating me with the respect I deserve. You asked me to meet Abraham and assess him. I did so. The fact that you may not like the result of that assessment is your problem. Not mine. A full report regarding Abraham's information will be with you later today once I finally get back into my office.'

'I see! Yes! My apologies, Boyd.'

'Careful, Phillip!' suggested Boyd. 'Someone may open an enquiry into your abilities if you admit a mistake.'

'You never miss an opportunity to hit back, do you?'

'True! But only when I'm hit first.'

Pouring more coffee into his cup, Phillip slackened his attitude and said, 'There's something else I want to discuss with you, Billy. At the end of our meeting in the Tate, Ushanka asked after Toni. I need to know if the Russians have her home address and whether she is safe.'

'What did he say that alerted you to a problem?'

'He told me to give Antonia his blessings. He used the name Antonia only, not her surname, or the name Toni.'

'Blessings!' replied Boyd thoughtfully. 'A term usually associated with the church and religion. I'm not sure. But it was hardly threatening, was it?'

'No, but I'm worried they have targeted her. I'd like you to take responsibility for her safety.'

'Why don't you use your people?'

'It's an abuse of power. I can't take advantage of my position as Director General to use my staff on a private matter.'

'But it's not a private matter if Ushanka mentioned it to you and you perceive it as a possible threat. You seem to think you can use me and my people for your own use,' challenged Boyd. 'And I'm getting tired of being used like a pawn in a game.'

'Apart from that,' added Phillip. 'We may have a leak in the organisation. Someone might have told the Russians about Antonia, or to be precise, told them more than I would like them to know.'

'You know all about Ushanka,' proposed Boyd. 'He'll expect that in his position. He'll know it. Maybe he was just throwing a name at you to see how you would react.'

'You may be correct. It's only the second time I have come face-to-face with Andrey Petrov. We coded him Ushanka because he's Russia's headman here and always wears a ushanka when he's out and about. He's no fool and looks the part. You are right about so many things. But now I ask you as a friend if you can help. I just need Toni to be safe and I don't want it advertised or well known in either the organisation or in government circles that we may have a leak or that I am overreacting to Ushanka. I need to portray myself as competent and in charge of the Russian bear, not afraid that he might degrade and humiliate me.'

Boyd set down his coffee and replied, 'I respect your candid attitude, but surely you can wrangle a way around the situation to come up with a protection operation using your people?'

'Not without jeopardising my position.'

'I'll accept what you say for now. Phillip. I'll arrange for Toni to stay with my wife until things are clear. Meg will be happy to accommodate Toni. They get on well. Does that suit?'

'A splendid idea. I'll let her know we have received some intelligence that concerns her safety and I need to make her safe.'

'And she'll access the Ticker Intelligence system and realise there is no such intelligence report because she manages the computer system every day. No! Leave it with me, Phillip. I'll speak with Toni and explain things. I'll make it my objective to secure her safety. There will be no paperwork and no digital record. It's your turn to play by my rules. Is that agreed?'

'Perfectly! Thank you, Billy.'

'My other objective is to find Jamil Volkov,' declared Boyd. 'And I'll be using Abraham in that endeavour.'

'Excellent,' beamed a happier Phillip. 'Yes! The Prime Minister called a COBRA meeting. The Cabinet Office Briefing Rooms are often well used when they need to be.'

'Good!'

'Authority has been given to terminate Jamil Volkov.'

'Purely as a result of information provided to you by Ushanka?' probed Boyd.

'Yes! Ushanka is a formidable opponent, but he has switched sides to help us catch an Al Qaeda-trained terrorist of Muslim extraction. Jamil was a member of the Taleban, was trained in terrorism by Al Qaeda, and is an ISIS warrior.'

'That's wrong,' disputed Boyd raising his voice to a pitch that surprised the Director General. 'You've not even read my report on Abraham's information from Solitude Beach. How can you support such a thing?'

'I did say your report should have hit my desk by now.'

'Ushanka has told you that Jamil Volkov is a Muslim terrorist trained by Jihadists to kill our prime minister. Abraham tells me Jamil's target is the Russian ambassador.'

'Ambassador Nikolai Lermontov!' remarked Phillip. 'Are you sure? Can Abraham be trusted?'

'Can Ushanka be trusted?' challenged Boyd.

'What a mishmash of an affair,' replied Phillip. 'Who do we believe and who do we trust? One set of government ministers will want Jamil terminated because he is an Al Qaeda terrorist. They'll want him prevented from murdering the prime minister; they'll prefer he works for us. They'll approve of the fact that he can continue killing the Russian military leadership. I'm going with my first thought. Locate Jamil and terminate. He is Al Qaeda. If you have a problem with that a phone call to Hereford will result in Special Forces being deployed to assist you in carrying out that order.'

'And I thought such things only happened in Russia,' mused Boyd before he replied loudly, "That's stupid. It's not the way forward, Phillip. No way!'

'You are relying on the word of a man that you haven't seen for twenty-plus years, Boyd.'

'And you are relying on the word of a man you have met twice.'

'Right now, I'm going with Ushanka, not Abraham.'

'Why don't you play the long game, Phillip?'

'What do you mean by that?'

'Stop thinking like the government ministers and the politicians who are famous for regularly changing their opinions. Put Ushanka's hat on for a moment. Don't you see? He's playing a game. The Russians want Jamil Volkov dead. Ushanka is moving you into a position whereby he wants to kill Jamil here, on British soil, to prove to the world how wonderful Russia is by saving the British prime minister.'

'You've lost me, Boyd.'

'Then find me again because if the Russians find Jamil before we do, they'll use him in a dozen different ways against us.'

'Really! Tell me one!'

'They find him. They manoeuvre him to a place where they know the prime minister is located. They kill Jamil having made it look as if he were about to assassinate the British prime minister. The Russians become lifesavers. They are heroes in the eyes of the international media and once the Kremlin know about Jamil, they'll be heroes in the Motherland too. Unexpectedly, the Russians aren't that bad after all. They reply by reminding everyone that their claim regarding Ukraine ought to be acceptable. They are right and we are wrong. It's another nail in the NATO argument. Another feather in the Russian cap as they change world opinion. How can they be an enemy when they are saving people like our prime minister from certain death? Think about it, Phillip. It's not beyond the realms of possibility. Indeed, it's quite complex but surely achievable.'

Phillip paused, nodded his understanding, and considered the matter.

'The truth is,' continued Boyd. 'Jamil is plotting to assassinate Nikolai Lermontov. He's the current ambassador. What's he like? What kind of man is Nikolai?'

'The ambassador is a dynamic individual who comes across rather well,' replied Phillip. 'Highly intelligent, sharp, quick-witted, mid-fifties with a slight paunch because he's always either out to lunch or dining out during the evenings.'

'Is he close to Ushanka?' questioned Boyd.

'Oh yes. Their working lives intermingle regularly because Ushanka is the cultural attaché. That doesn't make them friends by the way. But why is he the target?'

'Jamil is attacking the Russian State. He wants to murder the ambassador because he's against Russia sending Muslim soldiers to Ukraine to fight. If the ambassador is killed on British soil Jamil will be blamed and it will be seen as a further act orchestrated by the British who allow it to happen. Ushanka is no fool. He'll have something up his sleeve to twist the media to his way of thinking. A dead Russian ambassador on British soil only helps the reason for the war in Ukraine. A dead Muslim terrorist intent on killing a British prime minister killed by the Russians here on British soil is a point in their favour which may change the way other countries think of them and enhance their claim to Ukraine.'

'I've never heard anything so ridiculous in my life,' chided Phillip. 'What other fantasies did Abraham tell you?'

'That it might all change if Russia had a new president or if NATO talked peace and fully understood the Russian claims and the reason for them. He argues NATO should talk about peace instead of ramping up the war whenever they think it right.'

'No one would support those words right now, Boyd,' argued Phillip. 'Everyone from NATO to Ukraine to across the Atlantic wants that megalomaniac out of office.'

'Do they want a new megalomaniac instead?' queried Boyd. 'What guarantee is there we will get a different character?'

'The government won't go with Abraham's words, and I'd only ever describe Abraham to government circles as a highly placed sensitive source.'

'I'd better tell you what he told me about Shamash then.'

'Shamash? What the hell are you talking about, Boyd?'

'Shamash is an Al Qaeda operation happening right now in London. It's a fraudulent operation created by Al Qaeda to gather money from the Jewish community and give it to the Jihadist war machine. They're using a tiny number of Arab Jews to carry out the crime by pretending to be true Jews whilst working for the Jihadists.

'Good God, man! Are you telling me we have an Al Qaeda nest on our doorstep and we're unaware of it?'

'Yes! I am, or to be precise, Abraham is. He quietly evaluated me on Solitude Beach and told me I had been sent to assess him not receive intelligence from him.'

'Well! He was right about that,' agreed Phillip. 'He asked to see you. You knew him and were sent to assess him.'

'Abraham told me Shamash is a secret society based in London pretending to be Jewish. He said that he hadn't passed that intelligence to his Mossad handlers. It's his ticket out of the intelligence game into retirement. I believe him.'

Phillip fidgeted with a teaspoon, a saucer, and an empty cup, as he studied Boyd's face and eventually offered, 'Almost identical to Ushanka who told me his top-secret information was such that he hadn't passed it to the Kremlin.'

'Two sources of potentially high-grade lifesaving information,' remarked Boyd. 'Both about the same subject. One of them is lying.'

'I agree. But how do we work out which one is a liar?'

'Read my report, Phillip. It will be in your hands today. Meanwhile, I've tasked Abraham to visit Shamash. He's been a member since they started because he was identified by them as an Arab Jew who supported Al Qaeda and the Jihadist side of Islam. Abraham expects Jamil to get his killing gear from those who run Shamash. You see, Phillip, you sent me on holiday for a rest and I ended up with more objectives and more work than I've seen in a month of Sundays. My other objective is to take down Shamash and the Al Qaeda operation and arrest Jamil Volkov as opposed to killing him.'

Still fidgeting, Phillip looked Boyd in the eye and declared, 'Boyd! I've always trusted you. You are blessed with the ability to think outside of the box. You think like the opposition to beat the opposition. It sounds easy but it is difficult to achieve. Believe me. I've tried it to some effect, but you have mastered it. I've watched you mature into the best of the best and take so many others with you on that journey. But right now, I'm going to sit on the fence until I've read your report. I'll play your long game based purely on the fact that everything is up in the air. I need your report and the assessment of the government ministers I've spoken to. Only then will I decide based on the knowledge I possess and the instructions I am given.'

'You have the knowledge now, Phillip,' growled Boyd 'And the power! Make sure your government ministers are aware of the content of my report.'

'I will,' agreed Phillip. 'I'll refer to the source as having been derived from a secret and sensitive origin.'

'I would expect that of you, Phillip. Please remember, that when you first sat in that chair you were chosen to occupy it because of your abilities. Now you sit in it and listen to the politicians around you. Be an intelligence officer, Phillip. Not a government puppet.'

Boyd turned on his heel. He was gone from the office of the Director General of the Security Service leaving Sir Phillip Nesbitt biting his lip wondering who was right and who was wrong, and whether it had been such a good idea to reappoint Boyd.

An hour later Boyd signed off his report from the Abraham meeting on Solitude Beach, Porto Santo, and caused its secure delivery by hand to Phillip. Then he picked up the phone to speak with Meg to tell her of the impending visit of Antonia, and the reason for it. Lastly, he called Antonia and explained the full story concerning both Abraham and Ushanka, and the dilemma facing everyone at that time.

Meg indicated she had no problem with welcoming Antonia to the fold, and then reminded Boyd how right she had been about the outcome of the enquiry against him. Boyd acquiesced, listened to his wife's tirade of sound advice, told her he loved her, and then put the phone down. Antonia bucked and bellowed for a short time before Boyd told her the full story and reminded Antonia that she would have access to his office at home where she could tap into the Ticker system from a secure remote site. Like Meg, Antonia prattled on. Initially, she expressed annoyance at Phillip's desire to pass the problem to Boyd but then she decided a break was needed and rushed off to pack a suitcase.

Eventually, Boyd walked into the main office. It was deserted.

'Anthea!' he called but to no avail. 'Anthea!'

The duty detective manning the Commercial Desk appeared at the doorway and replied, 'Welcome back, Guvnor. Superintendent Adams is out on a job. Your informant *Ground Sparrow* phoned with information regarding the whereabouts of Robert Fitzpatrick: The robber outstanding from the post office job in Brixton. Unfortunately, you were not available, so she deployed the whole crew on duty. The cupboard is bare. Coffee, Guvnor? I can rustle a brew for you if you wish.'

'Thanks, Bob! I'll give it a miss if you don't mind. What did *Ground Sparrow* say and where are the troops now?'

'Clapham Common just off Brixton! Your man rang to say that Fitzpatrick is slumming it in a tent on the Common. Since you were suspended, Guvnor, Anthea has rattled every snout in the borough and beyond. They've missed him a few times, but her strategy is such that Fitzpatrick has run out of foxholes. He's nowhere to go and his pals have ditched him because Anthea has well and truly put the word out that anyone found harbouring him will be hung, drawn, and quartered. I reckon Fitzpatrick is holed up on the Common waiting for things to die down.'

'And Anthea has the area closed down completely?' queried Boyd.

'Oh, yes, Guvnor. She's driving the tactics now. Gradually closing in on the wanted man. Quite a few people camp out overnight on the common when the weather is good, but she's whittled the numbers down and has a target in sight. The superintendent took twenty-four armed officers with her plus Ricky and his drones. The Air Support Unit has been called in and the red blanket is down.'

'Never known the office so quiet,' remarked Boyd. 'Just you and me here. Am I right?'

'You are, plus a bank of phones and a Ticker computer system. Antonia is at home. She just rang to tell me she'll be operating from another base for a while.'

'That was quick,' chuckled Boyd. 'Turn the unit radio system up. Let's listen in.'

A finger and thumb turned the knob and the unit's radio network sprang to life with the words of Anthea rattling the airwaves, 'All units confirm your positions.'

The net was full of callsigns and locations before Anthea again radioed, 'I confirm we're locking down the target area. Drone coverage pinpoints the location of a green two-man tent beneath the trees and partially enclosed by bushes near Long Pond and Rookery Road. No sign of the target! He may be in the tent or the immediate vicinity. All units respond so far.'

Again, there was a bundle of responses on the net.

'I call a Trigger incident. The suspect is armed and dangerous. Mobiles, prepare to close Rookery Road. Teams One and Three, prepare to take closer order. Teams Two and Four, provide support. Bannerman has ground control. Try to negotiate with the target. Janice, you're Bannerman's backup. All units acknowledge.'

The network complied.

Boyd offered a smile to Bob who threw a chuckle back and added, 'She's not going to let him get away this time.'

'India Nine-Nine approaching the scene,' whistled across the airwaves when a police helicopter came into play and then radioed, 'Circling! I have the tent in sight. Wait one! Thermal Imaging Detector in use. Engaging!'

Boyd imagined a helicopter above Clapham Common slowing to a steady manageable speed and altitude with twenty-plus pairs of eyes looking upwards to the heavens.

'India Nine-Nine reports a positive thermal image detected at the tent. Hey, guys! I think your man is still at home. He is lying down. Wait one!' There was a pause and then, 'Confirmed! The subject is lying on his stomach in the tent and is pointing a long-barrelled rifle through the flaps. Advise caution.'

'I have that,' radioed Bannerman. 'I'm moving closer with the megaphone. Standby!'

'Sounds dodgy,' remarked Bob in the unit office. 'I hope he doesn't get too close. What's the firing range of a rifle, Guvnor?'

'Half a mile or more!'

'Would you send in the dogs?'

'I might.'

'Boss to Bannerman,' radioed Anthea. 'Two dog handlers are approaching from the other side. You may not see them yet.'

Bannerman took several giant strides followed by Janice who carried a ballistic shield and a rifle slung over her shoulder. The pair ended up behind a tree in a small copse about fifty yards from the tent. 'I have that,' radioed Bannerman who then switched on the megaphone and shouted, 'Robert Fitzpatrick! This is the police. You are surrounded. No escape this time, Fitzpatrick. Come out of the tent and stand tall with your arms held high.'

There was no reply.

Bannerman repeated his demands.

A bullet whistled from Fitzpatrick's rifle and slammed into the bark of a tree five yards from Bannerman's location.

'Hold your fire,' radioed Bannerman to the unit. He then lifted the megaphone again and said, 'Give yourself up, Fitzpatrick. You can shoot as many bullets as you want but you're wasting your time. Call it a day, buddy. Throw your rifle out of the tent.'

Another shot was taken and chipped more bark from the same tree followed by Fitzpatrick's voice booming, 'I'm not your buddy. I'm going to blast you to kingdom come.'

'Dogs!' radioed Bannerman. 'Let me hear them growl.'

Seconds later two dog handlers obliged, and a couple of Alsatians began barking incessantly in the distance.

'Hear those dogs, Fitzpatrick?' bellowed Bannerman on the horn. 'They're coming for you if you don't give up your weapon. Think about it, Fitzpatrick. If you come quietly now it might save you a year or two in prison if the judge so decides. Good behaviour and all that. Maybe even a touch of remorse at what you've done. Try to shoot your way out, Fitzpatrick, and that might just get you bitten here there and everywhere by those hungry growling police dogs. Throw the weapon down! Now!'

Fitzpatrick did not reply.

'India Nine-Nine, permission!'

'Go ahead,' replied Bannerman.

The thermal image shows the subject retreating inside the tent and leaving the weapon at the entrance. We are monitoring.'

'I have that,' replied Bannerman.

A short time later there was a flutter at the tent flap and Fitzpatrick appeared with the rifle in his hand.

Janice Burns levelled her rifle and took a bead. She was joined by every other armed officer at the site.

'Look around you,' voiced Bannerman. 'You're outgunned, outmanned, and out of time. Drop the weapon.'

Reluctantly, Fitzpatrick shouted, 'No chance!' He bent down, jabbed the rifle into his throat, and pulled the trigger.

One single bullet rifled along the long barrel, egressed the muzzle, and travelled directly into Fitzpatrick's skull at a speed of about seventeen hundred miles an hour.

The bullet blew the fugitive's head off.

Fitzpatrick's body wobbled. A messy vision of blood, blubber and bodily remains sat on the shoulders as the legs twitched, the knees capitulated, and Fitzpatrick's body tumbled to the ground in slow motion. A terrifying display of horror emblazoned the pitch.

'Holy Moses!' yelled Bannerman in astonishment.

'Goodbye, Mister Fitzpatrick,' offered Janice as she lowered her weapon and allowed the ballistic shield to drop. 'Well, we never thought he'd give in easily, but I certainly didn't expect that.'

'Did you hear gunshots on the radio?' queried Bob in the unit's office.

'I thought so,' replied Boyd. 'What happened?'

The radio came alive again from the scene with Bannerman reporting, 'Trigger incident closed. The suspect is down having committed suicide at the scene. Request the medical team to certify the death and carry out procedures. Lift the red blanket and inform Borough Command.'

Ricky replied, 'I have that. In progress!'

Anthea walked over to join her colleagues. The trio attended the tent, removed the rifle, made it safe, and then studied the remains of Robert Fitzpatrick.

'Incident closed,' reflected Anthea. 'The wanted man is no more. Bannerman, arrange a reception team for Borough Command and the Coroner's officer. Resume the dogs and the Air Support Unit. Request statements of evidence at the soonest possible juncture. Get a forensics team to examine the body, the tent, and the scene: the usual procedure, please. Secure any evidence that they find and stand down for a debrief. Let me know your time of arrival as soon as you have it. And, oh yes, ring Scotland Yard. I'm sure they'll want the press in on this one. By the way, in the event of their attendance, we are unable to comment since the matter is in the hands of the coroner.'

'Will do, Ma'am,' replied Bannerman with a grin. 'It was never going to be an easy one. He made it short and sweet.'

'His decision. Not ours,' replied Anthea.

Back in the unit's office, Boyd glanced at Bob and said, 'All that planning and Fitzpatrick took his own life. Still, it was only his life and no one else's. Yes, Bob. I think I will have that coffee now if you don't mind. Black! No sugar! Listening to all that was uniquely different from being on the ground with everyone.'

A phone at the Commercial Desk rang causing Bob to gesture to Boyd to make the coffee himself. Bob sat down, lifted the phone, and returned to work.

'Phones!' murmured Boyd. 'I wonder how Phillip is getting on. Good zoom or bad zoom?'

In the Director General's office, Sir Phillip engaged the computer screen via the Zoom software facility and listened to the argument. Maud Black, the Home Secretary argued for the termination of Jamil Volkov before he could ignite the underground Jihadist movement. Sir Henry, the Foreign Secretary, called for Jamil to be captured and recruited to work for British Intelligence. Preferably on Russian soil where he could continue his exemplary work in disposing of senior commanders in the Russian military. The Police Commissioner merely agreed with both parties and sat on the fence. Other cabinet ministers and Chief of Defence staff made similar challenges for both sides of the argument.

They were all interested to hear of Islamic Jihadists posing as Jews to extricate money from the Jewish community. The police commissioner suggested that Boyd be allowed to continue the investigation without interference from COBRA.

When it was clear that no progress was being made, Boyd's ability was questioned. Was he once again making mountains out of a molehill? Could Boyd be trusted so soon after reappointment?

After an hour and a half, Phillip called a halt to the meeting, thanked everyone for their input, and switched the computer off.

Phillip was no further forward. No one could agree on a way forward. The good, the bad, and the ugly were at play and whilst all the arguments formed some modicum of sense, none of them were attractive. Whatever the final decision, someone somewhere was going to be killed because of the power of the State.

It was even suggested that some credence ought to be awarded to the Russians. They had stepped forward to help British Society, so they perhaps weren't as bad as they were led to believe.

'Oh, for a magic wand,' thought Phillip.

~

12

Glenridding
The Lake District, Cumbria.
The following day.

An hour before dawn broke a campervan slid gracefully into the village car park near Greenside Road. The driver turned the vehicle around and reversed towards a row of houses. He switched the engine off and watched for traffic moving through the village. Only a post office van and a taxi flew through the rural sprawl, eager to take advantage of the fact that the road skirting Ullswater was almost deserted.

The driver checked his rear-view mirror and then his side mirrors. Content, he congratulated himself on his parking abilities when he confirmed that he had located the campervan directly opposite the fourth house in the row of quintessential homes that adorned this part of Glenridding.

Lowering the driver's window, he listened to the gurgling ripple of Ulls Water as it meandered through the settlement and into the lake known as Ullswater. The stream rose in two places on the heights of Helvellyn that dominated Glenridding. Divided by Swirral Edge, waters from Red Tarn and Brown Cove Tarn finally joined below Catstye Cam and rushed into Ullswater near the village sailing centre.

Blue curtains and rose bushes in the front garden confirmed to Mikhail that he was watching the home of Yuri and Svetlana Pavlova. They were Russians by birth but no longer tolerated by the Russian State. It was said they hurt Russia from within because of their political views. Indeed, many commentators noticed how anyone who opposed the State was a problem for the State to deal with. Some opposition politicians, for example, had been imprisoned for extremism by a system that was not considered to be a good example of a working democracy.

'The car,' thought Mikhail. 'Where is it?'

Mikhail clambered into the rear of the campervan, settled by the darkened rear window, and scanned the row of houses. The Mercedes was parked some twenty yards from Pavlova's house.

Ten minutes went by. Mikhail listened for the speech of humans, watched for the movement of people, and glanced at a delivery van speeding through the village towards Kendal.

'Nothing untoward here,' radioed Ivan. We are ready.'

'All clear! Come!' replied Mikhail.

'Travelling!' radioed Viktor.

On a layby a quarter of a mile away, Viktor pressed the ignition button on the motorcycle handlebar. The engine purred. He selected first gear and set off towards the village.

Minutes later, Mikhail radioed, 'No change! Come!'

Viktor turned into the car park and dismounted.

Opening one of the side panniers, Viktor removed a Matryoshka doll. Wearing his black leather skintight gloves, he opened the top of the doll and found a smaller doll inside. He removed the smaller doll and dropped the larger one into the pannier. Viktor continued to remove all the dolls. One by one, they decreased in size until he was left with a single complete doll. With the unused nest of dolls in his pannier, he opened the last doll and removed a cylindrical metal tin that was fitted with an aerosol spray. The device was the size of his thumb, and he handled the spray with great care.

'All clear,' radioed Mikhail.

'Proceed!' added Ivan.

Viktor, still wearing his crash helmet and leathers, strolled towards the Mercedes owned by the Pavlova couple, paused, and bent down by the side of the car as if to do up his boot laces.

Ivan sprayed the door handle with the contents of his tin and then made his way to the boot and passenger side where he again released the spray at key points of his choice.

Once he had completed that task, Ivan approached the Pavlova house, discreetly sprayed the handle on the garden gate and then sprayed the front door.

The spray was a soft hiss; the delivery hushed, speedy and clandestine. Released by a hand that had been trained in contaminating a target area with a lethal substance.

Viktor returned to his motorcycle, deposited the spray in the smallest of dolls, and rode north towards Penrith.

'All clear,' from Mikhail. 'Not even a twitching curtain.'

'Closed!' from Ivan. 'Resume!'

As the first sunrays of the day struck Ullswater, the Russian intelligence officers vacated Glenridding.

At a clearing beside Ullswater, Viktor stopped, opened the pannier, withdrew the doll, and threw it into the lake. Within seconds, the doll was submerged carrying with it what remained of a deadly substance wrapped in a nest of wooden dolls never to surface again.

By midday, Viktor was on a flight to Moscow from Manchester airport. He would be home later that day. Tomorrow, he would be in Yakustk: a port city on the River Lena in eastern Siberia. The metropolis is home to the Mammoth Museum where millennia-old fossils of woolly mammoths are exhibited in an underground laboratory at the Melnikov Permafrost Institute. For Viktor, Yakustk meant home. Far from the eyes of the global media.

Later that day, Yuri and Svetlana Pavlova left their home in Glenridding, walked down the path, opened the wooden gate that led to their vehicle, and unlocked the Mercedes. The couple drove towards Penrith admiring the view and talking of how beautiful the Lake District was. On arrival in Penrith, they parked the car and went to their favourite restaurant in the centre of town where they enjoyed a two-course meal and a glass of wine each. Relaxed, chilled, and enjoying life, Yuri held his wife's hand when he escorted her back to the car park. They again unlocked the vehicle, drove home, opened the wooden gate, walked down the garden path, and unlocked the front door.

The following morning, Yuri woke first, realised his wife was frothing at the mouth, and tried to wake her. Unable to do so, Yuri laid his wife on her side in the recovery position and went downstairs to use the telephone.

Ringing 999, Yuri quickly explained that his wife was seriously ill and in need of urgent medical care. Hurriedly, he described the symptoms, the froth at her mouth, the dampness of skin to the touch, and the paleness of her face when he had tried to wake her.

The call handler took notes and directed an emergency ambulance and the police to the scene.

Less than an hour later, the ambulance arrived at the house in Glenridding. Despite repeatedly banging on both front and rear doors, the paramedics could not gain entry.

Ben Parker, a police constable arrived. Stationed locally, he knew of the house and the occupants, knew a Russian couple lived there, and was aware they had been accepted by the local community. PC Parker looked through the windows of the house, checked the details of the phone call with the handler, and then broke a window. Ben climbed into the front room and found the body of Yuri Pavlova lying in the hallway. He knelt by the body, could not detect a pulse, and then ventured upstairs to discover Svetlana who had also passed away. Again, his fingers pressed her temple and carotid artery but there was no sign of life.

Puzzled as to the froth now drying at the edge of Svetlana's lips, and the sudden mysterious death of both individuals at the same time, Ben stood in the bedroom with his arms folded. There was no way he wanted to disturb anything that might be evidence. Experienced, Ben did not panic, did not make hasty decisions, but took time to reflect on the situation. He kept his hands in his pockets and wondered if he was at the scene of two sudden but natural deaths. Or was he the first at a murder scene?

'I need a doctor to pronounce death,' thought Ben. 'But there's something odd about the whole affair.'

Glancing at a pile of publications on the bedside table, Ben thought, 'They are readers. Books, newspapers, magazines.' He turned the first page of a book and saw the library imprint. 'Library books,' he remarked.

One magazine had been opened and then folded at a particular page. Ben pulled it from the stack and read the article. The piece related to the murder of Sergei Skripal, a former Russian military officer who became a double agent for British intelligence, and his daughter, Yulia. They were poisoned at their home in Salisbury in 2018. Reading the article, Ben discovered that one symptom of the Novichok nerve agent used in their murders was foaming at the mouth.

Glancing at the body of Svetlana and the remnants of foam at the side of her mouth, Ben contemplated whether he was contaminated with whatever had caused these deaths.

Once downstairs, the policeman climbed back out through the window and told the ambulance crew what he had found. The medics wanted him to go back into the house, open the door, and allow them inside to double-check that the two souls had truly departed. Or were they just unconscious? After all, it was said, the ambulance crew were paramedics, Ben was a policeman with a First Aid certificate.

Ben related the tale of Sergei and Yulia Skripal and of how they had been poisoned by a nerve agent. Recalling the magazine article from the bedside table, he suggested they remove their outer clothing in case they had been contaminated by a nerve agent. He recited the piece he had read indicating that nerve agents can spread from one person to another through clothing or skin by touch or unseen vapour. He removed his police tunic and watched as the paramedics removed theirs. Then he opened the boot of his patrol car, removed a bottle of water, and poured the contents onto his hands. He then splashed his face with water and, with what was left, handed the bottle to the ambulance crew.

'I don't know whether I'm right or wrong,' explained Ben. 'Maybe I'm overreacting. What I do know is that these two people are Russian. They seemed friendly enough although I heard tell the Russian government thought they were extremists. No one in my job ever told me they were spies on our side like the Skripals were. Am I being stupid or doing it right? What do you think?'

One of the ambulance crew replied, 'We've never seen anything like this before and I don't like it one little bit. We're with you but we need advice before we do anything else. I think we should examine the patients to make sure they're gone.'

'Oh, they're dead alright,' replied Ben. 'I'm not a doctor but I've seen many a dead body in my time. You'll have to take my word for it. We need to look after ourselves, not them. Sorry! It probably goes against all the training and all the protocols. I don't know but I'm forbidding you to enter the house and suggest we help cordon off the immediate area and call for assistance.'

Reluctantly, the ambulance crew agreed.

Making a call to police headquarters, PC Parker connected to the Head of CID: Max Johnston. Ben related the affair to the head of detectives. The event mushroomed immediately. Max activated the major response team as a precaution. All that Ben had considered was supported by Max. Within a few hours, an incident room had been set up at the Inn on the Lake Hotel in Glenridding.

A team of scientists from Porton Down (a science and defence technology site in Wiltshire) were dispatched to the scene. They arrived by helicopter dressed in biological suits. The response unit carried secure metal cases and was not identifiable to the media. The possible use of a nerve agent was such that a local doctor was not called to the scene in case of lingering contamination. Rather, death was certified by a senior scientific and medical expert from Porton Down who would give evidence of the deaths in a court of law if needed.

Porton Down is one of the most secret science and technology laboratories in the United Kingdom. Occupying 7,000 acres, most of its work is not known. Even parliamentarians and government ministers are not privy to the workings of this Ultra Top-Secret Agency.

With time on their side, the police closed the A592 between Matterdale and Windermere thus preventing media attendance in the early stages of the enquiry.

As the day progressed, Ben Parker and the ambulance crew were admitted to a specially prepared Isolation Ward at the Cumberland Infirmary, Carlisle, where they were monitored for the next month. Initially, they experienced headaches, runny noses, tight chests, and minor problems with eyesight, but overnight things worsened. The doctors placed all three on heart and lung machines and treated them with the drug *atropine*. It was touch and go whether they had caught them in time. It wasn't known if they would recover to some degree of normality. In the weeks that followed, the trio improved and eventually returned to a normal life. Despite that, they were each monitored for many years to come.

It was a medical fact that if diagnosed early enough, as in the case of the Skripals, and treated immediately, recovery from nerve agent poisoning was described as very possible.

Both the police car and ambulance were cleansed. Initially, the vehicles were scrubbed out by biologically suited operatives using hot soapy water which diluted any traces of a nerve agent. This was repeated and high-pressure hoses were used in every nook and cranny before the vehicles were again washed under instructions from the Porton Down experts. Eventually, the trio were released having suffered mainly from loss of energy, sickness, diarrhoea, and blurred vision.

In the afternoon, the Head of CID, Max, arranged to phone Boyd. He intended to inform him of the investigation taking place. As ever, Boyd may have been seconded to the Special Crime Unit in London, but he remained a Cumbrian officer. And Max Johnston knew the case would interest Boyd and the Special Crime Unit.

Whilst Cumbria police investigated events on the shores of Ullswater, it was a different story in London.

In Oxford Street, Bannerman swung the squad car around and took off in response to a call from the Commercial Desk that source *Abraham* had sighted Jamil Volkov in a department store.

From the passenger seat, DS Janice Burns glanced at Bannerman and said, 'Hoof it, Bannerman! We can get this man off the streets today if we're lucky Boyd tells me source *Abraham* has never been wrong in his entire life.'

'I know,' nodded Bannerman as he manoeuvred into the centre of the road, activated the siren and blue flashing headlights, and headed for Oxford Circus. 'All we've got is a photograph of this Jamil Volkov fella. I'd prefer it if I knew him. Up close and personal is always the best way.'

'Then today is our lucky day,' replied Janice. 'You can go nose to nose with him when we catch him.'

A taxi emerged from a side road, braked, and narrowly missed the squad car as Bannerman held his position and drove down the street. Here and there, pedestrians refrained from dashing across the road. Vehicles pulled into the nearside allowing Bannerman to guide their car through the heavy traffic at a reasonably safe speed. With two sets of traffic lights defeated, Bannerman was through the Bond Street junction with three more positioned to negotiate before arrival at Oxford Circus. The siren screeched horrendously as the London traffic surrendered to Bannerman's desires.

'Arab looking! Mid-thirties, tall, lean, long dark hair, and a beard,' declared Janice. 'He'll nay be wearing a kilt or a sporran,

Bannerman, but he'll hear our bagpipes when we get closer. With luck, he might think we're an ambulance.'

'I'll switch off when we hit the right street,' snapped Bannerman. 'If he's wearing a kilt, he'll be easy to spot but he might just have a dirk hidden in his sock. Now be a good passenger and keep a lookout. I'm doing the driving. You, your bagpipes, and your bloody sporran! Stow it, woman.'

At Oxford Circus, Bannerman snatched a lower gear, swung the steering wheel, and entered Regent Street. Almost immediately, he killed the siren and lights. The squad car crept slowly down the street as the duo checked out the faces.

The hands of the clock moved on a few minutes before Janice pointed and yelled, 'There! Near that shop. That's him!'

'Could be,' voiced Bannerman.

The target was on the other side of the street causing Bannerman to drive past the man of Middle Eastern extraction before glancing over his shoulder. The man's olive complexion, dark eyes and dark beard resembled the photograph that Janice clutched in her hand when she announced, 'That's him, Bannerman. Pull over.'

Bannerman activated his blue lights and flashing headlights as, against the flow of traffic, he swung the squad car across the road and slid to a standstill by the kerbside.

Janice was out of the car and approaching the target within seconds shouting, 'Jamil! This is the police! Stand still!'

The man faltered, saw the blue lights of the squad car, and turned around.

'Wait!' yelled Janice. 'Stand still, Jamil!'

Too late. Jamil retreated, spun to face Oxford Circus, and glanced over his shoulder at the approaching detective.

'Stay where you are!' ordered Janice.

Jamil was off, broke into a sprint, and pushed a postman out his way as he made good his escape.

Hot in pursuit, Janice set off after the Arab as Bannerman reversed the car trying to keep up with the chase. Surrendering, Bannerman carried out a three-point turn to the annoyance of a dozen motorists and joined the chase.

Jamil was tall, lean, and fit, launching himself across the street causing a bus to brake violently and a taxi driver to honk the horn.

Janice followed, jumped out of the way of a motorcycle, and collided with a woman pushing a pram before regaining her stride.

'All units, Oxford Circus area,' radioed Bannerman on the network. He passed the wanted man's description before adding, 'Made off north. Foot chase! We are in pursuit.'

The network filled with responses, but the Arab stole another yard or more when he stepped onto the highway and continued the race with Janice weaving in and out of pedestrians on the footpath.

Switching on the siren, Bannerman occupied the centre of the road, waved other motorists out of the way, and headed towards Oxford Circus intent on catching the escapee.

Jamil lengthened his stride and launched himself at a passing bus. He caught the handle of the boarding platform with Janice gaining ground when the bus crawled in slow-moving traffic.

The squad car burst past the traffic, swept in front of the bus, and brought it to a standstill.

As Janice jumped on board the platform, Jamil stole past her and jumped back onto the tarmac.

The Arab was off again with Bannerman now involved in the foot chase having abandoned the squad car.

In full flight, Jamil dashed into a department store with the detectives closing him down as members of the public got in Jamil's way when they heard Janice shouting, 'Police! Stop that man!'

Running through the store, Jamil made for the escalator and leapt aboard the third tread as it motored towards the upper floor.

There was an almighty crash when Bannerman brought the Arab down with a rugby tackle. A struggle ensued with Jamil kicking out and trying to escape Bannerman's clutches.

Arriving seconds later, Janice took half a dozen steps up the moving escalator and then dived into the fray landing on top of Jamil just as he was about to punch Bannerman.

Shoppers looked on in amazement. Some screamed. Mothers clung tight to their children, and shop assistants stood in awe not quite sure what to do.

The escalator continued with the trio struggling, writhing against the machine's motion, and then dodging the groove when the ride came to an end, and they were on the upper floor.

Jamil was first on his feet, tried to run away, and was snagged by Bannerman's outstretched hand. Falling, Jamil crashed headlong into a mannequin wearing a wedding dress. The dummy wobbled, tumbled into the groom standing beside it, and then crashed into the entire wedding party of mannequins that dominated the floor. Within seconds, a display of wedding dresses, bridesmaid dresses, veils, bouquets, posies, garters, top hats, kilts, sporrans, dress shirts and bowties became a battleground as the trio destroyed the entire exhibition whilst fighting amongst the pageant.

Wallop! Bannerman landed a punch in Jamil's face and the Arab collapsed like a sack of potatoes being dropped from a grocer's wagon. Within seconds, Jamil had been handcuffed, dragged to his feet, and pushed against the wall.

'Jamil Volkov! You're nicked,' bellowed Bannerman.

'I forgot!' yelled Jamil. 'I forgot to go so I just ran.'

'What do you mean forgot to go,' queried Janice.

'To court! I forgot to go to court,' explained Jamil as the detectives manhandled him towards a staircase.

'Jamil Volkov! You are held for questioning concerning the preparation of a terrorist act,' growled Bannerman.

'Who!'

Bannerman paused, slung Jamil against a wall and said, 'Jamil Volkov! That's you! Show him the photograph, Janice.'

'It's in the car,' replied Janice. 'But it's him alright.'

'Mustafa!' yelled Jamil. 'I'm Jamil Mustafa!'

'From Russia!'

'No! Lewisham! I was born in Lewisham!' replied Jamil with a London accent. 'I'm British! Oh, I know! I have my father's looks but I'm a Londoner.'

'Turn his pockets out,' suggested Bannerman.

A driving licence ended up in Janice's hands. She turned it over, studied the photograph and details on the licence and handed it to Bannerman.

Holding the licence against Jamil's face, Bannerman probed, 'Who did you say you were?'

'Jamil Mustafa! I'm not a terrorist. I'm wanted on warrant by the Lewisham cops for failing to attend court.'

'On what charge?'

'Burglary!'

Relaxing his hold on Jamil slightly, Bannerman glanced at Janice, then the driving licence, and then Jamil again before saying, 'Knew it was you. Come on!'

'I'm not a terrorist,' exclaimed Jamil.

'No! I reckon you're not,' replied Bannerman. 'Wait!'

Janice hit the digits on her mobile phone, passed details of Jamil Mustafa to New Scotland Yard, and then said, 'Wait one. We're checking now.' A minute later, Janice acknowledged the Yard, and said, 'He's wanted on a warrant for non-appearance at Blackfriars Crown Court. It relates to a burglary charge.'

'That's the one!' snapped Jamil. 'Blackfriars! I knew I was gonna get time with my record, so I made a run for it. You would have done too. You were just lucky you caught me when you did.'

Confused, annoyed, and dismayed, Bannerman and Janice led Jamil Mustafa out of the department store and towards their squad car which was now surrounded by both members of the public and other patrol cars that had arrived at the scene. Bannerman had blocked most of the road when he abandoned the squad car and those drivers honking their horns were making sure he knew they were not happy at being delayed.

A police transit van pulled up. The rear doors were opened, and Jamil was bundled into the back with a uniformed officer.

'We'll follow you to the nick,' said Bannerman to the van driver. 'We'll need to book him in.'

'Good lift,' replied the van driver. 'We've been on the lookout for him for months.'

The Transit drove away leaving Janice and Bannerman looking at each other in the middle of Regent Street.

'Well! It was Jamil,' revealed Janice.

'But the wrong one.'

'I told you he might be wearing a kilt and a sporran. I was right about that.'

'Best arrest today,' chuckled Bannerman. 'Come on! We need to lodge the prisoner at the nick and do the paperwork.'

'Only arrest today,' replied Janice. 'Let's go!'

The detectives slid into their squad car where Bannerman lifted the radio transmitter and reported, 'All units Oxford Circus! One in custody arrested on warrant for non-appearance at Blackfriars Crown Court. Resuming patrol. Thank you one and all.'

Bannerman fired the engine as the network responded and the detectives journeyed to the police station.

In the Special Crime Unit, Boyd listened to the radio network. He was interested in the possible detention of Jamil Volkov since the man had not committed any offences in the UK that they knew of. Boyd knew there was only Abraham's word that suggested he was here to kill someone, and he also knew that Abraham would never give evidence. Abraham's identity had to be protected at all costs. Yet Boyd was also pleased that Inspector Bannerman and Detective Sergeant

Janice Burns were back in the unit where they belonged. A spent day perhaps. But Boyd thought it good to see his comrades.

The phone sounded and Boyd answered. It was Max Johnston, Cumbria's chief detective who filled Boyd in on what had occurred in Glenridding. No assistance was required at the Ullswater location but now Boyd was up to date with events and the two senior detectives could liaise should anything further relevant to the investigation come to light. Both men discussed the possibility that those responsible must have travelled to the scene by either public transport or private conveyance. It was agreed that Boyd's unit would use its expertise in examining CCTV locations in the Ullswater area between Penrith and Kirkstone Pass.

Boyd thanked Max and ended the call before making another call to Ricky: the unit's technical wizard. Within the hour, Ricky was at his desk examining CCTV systems in the Ullswater area.

The phone sounded again. It was Antonia who said, 'I've been listening to the chase in central London, Boyd. The details of the initial report are on Ticker. Do you know what that means?'

'Tell me.'

'Abraham was wrong. It wasn't Jamil Volkov.'

'He's allowed to make the odd mistake,' defended Boyd.

'Not this time around,' replied Antonia. 'Your man Abraham has just destroyed any credibility you and he had with Phillip. You told Phillip that Abraham was trustworthy. Phillip put that argument to the COBRA committee and the government ministers. Now he knows Abraham got something wrong. He won't be impressed at all.'

'But Phillip will surely know about the incident that recently occurred in Glenridding. If he doesn't, he soon will. That event smacks of poisoning and you don't need to be a great investigator to point at the chief suspect: Russia!'

'That's the problem,' explained Antonia. 'Glenridding will send opinion one way. Abraham's mistaken tip-off will send it back again. The scales of opinion, if there is such a thing, are unbalanced.

Just thought I'd tell you. By the way, I love your office here in Carlisle. But you've no coffee.'

'Thank you,' replied Boyd. 'Why don't you buy some.'

'Cheeky! I will,' chuckled Antonia. 'Before I do that there's something I want you to know.'

'Go on!'

'Glenridding! It makes me wonder if some pro-Russian alliance is alive and kicking in Cumbria.'

'I'm sure there will be,' suggested Boyd. 'The world is full of critics who fill their lives disapproving of anything.'

'Of that I'm sure,' replied Antonia. 'Whilst my team was carrying out a surveillance operation on Ushanka they connected him to an Alexander Lowther of Windermere. Lowther had travelled to London by train to have a night out in a Russian restaurant in Soho with Ushanka and his pals from the embassy. He's in the intelligence file I created as a result. It's called *Supporters of Russia in Cumbria*. I'm sending you the file by email to consider along with the surveillance logs relevant to Operation Ushanka. I want a fresh mind to look at these papers. I'd be obliged if you tell me what you think about the Ushanka file and the *Supporters of Russia in Cumbria* file. Check out the piece on Alexander Lowther and his wife Sheena. They might be linked to Glenridding.'

'Full surveillance?' enquired Boyd.

'Technical only at this stage,' replied Antonia. 'I'm applying for the warrant today.'

'Good! I'll deploy a covert enquiry team to Cumbria, Toni. Something is going on that we should know about. It might be connected to the Glenridding poisoning or it might just be a mini spy ring of some kind flexing its muscles.'

'Are you going to take over the Glenridding enquiry from Max Johnston?'

'Absolutely not!' expressed Boyd. 'Max is more than capable of progressing the enquiry to satisfaction. I'm not the only detective in Cumbria, Toni. I've discussed my role with Max and how we can assist when needed. He's on the ground making all the enquiries relevant to a crime that is certainly going to be recorded as murder. I work in a different world studying espionage and the illegal activities of certain Russians living here in the UK. If the two meet, then Max will be the first to know.'

'How about putting him wise to Alexander and Sheena Lowther?' suggested Antonia.

'I suppose we could,' replied Boyd. 'But the connection links to your Ushanka surveillance operation and that is classified beyond Max's security level. Leave it with me for now, Toni. Let's see what a covert team can uncover.'

'Understood!' replied Antonia.

Boyd downloaded Antonia's file on *Supporters of Russia in Cumbria* from his email system and quickly scanned through the opening pages and various lists that Antonia had made. Ten minutes later, he grabbed a pen from the desk and began writing a list of officers he intended to deploy to Cumbria.

Boyd phoned Anthea, brought himself up to date with what was happening in the office, and told her what plans he had for those bound for Cumbria. Eventually, Boyd phoned a colleague.

'Bannerman!' growled the detective inspector.

'Boyd here! I want you to go to Cumbria and look at anything that might be Russian.'

'No problem,' replied Bannerman. 'I take it we're looking for connections to Glenridding?'

'Yes! Just turn the place upside down in the usual manner. You're an ex-Cumbrian officer so you'll find your way around alright. Got a pen or pencil handy?'

'Fire away,' replied Bannerman.

'I'm reading a file from Antonia's service. It's about possible supporters of Russia who live in Cumbria. Here's your starter pack.'

'Go ahead. I'm ready.'

'According to the 2011 census, approximately 73,000 Russians are living in the UK of which an estimated 36,000 live in England. The rest are in Scotland, Wales, and Northern Ireland. If you divide that number by the number of English counties and then acknowledge the geopolitical makeup of each county, it's thought that about 200 Russians may live in Cumbria. Tops! It's an estimate! A wild guess! Using *open-source material*, I want you to lead the team in trying to identify as many Russians as possible living in Cumbria.'

'Done this before with regards to Irish and Islamic terrorism,' replied Bannerman. 'We'll examine the electoral register, businesses in the area, check planning applications, village magazines, noticeboards, newspaper articles, council meetings – anything that is best described as *open-source material*. Then we'll look at restaurants serving Russian food, language courses, libraries, and anything open to the public. Russian cars, music, food, people, holidays, adverts, anything! You'll be surprised what will fall out, Guvnor once you rattle the cage. Leave it with me. Open, not covert! I'm on it. I'll take some shovels and dig around.'

'You have ground control! Split the team into three. One-third to concentrate on Ullswater, one-third on the Tarn Hotel area, and one-third on the rest of Cumbria.'

'I'll do the hotel,' responded Bannerman.

'Take Janice and the rest of the team,' continued Boyd. 'Anthea will be supervising the other teams in the office here. Don't forget Ricky. He's briefed with a CCTV operation to complete. If he needs help, make sure he gets it.'

'Will do,' replied Bannerman.

'Good luck!' Boyd cut the connection. 'Ground control!' mused Boyd. 'I can't wait to get out of this office and back on the ground. But what I need to do now is read the surveillance logs Toni sent me. Operation Ushanka here I come. A fresh mind, she said. A fresh mind? Of course! Fresh!'

Boyd paused for a moment, lifted the phone, dialled Ricky, and asked, 'How are you getting on with the CCTV challenge?'

'Give me a break, Guvnor. I've only just started.'

'On what?'

'Gathering details of CCTV systems in the Glenridding, Patterdale and Ullswater areas. I'll feed them into a computer program I wrote some years ago and wait for a result. I'm having trouble finding any CCTV that covers the A592 road. That said, I've located some shops, garages, the local Ullswater steamers, and one or two car parks that have CCTV systems in the target area.'

'Good! Do you need any assistance?'

'Nope! I've got two from another team with me. I'm showing them how to retrieve CCTV data. It's *on-the-job* training.'

'Excellent, Ricky. But I've been thinking I made a mistake when I briefed you. I asked you to examine systems in the Ullswater area. Now I want you to think like a killer.'

'How do I do that, Guvnor?'

'Go back to the basics. Whoever travelled to Glenridding to poison that couple must have known they lived there. Someone told them they lived at that address, Ricky, so my mind is talking to me again like it did before my suspension. It tells me someone is talking to the Russians and has identified those so-called dissidents living in Glenridding. Whoever it was told the Russians where Yuri and Svetlana were. Maybe they found Yuri and his wife in a gym, a cinema, or a place of regular entertainment enjoyed by the couple. Library books! Magazines! They were found by PC Ben Parker when he attended the home address in Glenridding. Get onto him and find out where the books are now. Which library are they borrowed from and what date were they taken out? Are any gym membership papers apparent? Any museum membership, swimming club, Pilates, yoga, stamp collectors, or yacht club membership? Anything at all? Not your fault, Ricky. Mine! All change. Can you do that for me? That's your starting point.

Somewhere specific where you might find someone following the victims. If someone in Cumbria discovered the Russian dissidents living there, I suspect they would have told the Russian embassy. Ushanka and his people would have been informed. You're looking for a starting point in that list I've just spouted. If you find Yuri and Svetlana on CCTV then ask yourself if anyone is following them. Got that?'

'I can moderate the computer program to accommodate that enquiry. Leave it with me, Guvnor. PC Parker is in hospital, but I'll get onto Max Johnston's team right away and follow it up. If the library books are from Penrith Library, I'll try and trace them on CCTV in Penrith. Hopefully, the books will be stamped with the date on which they were borrowed, or the lending library will have a computer record of that date. Maybe that's where the killers picked them up. It will be quicker to do it that way.'

'You read me loud and clear, Ricky,' voiced Boyd. 'Phone me when you get a hit.'

'I'm on it.'

Boyd returned the phone to its cradle and pulled the Ushanka surveillance logs towards him. Picking the first bundle, he said, 'A fresh mind it is then. Page one!'

An hour later, Boyd poured a jug of water into a glass, took a drink, and phoned Antonia.

'Do you ever sleep?' asked Antonia.

'Only when my mind is tired,' replied Boyd. 'Got two minutes for a remake of the killing?'

'I'm not with you. What do you mean?'

'I've read the papers you sent me. They are not time-connected and didn't all happen on the same day. They are complicated but here goes.'

'I'm all ears.'

'Alexander Lowther learns of Yuri and Svetlana Pavlova living in Cumbria. I don't know how yet but we're working on it. He tells the Russian embassy. Ushanka gets to know and invites Lowther to London, takes him for a slap-up thank-you meal, and wishes him well. He wants eyes and ears in Cumbria, so he looks after them. They are not spies in the way such characters are portrayed on film or television, but they are supporters of a regime that is known by us to be a hostile enemy state. They are the Lowther couple. They are the eyes and ears of Russia in Cumbria. Mini spies! So far?'

'I'm listening,' replied Antonia. 'Go on!'

'Ushanka sends a team to check their information out and house Yuri and Svetlana. The information is correct. Ushanka decides to terminate the couple. He contacts the Kremlin. Moscow authorises the use of a nerve agent and sends it to the Bulgarian embassy for delivery by courier to Ushanka. It's a one-way ticket. Ushanka meets the courier in a café at Gravesend. The courier hands over a doll that contains the nerve agent. So far?'

'I like it. Go on!'

'The courier is terminated, and an evidential link with the Russian embassy is destroyed. However, the murder of the courier becomes a circumstantial or intelligence link when you put the puzzle together. It's a jigsaw and part of it is the Bulgarian courier connection. The Russians, having housed their target in Glenridding, then deploy a team that sprays the car, gate, house, and windows, with the nerve agent. Death occurs. Job done.'

'If that is correct, we are on the way to proving it,' declared Antonia. 'Why didn't I see that?'

'You saw something that was bothering you or you wouldn't have sent those papers to me for analysis. Maybe you were just making sure I was up to the job following my recent problems.'

'No! The truth is something didn't feel right, and I'd read the papers so many times I wanted a second opinion.'

'We may not be right, Toni, but it is a possibility worth working on. Did you get the technical warrants?'

'Yes! Their phones are covered. The rest is in progress.'

'Do you dance, Toni?'

'You know I do but only at weekends. Why?'

'We think alike. You'd make a good dance partner.'

'I'd stand on your toes,' chuckled Antonia.

'Keep in touch.'

'I will. Thank you.'

Boyd cut the connection and gathered the papers.

The phone rang again. It was Abraham.

'We need to talk,' proposed the Arab Jew. 'I'm in Golders Green and ready for tonight. When can we meet?'

Boyd decided and ended the call.

Walking to a cabinet by the window, he slid open the second drawer, removed a bottle of brandy, and poured a three-finger shot. He sank it in one go, placed the glass on the top of the cabinet, looked out across the River Thames from his perch in the Special Crime Unit, and said, 'I'm back. At last. I know I'm back. Now to concentrate on Shamash. But as ever I have a hurdle to jump. Should I penetrate the target myself, with only me aware of what I am about to do? Or should I apply for a warrant and once again allow others to put Abraham under the microscope? That will take time and a presentation to a government minister responsible for such matters. Oh yes, they want Abraham's knowledge and his information, but only on their terms provided it sits well with them and doesn't go against the grain. The poor man makes a slight mistake, and the system stands against him and can't trust him. Yet none of them know him like I do. What should I do? Which way should I play the game and move forward?'

~

13

The Menorah Restaurant and Coffee Shop
Golders Green, North London
Later that week.

Golders Green is in the London Borough of Barnet in England. It was named after the Godyere family who occupied the area from the 14th century. Of medieval agricultural origins, the settlement began to flourish in the early 19th century. By the early 20th century, it grew rapidly following the opening of a London Underground tube station that was adjacent to the Golders Green Hippodrome which was home to the BBC Concert Orchestra. Golders Green is known for its large Jewish population as well as attracting many Jewish tourists from abroad.

It was early evening when Boyd and Abraham reached their destination having endured the constant drizzle of rain that had accompanied them throughout the day.

'Hanukkah!' exclaimed Boyd. 'We're here at last and this is where we part company for a while.'

'Pick me up in the bus shelter when I'm done,' relayed Abraham. 'It might have stopped raining by then.'

'Hope so! Strange name for a restaurant if you don't mind me saying so, Abraham. Hanukkah, Jewish?'

'Do me a favour! You know it is. The word is from the Hebrew language. Hanukkah is a festival that commemorates the recovery of Jerusalem and the subsequent rededication of the Second Temple at the beginning of the Maccabean Revolt against the Seleucid Empire in the 2nd century.'

'Wow! And I thought it was the name of a coffee bean.'

'Not funny, Mr Boyd. You know better than that.'

'Just trying to relax you, Abraham.'

'I'm quite relaxed, thank you. I'm sure you know Hanukkah is observed for eight nights and days, starting on the 25th day of

Kislev according to the Hebrew calendar, which may occur at any time from late November to late December in the Gregorian calendar. The festival is observed by lighting the candles of a candelabrum, commonly called a menorah. One branch is typically placed above or below the others and its candle is used to light the other eight candles.'

'The candle they call the shamash.'

'You're catching on,' chuckled Abraham. 'I'll convert you to Judaism yet.'

'I doubt it. I've no religion, Abraham. You got everything?'

'Yes!'

'Got the mobile phone?'

'Yes!'

'The button?'

'Yes!'

'Anything you're not sure of?' probed Boyd.

'Nothing! I know what I'm doing.'

'Need to recap on anything?'

'Not a thing,'

'In that case, I'll wait in the bus shelter for you.'

'I'll be an hour, no more,' revealed Abraham.

'Good luck! Nice and easy does it. Now remember what I told you to do. Okay?'

'Mr Boyd! I know what I'm doing, and I've done it before. Kindly give me some room and let me get on with it. The answer to your problem lies across the street in that restaurant. Get off my back and let me do it.'

'Okay! Off you go. I'm worried, that's all.'

Abraham stepped out of the shadows and into the moonlight. His leather shoes splashed in the shower that had dampened the road and obliged Boyd to take refuge.

Typical autumn weather, however, had not dissuaded Abraham from visiting the restaurant. He intended to visit the home of a secret organisation called Shamash. He had first learnt of its existence whilst working undercover as a taxi driver for Mossad in Dubai. The secret society enjoyed mysterious tentacles that stretched out across the globe and pretended to be supporters of the many Jewish communities that flourished throughout the world. It was a surprise to Abraham when he learnt that its headquarters were situated in Golders Green, north London. Without informing his Mossad colleagues, Abraham had charmed his way into Shamash by portraying his passion for the Arab world, revealing his love of the Islamic religion, and revealing himself to be a practising Muslim by exalting the Five Pillars of Islam. Except the truth of the matter was he was none of those things. He was a highly trained intelligence agent with the ability to act out any lifestyle he cared to imitate. And he found this part easy because he was already an Arab Jew. He joined Shamash and attended their meetings whenever he was in the UK. He saw the manoeuvre as an escape pod, a one-way ticket to get out of Mossad and the intelligence game and into another life. Joining Shamash was, in his mind, a passport to freedom. As an Arab Jew, he was a welcome addition to the club. It was the hub of fraudulent activity for the extreme Jihadist warmongers from the world of Islam. It was the place where information was passed by word of mouth, financial arrangements were made to support terrorism, and plans and rehearsals took place in which a handful of Arab Jews worked for their Arab bosses whilst pretending to be dedicated to Judaism. It was also the place where the Jewish community gave freely of their wealth unaware that their money was being fraudulently used by Jihadists.

Opening the restaurant door, Abraham stepped into a world of opulence, veiled religion, and mysterious characters when he was welcomed by the 'Front of House' and escorted to a table. A waiter was in attendance and guided Abraham into a comfortable leather chair from which he had an excellent view of others in the room.

A menu was offered, a meal was ordered, and a light beverage arrived for his consumption. The wine waiter appeared and displayed the list but was dismissed politely by Abraham who declined to select wine to accompany his meal.

The 'Front of House' made polite conversation before returning to his duties when guests arrived for their feast.

Abraham removed a mobile phone from his jacket pocket and placed it on the table with the charging point end facing towards a doorway in the restaurant. Above the door, a sign indicated that this was the entrance to a function room and conference facility. The door opened and a waiter carried a tray of drinks through the door and into the function room.

The mobile phone had been given to Abraham by Boyd with an explanation that the device was not just a phone. It was a covert video camera that recorded proceedings. The lens was at the charging point end of the phone. The capturing of images of customers was a necessity if Boyd was to learn who the patrons of the restaurant were, and this included those who entered the function room. Many of the customers would be law-abiding individuals who did not know that they were being hoodwinked into giving away their money. Others present may well be the fraudsters and Islamic crooks that Boyd sought to identify. But to do so, Boyd worked alone to preserve Abraham's identity. It was one thing for colleagues to know the name Abraham, and quite another to know Abraham himself and be able to identify him. Only a few people knew Abraham. They were Boyd, Antonia, and the two chiefs of MI5 and MI6. No one else was aware and neither Antonia nor the MI6 chief had physically met Abraham despite the status they enjoyed.

The evening wore on with Abraham enjoying his meal and the phone resting on the table doing its business. Abraham noticed a few people that he had met over recent months. Some entered the restaurant and were guided to a table for their meal. Others were admitted to the function room and conference facility. These were the ones that caught Abraham's eye, and the lens of the mobile phone.

In the restaurant where Abraham sat, a piano played and the chatter of innocent people enjoying good food, good company, and pleasant entertainment prevailed.

Eventually, the Front of House returned to Abraham. A bill was paid, and Abraham asked, 'May I see the menorah?'

'Of course, sir. You are expected at the meeting. Did you enjoy your meal?'

'Very much,' replied Abraham with a smile. 'It's so long since I treated myself, I thought I would have something to eat before the meeting. I hope you don't mind.'

'Of course, not sir.'

'Please extend my compliments to the chef.' Abraham handed over a twenty-pound note as a tip, pocketed the mobile phone, and followed the Front of House to the function room.

There was a long corridor ahead and the escort said, 'I believe you know the way, sir.'

'Yes, I do,' nodded Abraham who strolled along the corridor checking out various Jewish adornments that embellished the walls.

The corridor opened out into a room that was divided by a balustrade. On one side of the balustrade, a function room was apparent. It sported a bar, refreshment area, tables, and chairs, as well as a dance floor and stage. On the other side, there was a much smaller room which accommodated a score of guests engaged in idle chatter, pleasantries, and introductions.

Picking out some familiar faces, Abraham made his presence known, shook hands with friends and contacts, and met others whom he had heard of but never encountered.

In the middle of the room, there was a large mahogany table. A menorah sat in the centre of the table and dominated proceedings with its nine branches reaching out in that disciplined way.

A voice sounded, 'Gentlemen, please collect your drinks from the function room before we begin proceedings. Tea! Coffee!

Water! Even beer, spirits, or wine if you wish. Ten minutes! Please collect your drinks before we begin.'

There was a shuffle of feet, a chatter of voices, and a movement to the refreshment area as Abraham studied the menorah and reached out to touch the shamash candle.

'Beautiful, isn't it, Abraham,' voiced Ahmed: the chairman. 'Even though it's Jewish. Good to see you again. How was Dubai?'

'I've retired,' replied Abraham shaking hands with Ahmed. 'I've decided to move permanently to London and settle down as a part-time taxi driver.'

'Oh, I see. How interesting. That might be useful to us in the future. Coffee? Tea? What can I get you?'

'Water!' replied Abraham. 'I need to diet.'

'I'll be with you shortly. Don't drop that menorah whatever you do,' chuckled Ahmed.

As Ahmed joined the others in the function room, Abraham swiftly removed a metallic button from his trouser pocket. He turned the menorah over and attached the magnetic button to the underside of the menorah before replacing it in the centre of the table.

'What you doing?' asked Ahmed returning with drinks.

'Admiring the menorah,' explained Abraham who lifted it again and swung it towards the light shining from the ceiling. 'Such an extraordinary piece, don't you think?'

'I do. It's not fundamental to our Muslim beliefs but it's a big part of the way this business is presented to the Jewish community. Take a seat, Abraham. We have some new people tonight, but I think you know the important ones: Ali, Omar, Ibrahim, and Hamza.'

'Yes, indeed I do, Ahmed,' replied Abraham shaking hands with the group. 'Good to see you all again. It's been some weeks since my last visit.'

One of the elders, Omar, offered, 'Is it true you have left Dubai and are now living in London?'

'Yes!' confirmed Abraham. 'I've decided to settle here and get a job as a taxi driver. I'm learning their ways and the routes they use so expect me to pop up anywhere in the next few months.'

Omar returned an understanding smile and was about to speak when Ahmed tapped the table and announced, 'To business, gentlemen.'

Everyone took a seat.

Abraham hoped that the covert listening device he had just planted in the base of the menorah was emitting a signal that Boyd could pick up.

The group grew silent and listened to Ahmed who read out a long list of Jewish celebrations that had taken place during the last quarter. He then said, 'They'll be using this room, as usual, in the months ahead and during Hanukkah. Hence the nine-branched menorah. They love it. Fools that they are. May Allah strike them down when the great day falls upon us.'

There was a murmur of approval from around the table before Ahmed continued, 'Fifty per cent of all takings during the last quarter have been used to fund the restaurant, our wages, and future investments. I am delighted to tell you that the other fifty per cent, close to two hundred thousand pounds, has been transmitted to our headquarters in Islamabad. As you know, multiple fundraising activities are ongoing amongst the Jewish community. I thank you for organising them,' chuckled Ahmed who was immediately joined in laughter by the others around the table. The Arab Jew continued, 'Many of you here tonight will know more of our organisation in the future. It is within my knowledge that each of you sitting here has a speciality that we can use in our proposed ventures in the months ahead. It is only a question of time before you move from where you currently sit to a higher place where the in-depth business of Shamash is undertaken. Most of those transactions are confidential by nature and one-to-one in their function. Tonight, just become acquainted with each other, make yourself known to the top table, and take heed of what we are about. My friends, we need to continue to build on the financial successes I have mentioned. We shall do it quietly and deliberately for the good of our desires. *Remember, worldly life is short, so turn to Allah before you return to Allah.'*

Quoting from the Quran, Abraham replied, *'Allah is the Creator of all things, and He is, over all things, Disposer of affairs. To Him belong the keys of the heavens and the earth. And they who disbelieve in the verses of Allah - it is those who are the losers.'*

Ahmed declared, *'Glory is to Allah, and praise is to Allah, and there is none worthy of worship but Allah, and Allah is the Most Great.* Now then, gentlemen, in the coming weeks the following ceremonies, parties, and gatherings will occur.'

The business continued before Ahmed ended his deliberations and bid everyone farewell adding, 'Ali, Omar, Ibrahim, and Hamza, stay and take a drink with me. I have some pressing family news that I wish to discuss with you.'

There was an agreement from those concerned whilst the others made their way out of the conference facility and into the restaurant area.

Nodding farewell, Abraham gestured to the guests leaving and then returned to the restaurant. Moments later he was gone from the Menorah eatery making for a bus shelter to take cover from the rain.

A black taxi drew up. Abraham jumped into the rear and handed his mobile phone to Boyd with the words, 'Here you go! That went like clockwork! No problems.'

Boyd, who was wearing earphones, gestured his thanks and drove his source away dropping him close to a tube station entrance with the words, 'Well done, Abraham! I got it all. Ring me tomorrow. I'm listening in at the moment. I'll get the video sorted from the mobile too. Take care.'

Abraham was out of the taxi and into the tube station.

Boyd double-backed towards the restaurant. Parking five hundred yards from the building, he listened to the product of the covert snooping device hidden beneath the nine-branched menorah. The conversation involved Ahmed, Ali, Omar, Ibrahim and Hamza. They were all Arab Jews who leaned significantly towards the Muslim world and Islam and not the Jewish religion.

'Sounds like Shamash is at the forefront of the Jihadist financial movement. Heroes of Islam,' thought Boyd. 'As well as being a mix of Muslim spies within the Jewish community.'

Eavesdropping, Boyd heard contributors discussing matters beyond that of the meeting. He also heard the voice of a sixth man: a stranger. The new man had not been introduced to the other five participants but was now in charge of proceedings. Boyd sensed an air of leadership in his tone of voice.

'I intend to exterminate their top man,' revealed the newcomer. The accent was rich and guttural yet possessive of a defined beauty of which the Arab world was proud. 'I know from my private network that he is attending an international conference in Cumbria,' continued the visitor. 'Climate change is going to be discussed by various scientists, prime ministers, politicians, and ambassadors from various parts of Scandinavia and Europe. I'm sure they will also be discussing amongst themselves the war in Ukraine and may well mention how Russia is slowly emptying its prisons and sending convicts to the front. I have no time for such people. I will remove the top man.'

'How will Russia feel about that?' enquired Omar.

'They'll not mention the fact that they are now sending Muslims from Dagestan to the front. But by the time I finish, the whole world will know why this man was permanently removed from the face of the earth. They are in for a surprise I promise you.'

An audience of focused faces glided into a bright and cheerful mode when Ahmed drank from a glass of water and said, 'And you are with us tonight because you want help from ourselves, Jamil.'

'I have a list,' replied Jamil, the newcomer, who reached across and handed a piece of paper to Ahmed.

Ahmed read the list and handed it to Omar saying, 'I'm sure we can accommodate your request, Jamil. We will need time, of course, but we can arrange for the goods to be transferred directly to you if you wish.'

'Thank you,' replied Jamil.

'But I must point out,' remarked Ahmed. 'I would rather deliver the goods to a place of your choosing. Perhaps near the site of the kill zone. I can't be much more specific than that. What do you think of that course of action?'

'I say Allah is with us, Ahmed, and whereas you need time to gather my equipment together, I also need time to check the route and plan precisely the kill that I intend.'

'Good! We can work around that.'

'I shall not return to the Menorah restaurant, but you know how to contact me. I thank you all for being my fellow warriors. I shall not darken this restaurant again. A degree of security is required, and I respect your wishes in that regard.'

'Excellent,' replied Omar standing up to shake hands with Jamil. 'May Allah be with you and may He guide you to your triumphant destiny.'

Stunned, somewhat astonished, as he tapped his earphones in disbelief, Boyd heard the name Jamil, shook his head, and thought, 'It's him. It's Jamil Volkov. Abraham said Jamil would contact Shamash. What a stroke of luck.'

Boyd vacated the taxi and approached the restaurant on foot. The bus shelter provided an excellent location from which to watch the front of the restaurant and the detective duly slunk into the shadows watching and simultaneously listening to the meeting via his headphones.

'*Ma'a as-salaam*,' announced Jamil when he finished speaking to the organisers of Shamash.

'Peaces and blessings to you also,' replied Ahmed bowing from the hip in solemn gesture. 'Safe journey.'

'Thank you,' replied Jamil who nodded farewell and slipped out of the rear of the building into the back lane.

Outside, Boyd was kicking himself for doing things off his own bat. He wished he had applied for a technical warrant to eavesdrop legally on the restaurant. Had he done that, he would have deployed a surveillance team to cover the Menorah building and follow Jamil. Firstly, he cursed then reminded himself why he acted alone. He didn't want to jeopardise Abraham's safety in a hastily thrown-together surveillance operation. Something was bound to go wrong and possibly lead to compromising Abraham.

Boyd was on his own illegally serving his country for all he had witnessed and heard courtesy of the covert listening device was not admissible in evidence.

'Don't make it a problem,' thought Boyd. 'The problem is Jamil Volkov, not the evidence, and not Abraham.'

Ahmed, Ali, Omar, Hamza and Ibrahim left the restaurant by the front door and strolled towards a car park situated about a quarter of a mile from the building.

Boyd watched the five men leave, counted them all out, reckoned they were the people he had heard on the device secreted under the menorah by Abraham, and waited for Jamil to join them.

The seconds ticked by before it dawned on Boyd that Jamil had slipped out the backway. The detective shot across the road and ran to the corner where a back alley joined the main street.

The alley was clear but when Boyd spun around to scour the area, he saw a man walking away on his own.

'That's him,' thought Boyd who immediately fell in line and quickened his pace. 'I need to get in front of him.'

Boyd crossed to the other side of the street and lengthened his stride thinking, 'Mid-thirties, tall, lean, with a head of long dark hair, and a beard. He's all of that.'

Jamil paused at a road junction held by the road traffic at a pedestrian crossing.

Crossing the road well before the same junction, Boyd stole a march on Jamil and ended up parallel to him but on the other side of the street.

Boyd's hand slid into his pocket and seized the mobile phone. The phone went to his ear. His head turned. Boyd tilted the mobile phone slightly and videoed Jamil Volkov.

'At last,' thought Boyd. 'Got him on film! Now all I need to do is house him.'

Signalling a taxi to stop, Jamil leaned into the cab, gave the driver instructions, and climbed into the back seat.

The taxi drove off leaving Boyd stranded far from his vehicle. He dashed into the roadway and tried to signal a following car to stop so that he might hijack it for his use. The car swerved around Boyd abandoning the detective to his own devices as Jamil, unaware of the detective's presence, settled back into the rear seat of the taxi and left the area.

Returning to his vehicle, Boyd headed for the office and a late-night call to Antonia.

Listening intently to Boyd's story Antonia chuckled and said, 'Let's not get carried away with your illegal solo mission. No warrant means no evidence for the police but intelligence for us. And that's the problem, Billy.'

'What is?' queried Boyd.

'The top man!' explained Antonia. 'We've got Ushanka telling Phillip the target is our prime minister and your man Abraham telling us the target is the Russian ambassador. We're no further forward. Wait a moment.' Antonia rattled her keyboard and stated, 'Yes! The conference is at the Tarn

Hotel near Brampton in Cumbria. It's a new venue situated half an hour's drive from the Lake District and about the same from the Scottish border. It's close to Hadrian's Wall and I suspect it's marketing itself into the hotel and conference centre business. Both the Russian ambassador and our prime minister are on the guest list. The PM is a guest; the ambassador is listed as an observer.'

'Understood, but I heard Jamil say he was going to terminate the top man,' revealed Boyd. 'I took that to mean he was going to kill the Russian ambassador, not the prime minister. I heard him explain that the Russians were sending Muslims from Dagestan to fight in Ukraine. The target must be the ambassador. That's who Jamil has his gripe with, not our prime minister, and certainly not the British government. We were never mentioned. I'm sending you a clip of the video of Jamil Volkov that I took tonight. Run some copies off and make sure every member of the unit up there has a copy of Jamil's photograph in their possession. Tell them to study it hard because he's our target and his criminal history suggests that he'll turn up at the conference to do his evil bidding. Circulate his photograph to the protection teams.'

'Okay! I'll do that, but protection? Not my decision or area of responsibility,' remarked Antonia. 'I'd expect the powers that be will want both men protected to the hilt. I'll leave that for you to sort out tomorrow. Meg, Boyd! She heard the phone and she's just walked in. I'll put her on shortly.'

'Please do,' replied Boyd. 'She'll be pleased to know I'm coming home soon.'

'Before I do that,' continued Antonia. 'Ricky has been on the phone. The books in the Pavlova house in Glenridding are from the Ambleside library. He has the Pavlova couple on CCTV coming out of the library on numerous occasions over recent months. They are members there.'

'Ambleside?' queried Boyd. 'Not far from Windermere where the Lowther couple live. About five miles or thereabouts.'

'We're on the same wavelength,' replied Antonia. 'Dancing again! Checks reveal the Lowthers are members of Ambleside library. Now let's suppose they became aware of the Russian couple in the library, discovered who they were, and told their contact in the Russian embassy.'

'We thought they may be the eyes and ears of Russian intelligence in the Lake District. I recall discussing it with you recently. For me, that fits, Toni,' replied Boyd.

'And for me! Precisely!' agreed Antonia. 'Now fast forward to the last known visit of Yuri and Svetlana Pavlova to Ambleside library. They borrowed the library books found in their house in Glenridding. Ricky did a CCTV trail that day from Ambleside to Glenridding just as you suggested. The last CCTV sighting is in Ambleside where they took *The Struggle* over Kirkstone Pass. It shows them in their Mercedes. They were followed by numerous vehicles in the traffic flow but the next CCTV at the Inn near Brothers Water, on the approach to Patterdale, shows a motorbike, a campervan, and a salon car following. Nothing unusual in that until Ricky delves further and discovers all three vehicles are rented from a hire company in London.'

'By the Russian embassy?' queried Boyd.

'Listen to this,' suggested Antonia. 'The vehicles were paid for in cash by one person who used his driving licence. The address on the licence does not exist. Everything about it is false! But it gets better.'

'Go on!'

'Ricky tapped into the rental CCTV. The three drivers were all traced to the Russian embassy. We have details of the trio. They are all accredited employees of the Russian embassy.'

'They could well be the killers,' suggested Boyd.

'Yes! Agree! They are at least part of a conspiracy if nothing else. All we have on them is following the Pavlovas from Ambleside to Glenridding. That is not on the day they were poisoned but it surely puts them in the frame if nothing else. Ricky hasn't yet told Max Johnston, the head of Cumbria CID. He thought you should know first. What do you think?'

'I think Ricky is a hardworking superstar,' chuckled Boyd. 'I'll contact him tomorrow when I get home and thank him. Then I'll update Max as to what we've got and how we should deal with it.'

'Quietly and inhouse only?' queried Antonia.

'Yes!' replied Boyd. 'Anything else I should know?'

'Just Meg. Here she is?'

'Meg! I'll be home tomorrow. I have an idea.'

'Great! Can't wait to see you, Billy!' replied a happy wife whose voice bustled with excitement. 'You sound ten times better than you did last time you were home. And that, my darling, was when you were a pain in the proverbial.'

'I'm back in business one hundred per cent, Meg. A poisoning in Glenridding and now an assassination attempt in Cumbria. It's all go! I need your help. You're on the team as of now.'

'On the team?' chuckled Meg. 'Oh no! What do you want me to do this time?'

'Book a room at the Tarn Hotel for tomorrow night. We'll have dinner there too. Pick a good table. Plenty of vision. You know what I mean. Play surveillance officer for the night. Tell me what you see. I need a fresh mind on the subject. Think outside the box, Meg. Something is going to happen there soon.'

'I think I prefer it when you were suspended and panic-stricken, Billy. Why don't I make a meal to celebrate.'

'I'd rather you booked the Tarn Hotel,' suggested Boyd.

'New place!' replied Meg. 'Very expensive I'm told. Why not the village pub instead?'

'Because I'd like to take a good look at the hotel from inside and out. And I'll tell you exactly why...'

As Boyd explained, Meg placed her hand over the phone's mouthpiece, winked at Antonia who was listening in, and said, 'I've got him back. His brain is in top gear. Can you get me the number for the Tarn Hotel, Toni? The directory is on the table over there.'

~

14

~

The Russian Embassy.
That evening.
Simultaneous.

Ambassador Nikolai Lermontov smoothed the lapels of his pinstripe suit, straightened his tie, turned to his cultural attaché, and said, 'So there you have it, Andrey. I am no longer appreciated by the contacts I have made in my ambassadorial role. There was a time when I would have been asked to speak at the conference on climate change. Now I am merely an observer. I find it somewhat distasteful, but I have accepted the invitation albeit not what I would have expected or wished for.'

'I am aware, your Excellency,' gestured Andrey. 'Any reason why you have been downgraded to observer?'

'Obvious, I would have thought, Andrey. The war in Ukraine! They don't like the idea that our claim is historically based, legitimate in its design, and the Commander in Chief's overriding passion. What else could it be?'

'I think you are right, Your Excellency,' nodded Andrey.

'Excellency? My dear, Andrey,' smoothed the ambassador. 'We have been close friends for many years now. Please retain the nature of that address for when others are about. Nikolai will suffice when we are alone together. The conference! I would like you to attend with me. I've told the organisers you will be with me as you are my cultural secretary.'

'If you wish me to attend then I shall.'

'You need to know there are things I need to do and someone I need to speak to when we are in Cumbria. He is a close friend, and I shall take time out to visit him.'

'Good! Enjoy!'

'Now then, Andrey, I'm not supposed to be aware of your other remit here in the UK, but you know otherwise. I understand you are the resident and surround yourself with others in your role as cultural attaché. We both know your true role and you might be surprised to learn that very few within these walls are aware you are the resident working for the SVR. With that in mind, I need a security detail to protect me in Cumbria. My wife will not be joining me on this occasion, Andrey. She's returning to her home in Obninsk to visit her mother who is not very well. The conference is made up of numerous VIPs from Scandinavia and Europe. You have an ideal opportunity to take stock of who's who at the conference.' Nikolai smiled and added, 'Use your presence in my circle of friends and contacts in any way you see fit, Andrey. It is an excellent opportunity to assess others of high standing. I am aware you have a security interest. Perhaps your man Luka...'

'Is a good choice, Nikolai,' interrupted the resident. 'It is known inside the embassy that he is the chief security man and is responsible for embassy security. They think he is the night watchman with the keys and the lights out scenario. Few know he is with our intelligence service. I shall brief him. It's an opportunity to look the enemy in the eye.'

'Enemy! Be careful where you use such a term, Andrey. We're all good friends, don't you know. These conferences are full of ridiculous smiles, endless charm, idle chit chat, gin and tonics, and a knife in the back when you're not looking.'

'I'll be more careful, my friend. The fact is, Nikolai, that although the British have organised this event under the umbrella of climate change, I feel sure Ukraine will be high on the list of those at the conference. We will cover the event and learn what we can of those who may speak against us.'

'I thought you would. Now I must collect Natasha from her dressing room. We are scheduled to dine with a couple of professors from the language school. All very cultural. I'll make the arrangements. Keep in touch, Nikolai.'

'Of course! Have a good evening.'

When the ambassador left the embassy, Andrey Petrov called a meeting in the safe room.

Once the security protocols had been completed, Andrey sat down with Illya, Ivan, Mikhail, and Luka.

Wasting no time, Andrey enquired, 'The media, Ivan! You asked to raise the subject as a matter of urgency. Please do so now.'

'There's nothing specific and no concrete evidence mentioned in these press reports,' remarked Ivan as he spread a bundle of newspapers across the table. 'But if you read them carefully, you might share my opinion. I think the British are onto us.'

'In what way?'

'Glenridding! These two newspapers are the culprits,' remarked Ivan pushing a couple of broadsheets forward. 'Both refer to detectives liaising with British Intelligence regarding vehicles seen in the area where the Pavlova couple live. No mention of times or dates, but they suggest the vehicles trace to us.'

'The press in the UK is proficient at making things up if they are only given half a story,' replied Andrey.

'I knew we should have bought the vehicles at a car auction and not rented them,' replied Ivan. 'If they have traced the vehicles to us, then it's only a question of time before we are declared *persona non grata*. They might even arrest us for murder. I'm worried, Andrey. It's not what we planned, and I can't believe they've got onto us so quickly. I was sure we hadn't been seen. There was no one about when the spray went down. Even if they collected every piece of CCTV in the Lake District it would take them ages to view it and decide who the suspects were. If they've got me on CCTV then they've got Viktor and Mikhail too.'

'Viktor is safe,' replied Andrey.

'Mikhail and I are not.'

'You were only eyes and ears, back-up, supporters whilst Viktor carried out the mission.'

'I want to go home,' declared Ivan. 'So does Mikhail just to be on the safe side. Neither of us wants to insult the Motherland by being arrested or expelled from England in some diplomatic row about a murder sanctioned by the Commander in Chief.'

Mikhail nodded in agreement leaving Andrey deep in thought. Eventually, the resident replied, 'Very well! Like you, if the press reports are correct then I am surprised at the speed of the investigation. Make the arrangements, Ivan. Book flights back home at your earliest convenience. If the British are getting close, we need to lock the door to them. Go! Both of you. It may be weeks before they make a move but let's not dawdle and wait to be caught out.'

'Thank you,' replied Ivan, closely followed by Mikhail.

'Indeed, I suggest you leave now,' ordered Andrey. 'There's no need for either of you to stay at our meeting.'

The two men vacated the safe room leaving Andrey tapping impatiently on the table. Finally, he said, 'These events change everything, Luka. Where is Jamil Volkov?'

'We do not know,' replied the SVR man.

'I thought he was sighted outside the embassy. You told me it was only a question of time before he turned up again and you would be able to house him in London.'

'The man has never been seen since. We don't know where he disappeared to.'

Thoughtfully, Andrey looked Luka in the eye and replied, 'You disappoint me.'

'It is the way of the world,' replied Luka.

'Not my world,' challenged Andrey. 'Do you think the British have him?'

'I'm not sure. I must confess that I don't know.'

'If you don't know then we cannot complete our plan,' belittled Andrey. 'We cannot manipulate Jamil if we do not have him under our control. A new approach is needed.'

'I apologise for not having Jamil Volkov under control,' replied Luka. 'You were right that day when you told us we should have been onto him when we first saw him on CCTV outside the embassy. It's my fault. I should have known better. But I agree with you, Andrey. It's time for a new approach. Glenridding came at the wrong time for us. We concentrated too much on that when we should have focused on Volkov. If we don't have the man under our control, there is only one thing we can do.'

'And that is?'

'Kill him on sight and claim we saved the British prime minister's life by reacting to information received and expediting same in the name of freedom and democracy.'

'It is what we said,' agreed Andrey. 'It was one of the options we previously discussed. Okay! Yes! We know that Jamil operates in such a manner that he is likely to be physically present at the conference in Cumbria. Historically, as our records show, it's the kind of place where he carries out his attacks. Always an event of some kind. I don't know who his target is but with a selection of influential people there from Scandinavia and Europe, he has plenty to choose from. A military or police presence will not dissuade him. The man attacks without a conscience. Not even a regiment stopped him from blowing up Colonel Novikova in Dagestan.'

'He is a formidable terrorist,' remarked Luka.

'I agree. Our ambassador has instructed me to send a security detail to the conference. I'll be with him. I want you to put together a special protection unit and brief them to safeguard our ambassador. Cumbria Police cover the Lake District and the conference area. They will have little experience with people like Jamil Volkov. Liaise with them and find out how they will secure the event. They will be amateurs in comparison with the police here in London. Quietly block the gaps that you find without raising problems with them. Our ambassador will sail through the event without a problem. Understood, Luka?'

'Perfectly!'

'And Jamil!' continued Andrey. 'Brief the security detail to assassinate Jamil Volkov on sight.'

'I'll circulate Jamil's photograph to the detail.'

'Good!' nodded Andrey. 'He's the kind of man who will attract attention by the virtue of his presence in a crowd.'

'I expect he will stand out,' nodded Luka. 'He'll be the silent one at the back of the crowd of protestors who suddenly steps forward when the time is right, and he has the target in his sights. My men are trained to spot such people.'

'I wonder if the British are still arguing amongst themselves and if the MI5 chief that I spoke to is still a stressed-out man who doesn't know what to do next. He was a charming gentleman as I recall! Easily fooled in my experience. Luka, I want to throw Jamil's body onto the conference table and boast how we saved the life of the British prime minister. Do that for me. Understood?'

'Perfectly, sir,' replied Luka. 'Perfectly!'

'We shall remind the world how powerful we are, and I shall show our Commander in Chief why I am more than just the resident in the embassy. I am the next man into a seat at the top table in the Kremlin. See to it, Luka. When I sit in another place, it is people like you that I will remember.'

A drawer was pulled open by Luka.

The vodka was unscrewed; the bottle poured, a glass taken, and a toast was made by Luka, 'To the Motherland.'

'The Motherland!' toasted Andrey. 'Long may we enjoy the fruits of our labour and the power of our sword.'

Later that night, at a shooting gallery, Luka's unsteady hand lifted a Ruger pistol, loaded it, steadied the outstretched limb, and then fired at a target from close range. The bullseye was riddled with holes. Fifteen minutes later, from long range, his fingers curled around the trigger of a sniper's rifle, took aim along the sights, and fired. The bullet rifled along the barrel and spiralled into the bullseye leaving it riddled.

It was as if a war was about to start. The problem was the enemy was something of a mystery. Known in one quarter, suspected in another, and the subject of argument in government circles the nature of which Russian intelligence had carefully orchestrated.

It was the week of the conference. The British Establishment continued to debate who the target was, and what should be done to protect whomever. Should the conference be cancelled? Who trusted who in a game of life peppered with decisions to be made? Who empowered who and what did they want in return? Who abused power and why? Who would ignore instructions from the powerful and do their own thing? Who was powerful enough to decide on the best course of action to take?

In Cumbria, the response to the threat was met when the Commissioner of the Metropolitan Police phoned Boyd and ordered him to deploy the entire Special Crime Unit to Cumbria to bolster the prime minister's protection team. No mention was made of the Russian ambassador. As the Police Commissioner made clear, the ambassador was no concern of theirs.

Boyd did not argue, did not suggest that a mistake had been made, or more thought should be applied. He merely agreed that the all-powerful should be obeyed. For Boyd, in the final analysis, decisions regarding life and death were made in a split second without recourse to any direction from those above.

Time moved on and witnessed Boyd's welcome home and an update from Bannerman.

'What you got, Bannerman?'

'Lots of things, Guvnor. Mostly just blades of grass in the field. You'll be pleased to know we moved a flock of sheep before we found anything.'

'Okay! You've been busy. What did you find?'

'I followed your instructions. We began at the Tarn Hotel and Conference Centre then moved out in a circular pattern for an hour or so. I've found a nettle in the grass and it's open-source material.'

'And the nettle is?' probed Boyd.

'A Russian oligarch!'

'You're joking,' blurted Boyd. 'No way!'

'We ran a computer program into local estate agent websites and discovered that ten years ago Sergey Ivanov bought an eight-bedroomed detached house in Forest Head, near Brampton. It's a country mansion sitting on two acres of land between the villages of Talkin and Hallbankgate and it's called Seven Hills.'

'Seven Hills because of its location?' suggested Boyd.

'That's what I thought until I researched the name,' explained Bannerman. 'It might be a coincidence, but the house name bugged me because it doesn't match the locality. Forest Head is not a hilly or mountainous site that blasts seven hills in your face. I dug deeper. Did you know that Moscow was built on seven hills, Guvnor?'

'No! I did not,' replied Boyd.

'I wondered if there was a Moscow connection because of the name of the house. It sounds unlikely, but it led me to the owner Sergey Ivanov. The isolated dwelling overlooks Talkin Tarn which is close to the Tarn House Hotel and Conference Centre, and he's owned it for ten years.'

'Ten years!'

'Yes,' replied Bannerman. 'Ten years and he's never come to our notice, and our remit is counter terrorism and counter espionage. Anyway, I hit the Ticker intelligence computer system to access the MI6 files on Russians of interest. Ten years ago, Sergey was a student at the Red Banner Academy in Yurlovo near Moscow.'

'Where they once trained KGB officers until the Soviet Union collapsed and Russian Intelligence in the current format evolved into an enemy of unique and equal standing.'

'You got that in one, Guvnor.'

'Tell me how an intelligence officer for any country becomes a millionaire: an oligarch?'

'Utilities! Gas mainly! You know the story. Russian society changed. It evolved from a state-controlled communist regime into a Mafioso-type outfit exploited by the most powerful individuals in Russia and the former Soviet republics. They harnessed, stole, blackmailed, and utilised public services in a way that took them out of state control and into the private pocket. I accessed Sergey Ivanov's profile. He was once just a gangster, a gang leader, thug, and criminal in downtown Moscow. He took his chances, bullied his way towards the top, signed up to the Commander in Chief's dictate, and the rest is history.'

'Why hasn't he come to notice in Cumbria before?'

'The house stood empty for over five years, Guvnor. An estate manager took over responsibility for the running of the house at the request of the buyer. The manager kept it trim and tidy, looked after the garden and carried out routine maintenance work. They rendered it instantly accessible should the need arise. Sounds crazy but when you study the way criminals from organised crime gangs act out their lifestyles, it's not.'

'Go on, Bannerman,' pleaded Boyd. 'Not all oligarchs are gangsters. Convince me Sergey Ivanov is a crooked entrepreneur. Why did he buy a house and not live in it for over five years?'

'Because he wasn't quite in the money then, and he wasn't in the top team. Sergey got rich quick, didn't know what to do with the cash he'd made, saw the corruption and infighting that was taking place in the new Russia, and bought the house as an escape route. The first rule of a good burglar is to break in and find a way out before you search the house for anything worthwhile. For example, smash a window to get in but unlock a door to get out.

Good crooks always have their eye on an escape plan. I think Sergey knew that if things collapsed in an everchanging corrupt Moscow, he needed an escape route. He lived in a city where communism had collapsed, corruption, sleaze and exploitation were rife, and racketeers had taken over. Sergey eventually made the big time and now uses it occasionally as a holiday home. That, Guvnor, is why he's not come to notice in the UK before. He hasn't been here long enough to cause a stir.'

Boyd shook his head in astonishment and replied, 'Good work, Bannerman. That's an interesting nettle to find. I wonder if it stings. Do we know where he is now?'

'Windsurfing on the tarn,' chuckled Bannerman. 'I kid you not. I decided we needed to know more about him. I put one of the team on the job. DS Terry Anwhari is at the café at the tarn watching our oligarch sail up and down without a care in the world. We need to know more about him.'

'Excellent!' replied Boyd. 'And another possible target if I let my mind run amok. Deploy a drone camera and get photos of Sergey and a video of the Seven Hills house. I get your drift on the house name. He remembers his origins.'

'Drone coverage! I'm on it, Guvnor.'

'That makes my visit to the area more intriguing,' remarked Boyd. 'I wonder if Meg would like to take a walk.'

The following day, Boyd decided to deploy the unit's response helicopter to Cumbria. After all, he'd been ordered by the Commissioner to deploy the entire Special Crime Unit to Cumbria to bolster the prime minister's security team. The unit consisted of one covert unit and four operational units. The total strength of the unit fluctuated between 60 and 70 detectives depending upon sickness and availability.

Boyd flew home with others in the response helicopter. 'Callsign Charlie Tango Charlie' was an Agusta 109 helicopter with a maximum speed of 180mph. It didn't take long before Commander Boyd touched down at Carlisle airport where Meg picked him up and they drove home.

That night, Meg and her husband drove to the Tarn Hotel near Brampton. They enjoyed an excellent but expensive meal and stayed the night in a room on the upper floor. It was a five-star hotel the nature of which suggested a five-star protection plan would be needed for the conference at the end of the week. The hotel staff were already preparing to hoist the flags from various countries whose representatives were attending the convention. Furthermore, a police command-and-control centre in the shape of a long wheel-based vehicle had arrived. The vehicle enjoyed a double axle made to carry the weight of the contents therein. Boyd knew that meant a sophisticated computerised system with the potential to deploy a local CCTV network to aid security.

'My office,' he thought. 'Or at least it will be soon.'

The following day, when the couple knew the hotel inside out, Boyd suggested a stroll around Talkin Tarn and coffee at the café followed.

The beauty of it all was that Meg agreed. Boyd spent his day off looking at expensive detached houses and walking in the picturesque area that was known locally as Geltsdale: a gorgeous scenic gem lying in the hills south of Brampton.

By nightfall, Boyd had the outline of Seven Hills in his mind.

~

15

The Tarn Hotel, Talkin Tarn.
Near Brampton, Carlisle, Cumbria.
The day of the conference.

Brampton is a market town situated 9 miles east of Carlisle, Cumbria, and 2 miles south of Hadrian's Roman Wall. The A69 road bypasses the settlement and on the day of the conference witnessed a host of saloon cars under police motorcycle escort. Each vehicle contained a dignitary attending the conference close to Talkin Tarn Country Park.

The township was founded in the 7th century as an Anglian settlement. The placename 'Braunton' is first shown in an administrative record created by a medieval chancery in 1252 (*The Charter Rolls*). The record refers to what we now know as Brampton. In 1291, in a database referring to the valuation for the taxation of churches in England, Wales and Ireland (*the Taxatio Ecclesiastica*) the community finally appears as Brampton. However, a study of the name derived from the Old English would highlight the name 'Brōm-tūn': a settlement where broom grew.

Its original church survives a couple of miles away to the west as Brampton Old Church. It's on the site of a Stanegate Roman fort. The town is overlooked by the large medieval motte known as The Mote. Historically, during the Jacobite rising of 1745, Bonnie Prince Charlie stayed in the town for one night. His presence is marked by a plaque on the wall of an antique shop in the town.

The octagonal Moot Hall, which is in the centre of Brampton and houses the tourist information office, replaced a building which in 1648 was once used by Oliver Cromwell to house prisoners. To the right of its door lies the old iron stocks fixed to the pavement.

Talkin Tarn lies two miles south of Brampton. The tarn is a kettle hole formed 10,000 years ago by glacial action. There's a boating club, sailing club and rowing club as well as a tearoom and shop. The Talkin Tarn Amateur Rowing Club celebrated its 150th anniversary in 2009. Rowing races were first held on the tarn in the 1850s, and the rowing club was formed in 1859. It is the second oldest rowing club in the North of England. The location is steeped in history and is a treasure.

As far as the various police services, and the Tarn Hotel and Conference Centre, were concerned, Commander Boyd had assumed overall command of the security and protection zones. The Metropolitan police protection team was responsible for the safety of the prime minister whilst Cumbria police assumed security of the venue and its surroundings with uniform officers and a scattering of dog handlers at key points. Cumbria mobile support also undertook the escort of all VIPs to and from the venue either by motorcycle escort or signed police patrol car.

Boyd briefed the Special Crime Unit about the conference and the reason for their unplanned deployment to it. He was annoyed that the task had been dumped in his lap at such short notice. Normally, his unit would have enjoyed a longer planning scenario and total control over all aspects of an event at risk. But Boyd knew he had to get on with it and work with all concerned.

Circulating photographs of Jamil Volkov, Boyd revealed, 'This is the target. He is a highly trained killer and has worked with Al Qaeda, ISIS, and other Islamic Jihadist groups. He has a long history of killing military figures in Russia where he is wanted by the police. He can kill by hand, by gun, by knife, by bullet or by bomb. His name is Jamil Volkov, and he is a Russian Muslim. Study his photograph and commit the image to your mind. Your controllers are Anthea who will take charge of the snipers and covert teams in the woods. Janice will oversee the sniper teams on the hotel rooftops, and Bannerman is responsible for security and close protection in the conference area. I'll float as usual. Our headquarters for the operation is the command-and-control vehicle in the car park. You have your weapons of choice. Remember your arcs of fire and rules of engagement and always check your backgrounds. It's a venue where the delegates need looking after. We've done dozens of such operations previously. There's nothing new other than the fact we know who we are looking for. Any questions?'

A line of bodies remained head down studying the photograph. There was no response.

'Okay!' voiced Boyd. 'Let's go find Jamil. He's out there somewhere. Body armour on and load up.'

The briefing gradually dispersed.

Cars containing VIPs, and their security escorts left the bypass and travelled down a minor road which took them to a railway level crossing near Brampton Golf Club. Here, approximately one hundred demonstrators were present. Many held placards whilst others shouted slogans pleading for the planet to be saved and the climate problems to be addressed. A minority just shouted abuse at the delegates who sat behind the blacked-out windows and ignored the activists.

The police response thwarted the first line of demonstrators gathered near the level crossing hoping the convoy of cars might be brought to a standstill by the passing of a train on the Newcastle-Carlisle line. Discussions between the rail operators and police resulted in a constantly open highway for the security convoy to pass over and remain in motion. Upon realising this, the campaigners regrouped near the turn into the country park where they were met by a contingent of uniformed officers who formed a human barrier preventing public access to the security zone. The junction was formed of a line of blue uniforms holding back a mass of noisy and potentially violent people.

The convoy turned into the country park and headed for the Tarn Hotel where they were met by more uniforms who guided them into parking areas before the occupants walked into the hotel.

The flags of more than a dozen countries flew from the flagpoles surrounding the car park and witnessed the so-called great and good of the northern hemisphere.

Boyd checked his list and ticked off the actions that had taken place to secure the event. The narrow lane to the park had been walked, searched, and declared safe. The fields running parallel to the lane had been searched by police sniffer dogs and their handlers. The same dogs had been used in the search of the hotel and conference centre. Every room had been visited and examined. A 24-hour presence inside the conference hall had been maintained, and the woods surrounding the building had been searched by police and sniffer dogs trained in rooting out hidden explosives.

Boyd ticked another item in the long list of security actions that he had agreed with the prime minister's principal personal protection officer and his close protection team.

There was no sign of an intrusion and no sign of Jamil.

Turning a page in his notebook, Boyd radioed the Special Crime Unit teams. He checked that Ricky's drone coverage was operating and noted the area appeared to be safe. He spoke with the camouflaged team that occupied the woods and the sniper teams on the high ground that surrounded both the tarn and the hotel. Then, worried that something might be amiss, Boyd visited the sniper team on the hotel roof and checked that the pathway around the tarn was closed and devoid of people.

On returning to the command-and-control vehicle Boyd radioed his team to confirm their location.

'All secure!' came the reply.

The event was secure. There were no problems. But Boyd kept searching for Jamil Volkov and the attack he knew would come. He felt it in his bones and those bones told him more than any other thing he had ticked on his list that it wouldn't be over until Jamil had made his move.

'Give it a rest, Guvnor,' suggested Anthea. 'I can see your mind is working overtime. There's no sign of him. It's a good result. Have you ever thought that all the hard work we've put into securing the event has put him off?'

'If that was the case, I'd need to see the back of him,' replied Boyd. 'So far, there's no hide nor hair of him. Has it occurred to you that he might be too good for us, Anthea?'

'Papa Mike is approaching,' rattled across the radio network and interrupted the two detectives. 'Two miles and closing. Also in the convoy is Romeo Alpha approximately one minute behind. Status update required at the venue.'

Boyd recognised the voice of the prime minister's principal personal protection officer, imagined him in the passenger seat of a black Jaguar car, and reckoned the prime minister would be on site within the next five minutes closely followed by callsign Romeo Alpha: the Russian ambassador.

Focusing his eyes on the temporary CCTV systems, Boyd scanned the level crossing, the golf club, the turn into the park, and the run-up to the hotel entrance.

On the CCTV, Boyd realised the Russian ambassador's vehicle was gradually closing with the prime minister's Jaguar. Thirty seconds separated the passage of the two vehicles.

Lifting the radio transmitter, Boyd replied, 'All secure! Come! All units, stand by. Papa Mike is on the plot. Romeo Alpha is close behind. Full alert status!'

The network responded with acknowledgements as Boyd's eyes double-checked the protestors gathered at the turn into the park. His eyes scanned the bodies the CCTV transmitted leaving him to wonder if the CCTV link had been hacked and a false transmission substituted. But it was too late to check the wiring, too late to ask Ricky to convince him the link was secure, just too late.

An egg was thrown from the crowd. Boyd's heart rate quivered but he knew the Jaguar was fitted with the TALOS system. The egg missed the prime minister's car and smashed into the tarmac splattering yoke across the highway.

A police officer launched into the crowd and took a protestor to the ground. It was the culprit. The egg thrower was arrested as the Jaguar's tyres spit gravel from the rear when the driver accelerated away from the incident.

The Russian ambassador's car came into view. The cultural attaché sat next to the ambassador in the rear seat and Boyd noticed that, as authorised, a car containing Russian bodyguards followed the ambassador's car as support in case of attack.

Boyd's mind twisted and turned. Somewhere out there lay Jamil Volkov. Or had Abraham been wrong with his tip-off that Russia's top man was the target for assassination? Were the Russians right when they told Sir Phillip the target for the assassination was the British prime minister? Were the government ministers right and Boyd wrong?

'How many times do I have to think this through?' asked a troubled Boyd. 'My brain is in turmoil.'

'I know what you're thinking,' remarked Anthea.

'I'm not surprised,' replied Boyd. 'Not after all the years we've worked together.'

'Has anyone ever succeeded in making us look fools?'

'A few over the years,' chuckled Boyd. 'But we always ended up winners. I feel like we are going to lose today.'

'Let's play for a draw at least then,' proposed Anthea.

'A draw?' queried Boyd. 'You know what they say about a draw. Second place is the first loser. We never play for second place.'

'Try and relax,' consoled Anthea. 'Right now, we're winning.'

Gesturing his thanks, Boyd noticed the prime minister's Jaguar swing left from the minor road into the country park. The back end twitched slightly when it accelerated, outwitted the demonstrators, and spat another load of loose gravel from its rear tyres. The armoured vehicle cruised towards the venue.

Moments later, a radio transmission informed, 'Papa Mike is at a Stop! Stop at the venue. We are Out! Out of the vehicle. Wait!'

Seconds ticked away as Boyd watched proceedings from his control point and heard the principal personal protection officer radio, 'We are at the venue. Wait!'

The principal personal protection officer was at the prime minister's car door. He paused, held his hand tight on the door handle, glanced around, and then opened the door saying to the prime minister, 'Come!'

As Britain's top man shuffled in his seat, the protection officer activated a button radio device in his hand and transmitted, 'Papa Mike is on foot moving into the venue.'

The prime minister, dressed in a dark pinstripe suit set off by a white thinly striped shirt and matching tie, stepped out of the Jaguar. He waved to a collection of photographers standing in a nearby police-controlled security zone.

Journalistic fingers moved frantically. Cameras flashed, photographs were taken, and within minutes the internet was full of emails being sent to tabloids and broadsheets across the globe. The conference was tomorrow's headlines.

Following behind, the prime minister's assistant carried his briefcase and ignored the cameras.

The Russian ambassador's car drew nearer moments later. It was a black six-litre BMW 7 series fitted with diplomatic number plates and a state-of-the-art TALOS bomb detection system identical to that of the prime minister.

A blue and yellow Ukrainian flag was hoisted from within the group of climate protestors and political activists. Cameras flashed at the turn-off where demonstrators stood. There was no further reaction from the activists. No one seemed to know who the car belonged to. Any protest against the war in Ukraine started and ended with a flag. The group was committed to climate change and lacked an anti-Russian heart.

The BMW came to a standstill outside the hotel. The doors of the backup vehicle swiftly opened. Four plainclothes operatives quickly abandoned their vehicle and cocooned the ambassador and the cultural attaché as they made for the hotel lobby.

Russia's top man - the ambassador - sported a dark grey suit, white shirt, and red tie. A dark-coloured overcoat hung over his arm. Andrey - the cultural attaché - wore a knee-length black overcoat covering a dark suit topped off by his favourite ushanka that proudly adorned his head for all to see. The hat was made from real black fox fur. It was soft and unique in its design and carried, as a centrepiece, a prominent Russian military badge.

The prime minister and the Russian ambassador had arrived safely at the hotel.

An anxious Boyd lifted binoculars to his eyes and scoured the surroundings before radioing, 'All security units hold position. Remain vigilant. Out!'

The day wore on with the conference in full swing as ministers and invited speakers moved from their seats to the rostrum on the stage to deliver their speeches.

A break was scheduled. Coffee and tea arrived. Drinks were taken. Smiles and pleasantries were observed, and Boyd and Bannerman watched it all from opposite corners of the conference room. The Russian ambassador and the prime minister shook hands. The cultural attaché was introduced to the prime minister. Their conversation began pleasantly and subsequently led to friendly gestures, smiles and laughter. The minister from Sweden joined in, introduced his counterpart from Norway, and seemed to accept the Russian presence. There was no mention of the war in Ukraine just a veiled understanding that it was not on the agenda.

It surprised Boyd who had expected that the Russians may have been vetoed from proceedings. Perhaps it was the nature and title of the conference. He did not know and was puzzled at how delegates in the assembly seemed to move effortlessly between each other. But then Boyd had little experience of political proceedings at such conferences and merely watched the posturing taking place. Continuing to observe, he studied the fluid body language on display. He tried to understand the ethics and conscience of high-flying politicians. Smiles beamed, became the order of the day, and made a mockery of those gathered to discuss climate change when the war in Ukraine was an unspoken downside to proceedings. Sensing the atmosphere, Boyd felt his fingers curl around the trigger guard of a Gloch 17 handgun secreted in his suit.

The conference hall doors opened wide and a line of smartly dressed waiters trooped into the room carrying trays of hors d'oeuvre that were offered to the delegates. Stuffed mushrooms, prawns, cucumber, and sliced pickles were savoured and washed down with white wine.

Half an hour later, a bell rang, and the representatives returned to their seats. The conference continued with a scientist from France providing a PowerPoint presentation.

Agitated, Boyd stepped outside, paced the lobby and corridor, and then went to inspect the vehicles the delegates had arrived in. Still parked in the same positions, the drivers had stayed with the cars throughout. As Boyd cast his critical eye around, he noticed some of his teams were close to the parking area. Everything is going according to plan.

By late afternoon, the conference ended. Final speeches were made, hands were shaken, promises made, photographs for the media taken, and gradually the delegates left the hotel and returned to their vehicles.

The security zone reawakened when delegates returned to the junction, faced the noisy protest, negotiated the level crossing, and embarked on the journey home.

The Russian ambassador's BMW travelled to the junction, turned left, and set off in a different direction from the others. Nikolai Lermontov was gone from the venue.

Nevertheless, Boyd was sufficiently worried to seek out the prime minister's principal personal protection officer. He told the chief bodyguard that security arrangements had to be tightened and then called the unit's response helicopter. The whirlybird landed in the car park and the prime minister was escorted onto the flight. The helicopter took off and was gone from the area within minutes.

The prime minister was safe.

Boyd radioed, 'All Special Crime Units, stand down! Muster to the conference hall in the hotel. Five minutes!'

The network acknowledged.

'Network now closed to Special Crime Unit personnel,' radioed Boyd as he walked towards the hotel and a mug of coffee he was looking forward to. 'Cumbria only. Thank you!'

The phone rang and was handed to Boyd by Bannerman with the words, 'It's the Home Secretary, Guvnor. It's Maude Black.'

Boyd took the phone and paused for a moment before finally replying, 'Maude Black!'

'The Home Secretary, Guvnor. I think you know her.'

Boyd crooked his index finger and gestured Anthea, Bannerman, and Janice closer before pressing a button on the telephone that enabled speech to be audible to all present.

His colleagues drew near. Boyd announced his name.

'Commander!' urged the Home Secretary. 'William! It's your good friend Maude Black talking to you from my desk in the Home Office. I've just taken a phone call from the prime minister who expressed abundant gratitude for the professional way his protection team, and your security detail, conducted themselves today and safeguarded so many important political contacts throughout Europe and Scandinavia. You will be aware, Commander, that I have long supported you and the Special Crime

Unit. Your Home Secretary has always been thankful for the work you have delivered over many years.'

'Thank you,' mumbled Boyd incoherently.

'His Majesty's Government is deliriously happy that all went well, Commander Boyd,' continued the Home Secretary. 'You should feel proud.'

'Mmm...' from Boyd. 'I see.'

'However, I need to discuss something with you.'

'I'm listening.'

'It seems that the highly placed sensitive and secure source that has been spoken of was wrong all along,' suggested Maude Black. 'His intelligence was wrong and drove us to distraction, Commander.'

'I've never indicated whether the source was male or female,' declared Boyd.

'Indeed, Commander Boyd, it's time for the truth. Is the source a man or a woman? Is the intelligence from a technical deployment following an authorised warrant? A phone intercept or a postal interception? Perhaps a bugging device of some kind? I'd like to know, strictly between you and me only, of course. You know you can trust me, Commander Boyd. I am your ally.'

Denying a proper reply, Boyd merely mumbled a cough as he wondered how he should respond to an unwanted phone call. He had long enjoyed the support of Maude Black, knew her well, and felt content in her company. He even recalled presenting her with a bottle of Bushmills Irish whiskey on her birthday once. Today, he wasn't in the mood.

'I think you'll agree that you need to re-appraise the quality of the sources that are in use in your line of work and how the content is assessed,' continued the Home Secretary. 'Don't you think so, Commander Boyd? I ought to tell you that the Foreign Secretary, Sir Henry Fielding agrees. He sends his heartiest congratulations to you for the way you have orchestrated special security today. He'd like to be remembered to you, as always.'

Boyd offered a mild grunt.

'That said, I find myself under pressure from ministerial colleagues. It's only a short time ago that you were reinstated following an incident in Brixton. Yes! You were cleared but there were some discrepancies as I recall. It occurs to Her Majesty's Government that yet again you appear to have made another mistake. Your highly placed sensitive and secure source was wrong. You chose to believe the source, not the advice we gave you. What's more, you tried to convince everyone of the veracity of the source. You were wrong, Commander. I agree the Russians were also wrong, but they don't work for us. You do. Is it time for you to retire while the going is good, Commander? People are asking.'

Boyd held the phone to his ear and reflected on the job. He'd placed so much trust in Abraham right from the beginning. He knew Abraham had provided an abundance of intelligence to him, M15, M16 and Mossad over the years. So, he'd made a mistake. Should that destroy Abraham's credibility after all those years? Boyd wasn't listening to the voice prattling away on the phone. He was thinking about Abraham, how it had all started, how it was all finishing. Boyd's brain was still wondering where Jamil Volkov was hiding. He had no time for the Home Secretary.

'Commander!' remarked Maude Black. 'Commander Boyd, are you there? Speak to me Goddammit, man!'

Boyd dropped the phone onto its cradle, looked Anthea in the eye, and said, 'The top man! It's the top man, Anthea! Not the prime minister and not the Russian ambassador. All those bigwigs being nice to each other. Talking climate change, tittle-tattle, and irrelevant chatter whilst eating stuffed mushrooms and shrimp cocktails. Not one person talking about war. Only thinking about it. Who was the only one wearing military insignia?'

'Military what...?' queried Janice.

'No one,' ventured Anthea. 'There was no military present.'

- 238 -

'Come on!' snapped Boyd. 'He wore the Russian military badge for all to see.'

'Andrey Petrov!' cried Bannerman. 'On his ushanka!'

Setting off at a pace, Boyd glanced over his shoulder and said, 'Who is the top Russian in the UK, Anthea?'

'The ambassador: Nikolai Lermontov.'

'No! The hat, Anthea! The ushanka! The top man wears the hat, not the ambassador.'

'You mean...'

'Yes! Ushanka! Andrey Petrov is the target, not the ambassador. Andrey has more power than any other Russian in the country and that's why he wears a military badge on his ushanka. He's the top spy and one of his tasks is to find out what our government is up to and tell Moscow. Got it?'

'But Nikolai Lermontov has the ear of the Kremlin.'

'But he's not a spy. He's not fighting a war. He's not plotting to kill dissidents in Glenridding. Ushanka is. That's what he does. He runs agents, like the Lowther couple, so that can he finish Moscow's work when he needs to and find out what we are up to. He's fighting a war every day except there are no bullets or bombs in his line of fire. Spies are the secret weapon in war. Where is he? Which way did he go?'

'Andrey Petrov is on his way to Seven Hills. That's the home of Sergey Ivanov, the oligarch I told you about,' explained Bannerman. 'There were so many of us in the security area today that I left Terry Anwhari watching Sergey. Terry is alone and tells me Sergey has never left the house all day. You wanted to know more about Sergey Ivanov. Terry would tell you he is the most boring man on the planet. If he's not windsurfing on the tarn, he's at home.'

'Because he doesn't want to advertise his presence perhaps,' offered Anthea. 'That makes sense if he doesn't want people to know about his connections in the Kremlin.'

'All three!' barked Boyd. 'Jamil is after all three. Hit the road!'

Dashing towards the entrance, Boyd reached the front door with Anthea, Bannerman and Janice running alongside him.

A voice from the lobby yelled, 'The phone, Guvnor! It's the Home Secretary! She's as angry as hell! You'd best take the call.'

Glancing over his shoulder, Boyd shouted, 'Later! Tell her I'm busy! Tell her the target is Andrey Petrov! She won't believe you but tell her anyway.'

A lone suit appeared at the hotel doorway as Boyd and his colleagues rushed towards the nearest squad car. Holding a telephone trailing a line behind it, the figure lifted the handset to his mouth but didn't know what to say.

Boyd dived into the driver's seat of the squad car. He fired the engine. Anthea took the passenger seat. Bannerman and Janice took the rear. The back end twitched and splattered a mix of gravel and soil from the rear wheels when Boyd's foot slammed the accelerator to the floor and the rear tyres sizzled across the ground.

'Where are they now?' yelled Boyd as he drove the car hell for leather from the car park towards the main road and the junction where the protestors had spent the day.

On his mobile phone, Bannerman replied, 'Still inside the house. Terry tells me there are four cars on site. One belongs to Sergey, one is his wife's, and the other two have just arrived. Two black BMWs. I'd say Ushanka and his bodyguards are at Seven Hills. What do you think?'

'Sounds like it,' replied Boyd. 'Anthea! Get hold of Ricky! Drone coverage over Seven Hills!'

'Already asked,' voiced Anthea stowing her mobile. 'He's out of time! No battery life! No replacement! We're on our own.'

The click of two cartridges being slid swiftly and majestically into a side-by-side 20-inch double-barrelled Viking shotgun was accompanied by the raw accent of Janice's Scottish voice when she added, 'Och! I wouldna say that! I've got ma wee pal here.'

'Oh dear,' replied Anthea as the squad car bounced around the junction and swung towards the road to Forest Hill and the home of Sergey Ivanov.

'You're on loudspeaker, Terry,' from Bannerman holding his mobile phone up for all to hear.

'Two men went into the house together,' revealed Terry Anwhari. 'Andrey Petrov and Nikolai Lermontov were welcomed by Sergey Ivanov and a woman I presume to be his wife. A manservant escorted four other males in dark suits from a black BMW that followed Andrey and the ambassador. I reckon there may be a few more other suits already in the house and suggest they are dedicated to Sergey. Could be a manservant, domestic staff, people like that.'

'And bodyguards?' queried Boyd.

'I think so. They're all inside the house.'

'Anyone else in attendance?'

'No! Other than three gardeners piling logs and brushwood against the wall that surrounds the house. On the inside of the wall, there is a conservatory but there's no one in it that I can see. The gardeners have been here for about an hour. Three males all dressed in dark blue overalls. They appear to be known to Sergey who waved at them when they arrived this morning. It looked to me as if they were regulars on site and he was happy they were looking after the garden.'

'Any of them resemble Jamil?'

'No! I have a good line of vision with my binoculars. Jamil is not in sight, Guvnor. Nowhere to be seen.'

'Got that!' from Boyd who gunned the squad car along the road towards Seven Hills and replied, 'The wall, Terry! What part of the wall do you mean?'

'West side just through Talkin village. Near Hare Beck!'

'Got that,' from Boyd as the four detectives glided through Talkin with Boyd decreasing speed on the approach.

'You know it?' queried Anthea.

'I've walked past the house with Meg,' chuckled Boyd. 'We were on the path that takes you to Forest Head. You can look down on the house from there. It sounds like Terry is on the same pathway. A wall encircles the entire house except for the front entrance where a wireless operated iron gate is situated.'

'Where you at precisely, Terry?' probed Bannerman.

'Lying on the grass near a pathway that takes you halfway up the hill at Hare Beck and behind the house looking down on the building through binoculars. More brushwood is being piled against the wall. I don't get it, Guvnor.'

'Me neither,' replied Boyd bringing the squad car to a standstill near a field gate. Swinging around in his seat, Boyd spoke aloud to Bannerman's mobile phone saying, 'Okay! We've stopped about one hundred yards from the house on the Talkin village side. Can you see us, Terry?'

Terry rolled from his stomach onto his back and then onto his stomach again some yards from his original position. Bringing his binoculars into play, he replied, 'Four of you in sight. Confirm?'

'Confirmed!' replied Boyd. 'We are four and it's quite breezy down here! We'll go through the gate into the field and approach the house line abreast. I want us as close as possible to Seven Hills. You are our eyes and ears, Terry. Guide us in safely.'

'All clear at the moment,' reported Terry. 'Proceed!'

The detectives abandoned the squad car, hunkered down into the field, and headed to Seven Hills. Here and there, the topography of the countryside pitched up in their favour allowing them to make progress. In other places, the land dropped and exposed them to anyone watching from Seven Hills.

Fifty yards in, Boyd brought his binoculars to bear, gestured to Bannerman for an update from Terry, and learnt it was plain sailing as they approached the house.

Boyd's heart rate increased when he saw the bearded Jamil Volkov emerge from the copse next to Seven Hills.

Jamil lugged holdalls which he placed on top of the pile. He then went back to the wood and returned with two more holdalls which he laid on top of the pile. Jamil gestured to the gardeners to go to the front of the building.

'What are they doing?' queried Anthea. 'Setting a fire?'

'Or is it a wee bomb?' suggested Janice.

'Might be either,' declared Boyd. 'That's Jamil on the plot and he's up to no good. Whatever is in those holdalls is heavy. He made hard work of carrying them from the wood. But I just don't know what the hell he's doing. He's not preparing to take a rifle shot at anyone, and I don't get how starting a fire from brushwood is going to pose a threat.'

'It's all from the thicket in the neighbouring copse,' observed Anthea. 'He must have a vehicle somewhere. Can you see a car, Terry?'

'Nothing seen!' replied Terry. 'Probably hidden from me by the trees.'

'I wonder what is in those holdalls,' continued Anthea.

Glued to the mobile phone, Bannerman announced, 'From Terry, he too confirms Jamil Volkov is on the plot and whilst Jamil is fussing with the brushwood, he's pointing to those three gardeners to move away. They're going towards the front entrance. What are they doing?'

Boyd raised himself onto his haunches in the grass and declared, 'Shamash!'

'What?' questioned Anthea. 'What do you mean?'

'The secret Arab Jew organisation in London. Those three so-called gardeners are three of the men I saw when Abraham covered the meeting for me. Jamil is not alone, folks! It's a four-hander, guys! Jamil plus three!'

'Well, I'm all for equality,' chuckled Janice. 'Everyone should play the bagpipes and wear kilts but that will never happen. But it's four apiece so we're even. Tell me though, what the hell is he doing?'

'Connecting a piece of cord to a device inside one of the holdalls,' ventured Boyd who was still glued to his binoculars.

'It's a bomb then,' suggested Janice. The wee man is going to make a big bang, so he is.'

'To blow a hole in a garden wall?' argued Boyd. 'I don't think so, Janice. But something isn't right.'

Stumped, and suspended in mid-operation, the four detectives were at a loss to explain what was happening. And then it dawned on Boyd who gasped, 'Of course! He's sent Shamash to the front of the building because he's making a diversionary attack at the rear.'

'Exactly! Look!' pointed Bannerman.

With the three Shamash so-called gardeners now at the front of Seven Hills, Jamil unrolled a long piece of clothesline behind him as he disappeared into the wood.

Boyd stood up and studied the clothesline through his binoculars. He scrutinised its composition, considered the connection to the holdalls lying on the pile of brushwood, and then realised what it was. 'I think it's a phosphorous high explosive attack!' mouthed a stunned Boyd. His jaw dropped for a second before he continued, 'He's jammed a detonator into one of the holdalls. No finesse. It's not as if he's had to carefully thread a detonator into a particular device. He's rammed the end of the cord into whatever is in that holdall. I'm guessing it's phosphorous.'

'You never guess at anything, Guvnor,' ventured Janice. 'Your brain has always been your best weapon and you're thinking like a killer again. What's he doing now?'

'He's going to cause an explosion at the rear of the house to drive the occupants out of the front door and into the Shamash line of fire. It's a diversionary tactic. Call for back up, Bannerman.'

Bannerman hit the digits on his mobile.

Jamil lit the clothesline.

'Get ready, guys!' ventured Boyd.

The clothesline was a cord that contained pentaerythritol tetranitrate (PETN). The explosive substance is the main ingredient in a plastic explosive called Semtex. It travelled along the line at a furious unstoppable speed of four miles per second and ignited the white phosphorous in one of the holdalls piled on the stack of brushwood. What appeared to be a perfectly innocent pile of garden rubbish and kindling erupted immediately. White phosphorous exploded and destroyed the canvas holdalls that contained more phosphorous. Two holdalls were packed with ball bearings, old car batteries, and scrap metal as well as phosphorous. The explosion scorched the firewood and propelled logs, wooden branches, and countless metallic parts into the air. Burning phosphorus caused a hot, white smoke - consisting mostly of phosphorus pentoxide – to dominate the area in a huge cloud of breathtaking fumes that consumed every speck of oxygen in the vicinity. The air burnt and the smoke circled like a deranged devil with a mind of its own determined to shut down life inside Seven Hills.

The sound of breaking glass followed when it rained ball bearings, car batteries, branches, and everything else that had been piled up against the wall. Falling through the conservatory roof, the burning debris scorched the floor and then snuffed out the oxygen in the room. Burning white phosphorous snaked its way through Seven Hills setting fire to anything inflammable whilst simultaneously suffocating the air to deny the occupants the chance to breathe.

Phosphorous attacks the lungs. The devil was inside Seven Hills and mounting a blistering attack on anyone standing in the way. Jamil Volkov, the self-taught pyrotechnic engineer, had used the breeze and his knowledge of advanced pyrotechnics to create a humongous explosion which drove the occupants out of the house because of the noise, the burning air sensation, and the sheer fear of the fireball that mushroomed above the building.

Inside Seven Hills, panic took over. Screams rent the air. People's hands rushed to cover their noses to stop the burning sensation threatening their very existence. Stinging eyes dominated everyone's body. The feeling of blistering heat tingling on the skin and then reaching a petrifying crescendo of red-hot roguery caused a rush to the front door, freedom, and the chance to breathe freely.

The occupants ran to escape the phosphorous torment. Andrey dived beneath a dining table and felt the pitter-patter of debris bouncing on top of the oak structure. Nikolai scurried to a window where he coiled a long velvet curtain around himself in the mistaken belief that it would protect him from the gruesome onslaught. The fabric caught fire. Nikolai felt it burn his clothes and singe his body. That was when he began screaming and cavorting on the floor trying to disentangle himself. Sergey and his wife followed the panic-stricken servants and bodyguards out of the building into the front garden. They were hurrying, running for their lives, knocking over chairs, coffee tables, and ornaments in a frenzied bid to escape the demon's claws.

Ali, Ibrahim and Hamza, from Shamash, leaned across the garden wall and released a barrage of rifle shots that took the first three manservants to the ground in a matter of seconds. Three bodyguards hit the deck, rolled either behind or under the two parked BMWs, and withdrew their weapons. It took a few seconds for them to activate their stinging hands and return fire.

A firefight ensued.

Ibrahim unshouldered a submachine gun and let rip a salvo of bullets that took down Sergey's wife when she appeared at the door. From head to toe her body was riddled with bullets and her life ended tragically far from the country in which she was born and bred. She died instantly on the porch of Seven Hills. The very heart and soul of a woman born in Moscow had been murdered in a far-off place named in recognition of her birthplace.

More bullets raked across the frontage of Seven Hills peppering the BMWs, blasting garden ornaments to kingdom come, and wreaking havoc on the occupants of the building.

Boyd yelled, 'Engage!' and led his team forward towards the house with his hand outstretched firing from his Gloch at the three Shamash gunmen.

Suddenly, the phosphorous cloud dissipated. Having burnt up the oxygen in the house, there was nothing to consume. The white smoke frittered away with only the odd wisp spiralling unchallenged into the atmosphere where it died an instant death. Smouldering pieces of inflammable substances had caught fire, burnt, and scorched, but failed to spread because the phosphorous was gone from Seven Hills.

Yet the damage had been done. Jamil Volkov had successfully emptied the house and driven the occupants into a lethal firing line that equated to cold-blooded murder.

At the side of the house, close to where the pile of brushwood had been laid to stage the diversionary attack, Jamil emerged from the wood, slithered watchfully over the wall, and crept towards the front door of the house to see the dead body of Sergey's wife lying in the porch.

A bodyguard glanced over his shoulder, aimed at Jamil, and was killed by a succession of rifle shots from Ali.

At the rear of Seven Hills, safe and untouched from the horrific attack, Luka heard and saw the explosion, felt a blast of hot air whizz past him as he ducked low, and then dived into a hollow in the ground. The cloud of white phosphorous smoke swept over his body and died in the breeze moments later. To British Intelligence, Luka was FEDORA and was second in command to USHANKA. He relished powerful contacts in the Kremlin. In years gone by, when the Soviet Union was alive and kicking, the KGB deployed undercover political officers to covertly oversee the actions of those in authority. Luka was such a man in the new regime. Dressed in a black suit, sporting a white shirt and black tie, the member of Russia's Foreign Intelligence Service (the FSB) quickly worked out what had happened. He stole into the nearby copse where he found a dark blue Transit van adorned with the fictitious name of a gardening company on its side. Hearing the gunfire, Luka hit the deck and crawled to the van determined to escape the firefight.

Noisy, chattering machine guns turned their attention to Boyd and his team allowing the bodyguards that were still alive time to reload and move closer to the wall of fire they had experienced from the Shamash operatives.

As Janice stood tall and walked towards the trio of gunmen attacking the bodyguards, Jamil closed on the house, saw Sergey rush to the body of his wife, hold her close, and then shot him dead from ten yards with a single bullet to the skull. Still holding the gun by his side, Jamil strolled towards the house and casually fired another round into Sergey's head as he stepped over him. The fearless killer then turned into the lobby of the house and confronted Nikolai with the words, 'You can run but you cannot hide from me. You represent the Kremlin, but I am the Muslim ambassador in the service of Allah. I come to remove you from the life you lead. Do you understand me, Nikolai?'

Staring nonplussed at Jamil, Nikolai was still smarting from the effects of the phosphorous. The ambassador's mind was still warped by the mild blisters forming on the back of his hands, still panic-stricken and overawed by it all.

Jamil yelled, '*Allahu Akbar!* Allah is the Greatest! Allah commands that you do not send Muslims to the war in Ukraine! Allah has spoken.'

'It's...,' from the dumbstruck ambassador who had no other words to offer other than a grey paling face and a softly murmured, 'It's not my decision. It's the Kremlin's decision. Don't shoot me!'

'*Mashallah!*' declared Jamil.

The fanatic drilled two bullets in quick succession into the chest of the ambassador. Jamil then walked forward, stood astride the dying man, and fired two more bullets into his forehead saying, 'God has willed it! *Mashallah!'*

A traumatised Andrey Petrov watched from beneath the oak dining table, witnessed the final seconds of the ambassador's life, and then retreated into the heart of Seven Hills. He carried no weapon, enjoyed no bodyguard, and sought only to hide from the irrepressible fiend that was Jamil Volkov: a determined man whose bloodstream carried pure cold hatred.

Jamil heard Andrey's feet scuttling into the depths of Seven Hills. Entering the house, he was resolved to kill the man he considered to be the top Russian in the UK. Jamil waged a private war with Andrey Petrov.

Outside, the battle raged with the Shamash trio annihilating those who escaped Seven Hills in the belief that the air outside was good and they would live again. The three Arab Jews turned their attention to those who had escaped the house. One by one, they picked them off.

One bodyguard remained beneath a BMW. Ibrahim fired scathingly into the vehicle's bodywork. The car blew up, erupted with a punctured fuel tank, and rose into the air before crashing to the ground in the same place.

There was a slow moaning from the last bodyguard followed by a final twitch of his arm, and then he died.

Rushing into the fray, Boyd, Bannerman, Anthea, and Janice ducked and dived, used the sunken hollows in the field to draw nearer, and then finally stood together to unleash an unforgiving torrent of gunfire on the Shamash enemy.

Firing from the hip, Janice pulled the trigger and watched Ibrahim crash to the ground out of the game.

Bannerman vaulted the wall, rolled towards the burning BMW, and simultaneously shot Hamza in the chest.

Following suit, Anthea engaged the trio and clipped Ali with two bullets that ensured he fell to the ground writhing in agony.

Janice reloaded, felt Ali's final bullet zip past her head, and then returned fire powering two more slugs into Ali.

It was over. Only the smell of cordite mixed with the slight lingering odour of dying phosphorous infiltrated the battle zone.

Boyd hurdled the wall, sprinted past numerous bodies that littered the car park, and scrambled up the steps into the porch area where he slammed himself against the concrete column. Regaining his breath, he took stock of what lay ahead. Eyeing the interior of the house, Boyd scanned the floor looking for signs of Jamil but heard only the clatter of footsteps when someone inside fell to the ground. Filling his lungs with air, Boyd felt unease in the pit of his stomach, sweat on his brow, and the growth of fear in his mind.

Anthea, Janice, and Bannerman appeared at Boyd's shoulder.

'Reinforcements are on their way,' remarked Bannerman. 'Terry Anwhari is also covering the rear of the house.'

'Good!' nodded Boyd. 'I'm going in. Stay here! Surround the building. Jamil is trapped, but I want Ushanka.'

'Guvnor!' exclaimed Anthea. 'You have a face gone white. No colour. Don't do it! Let them kill each other and then we'll go in and recover the bodies. They're not even on our side.'

'Not yet,' barked Boyd. 'Do as I say, Anthea. I've something to do that is just between Ushanka and me.'

'What?' queried Anthea. 'What's going on?'

'The less you know the better,' replied Boyd. 'Something I promised Phillip that if I ever got the chance I would do it. Well, now I see the chance. Look, Anthea, if I don't come back, tell Meg and the kids how much I love them. You have ground control, Anthea. It's your command. Lock the plot down!'

'No! Billy!' screamed Anthea. 'Billy...' voiced in despair, muffled in the breeze, lost.

Boyd was gone from his colleagues, sprinting to an overturned chair that offered little protection, then sliding across the floor on his belly to an open door.

'You heard him,' barked Bannerman. 'As long as he lives and breathes, I will support him. He knows what he's doing. Stay here! Janice, take the rear exit with Terry. Anthea!

But Anthea was mesmerised, dumbstruck, and riveted to the spot. Her public facade masked private despair as she wondered why Boyd had abandoned the team and rushed into a hellhole from which he might never return. He was going after one of the world's most prolific killers. She shook her head and tried to free her mind from the turmoil of potentially losing a lifelong colleague and friend.

Bannerman shook Anthea growling, 'It's your shout, Anthea. It's your command and you need to close the plot. Lock down Geltsdale, Forest Head, Talkin, wherever we are. Work it out! When Boyd shouts 'lock it down' it's because we're not finished yet and there's more to play for. Don't ask me what because I don't know. You've got the authority. Reinforcements will be here shortly. Do it, Anthea. Lock down the patch. No questions asked.'

Anthea's eyes searched the inside of the house as far as she could see, and then nodded at Bannerman with the words, 'Okay! Agreed! Close the plot. Use all teams to close every inch of movement. Roadblocks to prevent access to the plot. I'll make the call to Cumbria's chief. Whatever happens, Bannerman, we're carrying Jamil out of this building in a box.'

Bannerman dropped to one knee and pointed his weapon in a wide arc covering the porch, lobby, and visible innards of the building. Janice moved to the rear of the house and Anthea stepped over the body of Sergey's wife, stepped outside, and stepped towards the electronic gates that fronted the house to welcome and deploy the reinforcements. Locking down a London borough to prevent a getaway was routine, but not in the massive county of Cumbria which had little experience with such actions.

Midstride, Anthea stopped. She heard the thunder of sirens rushing closer, picked out the reflections of rotating blue lights approaching Seven Hills, and let her Gloch drop to her side before concluding, 'I'm finished. I should be at the front leading the way not waiting to tell people which queue to stand in. My mind has gone. Is this how Boyd felt in Brixton?'

Sinking to her knees, Anthea Adams dropped her head forward and allowed her long auburn hair to cascade over her crown and tumble like a waterfall before her eyes.

Inside Seven Hills, shards of loose glass disturbed by the phosphorous attack continually fell to the floor, shattered, and exploded in a cacophony of unexpected sounds. Simultaneously, long velvet curtains hanging in front of the windows finally collapsed, gathered on the ground, and added to the mayhem still apparent throughout. It was the force of the explosion when the phosphorous had detonated that had brought instability to the fragile ceiling of the building.

Jamil kicked over a stool that was in his way, grabbed at a door handle, and entered the drawing room to see Andrey's legs scuttling behind a sofa. Laughing, Jamil shouted, 'I've said it before; I'll say it again. There is no escape from the will of Allah. Andrey! Oh yes, Andrey! I know who you are. I know all about you.'

A bullet fired by Jamil deliberately missed Andrey, plummeted into the leather sofa way above Andrey's head, and exited to the rear of the room.

Roaring with laughter, Jamil drew closer to the sofa and walked indifferently to the rear of the leather pile voicing, 'King of the Kremlin's spies in Britain. A man of war, are you not? A killer of men and women who despise you and all you stand for. A man who loves the Commander in Chief in Moscow. You love the thrill of enjoying levels of power not experienced by mortals like me.'

Andrey began to rise and felt the breath of the devil breeze across him.

'It is people like you,' continued Jamil. 'That support the war in Ukraine, cheer when my Muslim blood brothers are despatched there and shed not a tear when they are killed on foreign soil far from home. It is a Godless wasteland to which you send them, and then abandon them.'

Andrey launched himself at Jamil, but the Muslim envoy drilled a bullet into his shoulder as he dodged Andrey.

'*Allahu Akbar*,' professed Jamil. 'God is Great! Allah is my God. Your time is over. You are a garbage can of a man.'

More gunshots from Jamil's weapon but they all missed when Andrey catapulted himself out of range slithering to a stop with blood oozing from a shoulder wound.

'Enough of you! I have work to do!' voiced Jamil who took a couple of steps forward and stood astride Andrey with his gun pointed at his head before saying, 'For Allah and my kin, I kill you. To hell you go. To hell I send you!'

'Jamil!' yelled Boyd bursting into the room. The door moaned at its hinges.

The Muslim murderer swung his head towards the voice, saw Boyd airborne, and aimed at the detective.

Midair, Boyd fired from his Gloch before crashlanding on the floor next to Andrey who was writhing in pain.

Hit by the first bullet, Jamil faltered, fell back, realised he'd been shot in the hip and returned fire.

Boyd rolled over and felt the heat of Jamil's bullets when they scorched the floor behind him. The detective delivered another two shots at the deranged terrorist. They both missed. Firing again, Boyd realised the chamber was empty. He was out of ammunition.

Hugging his hip with his free hand, limping badly, Jamil approached the pair lying on the floor close to each other.

'And then there were two,' said Jamil as he aimed Boyd.

Door hinges creaked in protest at another intrusion. Anthea barged in, saw Jamil standing over the bodies of his next victims, and let off a salvo of bullets from a submachine gun as she flung herself into a corner and rolled into a ball. The bullets peppered the wall, ceiling, and furniture before hitting Jamil in the upper body.

Jamil turned awkwardly, crumpled, paused in a violent death throe, staggered towards Boyd and Andrey pointing his weapon, and then felt the wrath of Janice when she entered the battle and blasted Jamil with her shotgun.

The Muslim terrorist tumbled unceremoniously to the floor.

'I thought I told you two to stay where you were,' offered Boyd in sarcastic tribute. 'You can't be trusted, can you?'

Twitching, Jamil tried to level his gun, heard the trigger pull, and took the final lethal slug in the chest from Janice's shotgun when she ended his life.

Jamil Volkov did not hear Janice remark, 'Och! No! I cannae be trusted but ma wee pal here can.' She patted the shotgun stock.

Boyd shook his head in disbelief when Janice added, 'We done now, Guvnor?'

'You okay, Anthea?' queried Boyd.

'Had better days, but getting there,' replied an auburn-haired detective who had suddenly lost then found her feet.

The ceiling quivered. A thick pointed shard of glass hurtled downwards from the remnants of the conservatory roof. The long spike thundered into a glass dining table, broke into a dozen smaller pieces, and caused a cascade of glass slivers from the table to explode here, there, and everywhere in the room.

One slender piece of glass hurtled towards Boyd and his crew and lodged itself in the shoulder joint of Andrey Petrov who screamed in pain. Blood from his wound spurted everywhere as Andrey screamed in agony and the glass attack finally ended with a scattering of flakes spreading across the floor.

Boyd stripped off his jacket, stuffed it into Andrey's shoulder joint, and screamed, 'Ambulance!'

Hitting the digits on her phone, Anthea waited for a reply as Janice used hers to summon the unit's helicopter currently flying south with the prime minister on board.

'Thirty minutes,' from Anthea.

'No show,' from Janice. 'Too far south to turn back. Insufficient fuel, Guvnor.'

Pressing into Andrey's shoulder, stemming the blood flow, Boyd started into Andrey's eyes and said, 'It's over, Andrey. You're finished! If I release pressure on your wound, you'll be dead within fifteen minutes at the most.'

'The ambulance! What about the ambulance?'

'All tied up. Never going to happen.'

'Help me! Whoever you are, help me.'

'You know who I am,' replied Boyd. 'We've never met but you know who I am, Andrey. You'll have a file on me, and we've got a file on you. Isn't that right?'

Andrey did not reply.

'I know who you are, Andrey. 'You are the resident.'

Convulsing in pain, Andrey stared into Boyd's face and replied, 'I don't live here.'

'Of course not,' chuckled Boyd. 'Sergey and his wife live here. They're both dead and so is Nikolai, the ambassador. You live in the Russian embassy, Andrey. You are Russia's top spy in Britain.'

'Get an ambulance! I'm bleeding to death.'

A stream of dark red liquid seeped from beneath Andrey. There was more than one shoulder wound to tend.

'I can save you, Andrey,' nodded Boyd. 'I'll keep the pressure on until the paramedics arrive and cart you away in an ambulance. That's your problem, Andrey. You will live and your life will be over. Moscow won't want you back. You failed them. Every single person in Seven Hills has been killed by Jamil Volkov and his gang of three. Do think the Commander in Chief will welcome you back to Moscow as a hero? Tell me, Andrey, were you in charge of security here and at the conference in the hotel?'

Unsure of how to react, Andrey squirmed.

'Were you the one responsible for keeping the ambassador and the oligarch alive? Of course, you were Andrey. But you failed. The man in the Kremlin will not welcome you home. He might nod and smile but how long do you think it will be before you have a mysterious accident in Russia and die, Andrey?'

'Get that ambulance here. Now!'

'A week, maybe two, am I right? The man in the Kremlin is not famous for looking after people, Andrey. When they fail him, he fails them. Am I right?'

Andrey's eyes flickered in recognition of the truth.

'You know I'm right. You're living on borrowed time.'

'I know.'

Another drop of blood squeezed out of Andrey's body causing Boyd to increase the pressure on Andrey's wound. Boyd glanced at Anthea and gestured with his head.

'Bring the car round, Janice,' ordered Anthea. 'To the front door. Bannerman! Clear a path between here and the front door. Move those bodies. And kick the glass out of the way if you can. I don't want anyone falling over the dead. Bring me a first aid kit.'

'Where from?'

'Find one!' growled Anthea.

Boyd nodded his thanks and said, 'You're a dead man, Andrey. Here or in Moscow. Where do you want to die?'

'Not on this Godforsaken floor, that's for sure.'

'I have a contract for you,' ventured Boyd. 'We can report you dead and at the same time, we can save your life and let you live with us in safety. What do you think of it so far?' chuckled Boyd.

'What do you want?'

'Everything,' persuaded Boyd. 'You tell us everything you know about your spy networks in Britain and elsewhere and we lock out the media from Seven Hills. All they need to know is that there was an explosion in the house when you were all visiting a friend. A cooker in the kitchen exploded. People were having dinner in the conservatory when the ceiling collapsed because of the explosion. There was a fire. Nothing to do with Jamil Volkov. Never heard of him. You can make it up yourself, Andrey. You are the only one alive here. All your friends are dead. The ambassador, the oligarch, the manservants, and the bodyguards, are all dead. There's no one left to argue with you, no one to talk to. Understand?'

The car door banged closed when Janice brought the vehicle to the front door.

'The world will be told that you died here today. Your body was so severely burnt that it will never be formally identified. You die today, Andrey, and that's the message that goes to the Kremlin. The reality, however, is that you live today, Andrey. I'll take you to the nearest hospital where you'll be treated anonymously as a matter of urgency. We'll never lose sight of you. Within a couple of hours, we'll take you to a private hospital where you will recuperate in our presence. That's the offer, Andrey. Your life for the information you hold in that brain of yours. One day you will be free. We'll find somewhere for you to live in peace.'

'Plastic surgery?'

'If that's what you want, yes.'

'I have little choice,' murmured Andrey. 'You can leave me here to die or you can save me and send me home where I shall be murdered by the State.'

'Your choice,' remarked Boyd. 'I'm just pressing into your shoulder and stemming the flow of blood. Up to you.'

'I want to defect!'

'Then you have a deal,' replied Boyd.

'In that case, can you get me out of here before I bleed to death all over the floor?'

Bannerman arrived, broke open a first aid kit, and helped Boyd apply dressings to both shoulders.

Anthea held her mobile phone, studied Boyd, and queried, 'Antonia?'

'Yes, please,' replied Boyd. 'Let her know that Ushanka has come over. Tell her 'Code Zero Clear zero'. She can take it upstairs. Nothing happened here today. Get the ball rolling. We need a clear-up team as soon as possible. Zero Clear Zero! She'll understand.'

'I'm on it,' replied Anthea.

Boyd and Bannerman gently hoisted Andrey to his feet and guided him to the waiting squad car.

'I'll drive,' remarked Boyd. 'Bannerman, take the passenger seat. Janice can tag along behind as backup and Anthea can manage the clear-up squad when it arrives. Let's go.'

They were on the move and the casualty was now also a defector intent on living rather than dying.

~

16

~

The Irish Gate 'Millenium' Bridge.
Castle Way, Carlisle.
Later the same day.

Irish Gate Bridge was constructed as a pedestrian bridge over the busy dual carriageway known as Castle Way. It is named after one of the early medieval gateways that formed an entrance to the border city. The bridge links the city centre with Carlisle Castle. It is a Millennium Bridge in that its creation was funded by the Millennium Commission and was opened in 2000.

It was to this location that Boyd drove the squad car with Andrey Petrov as his front-seat passenger. Bandaged across his chest and shoulder, Andrey grimaced as Boyd hurtled down Brampton Road. His headlights were on full beam and his foot caressed the accelerator. They would soon be approaching Eden Bridge, Hardwicke Circus, Irish Gate, and the Cumberland Infirmary.

The road was clear. Boyd made progress.

Andrey grimaced and complained, 'There were ambulances on standby at the conference. Why couldn't you put me in one of them?'

'Because they'd left the area, Andrey. The conference was over when you were wounded, and the nearest ambulance was twenty minutes away. I can get you to the hospital in that time. Apart from that, the less people know about you the better. We don't need to involve paramedics and the ambulance service. One of my colleagues is making arrangements with the infirmary. You won't exist today, Andrey. You're dead. Remember?'

'This isn't Russia. Can you do that?'

'We're doing it right now,' replied Boyd. 'You still in pain? We'll be there soon.'

The squad car hit the city boundary and Boyd reduced speed and cruised towards Stanwix Bank.

'I don't know what that big man gave me back at Seven Hills but I'm all numb and a little drowsy.'

'Bannerman?' queried Boyd. 'He gave you a pain killer: an opiate that paramedics use to treat pain.'

'I think it's starting to work,' replied Andrey gasping, wriggling in his seat, and comforting his shoulder.

'I'm no medic,' explained Boyd. 'But I think you have two bullet wounds. One slotted straight through you and the other is lodged an inch or two below your collarbone.'

'I can feel it,' nodded the defecting culture secretary. 'How long before the hospital?'

'Soon!' said Boyd. 'I think you might also have glass splinters in your shoulder. None of us expected the ceiling to collapse.'

'Volkov!' ventured Andrey aggressively. 'Dead? I take it you were pleased to kill him?'

Boyd swung a sideways glance at Andrey and said, 'I'm not paid to kill people other than in self-defence. You, on the other hand, have a track record of murdering people. Take Glenridding, for instance.'

'I didn't spray the place with poison, and I've never pulled the trigger and killed anyone.'

'That's because you don't have to with your status,' replied Boyd. 'You might be Russia's culture secretary but you're also the Head of Station: The resident! The lead spy and warmonger in the Russian community here in England.'

Andrey remained silent as Boyd slid through the traffic lights at Stanwix Bank and began to glide over the Eden Bridge.

'Why did Volkov come to England to kill me?' probed Andrey now easing himself back, trying to find a more favoured position in which to comfort his shoulder.

'He killed a colonel, and others, in Dagestan,' revealed Boyd. 'You'll know that and don't pretend you don't, Andrey. Jamil Volkov spoke for thousands of Muslims all over the world when he bombed the life out of that colonel and made it clear to the Kremlin that Russia needs to stop sending Muslims to the war in Ukraine.'

'Did you know we release prisoners and criminals, enlist them in the army, and send them and mercenaries to Ukraine to fight the war?'

'Yes,' replied Boyd. 'But you asked about Volkov and that was his reason. No more Muslim soldiers to Ukraine.'

'We've got enough problems,' suggested Andrey. 'Ukraine has them too. Thousands of young men have crossed the borders of Ukraine into Poland and Hungary. Do you know why?'

'No! Tell me, Andrey!' demanded Boyd.

'They are all conscripts, but they don't want to fight for their country. They get out of Ukraine before they are called up. They want to escape the war.'

Crossing the bridge over the River Eden, the squad car negotiated the roundabout and headed along Castle Way towards Irish Gate Bridge and the Cumberland Infirmary beyond. The safe hands of a casualty doctor and surgical team waited patiently when the chief executive received orders from above and promptly oversaw their execution.

'No one wants to fight a war,' remarked Boyd as the squad car climbed the slight ascent towards Irish Gate.

In a car park, known locally as Devonshire Walk, a Transit van bearing the name of a gardener's company that did not exist was parked with its front facing outwards towards Carlisle Castle ready for a quick departure.

On the pedestrian bridge that crossed Castle Way, Luka withdrew an SRS-A2 Covert sniper rifle from his jacket. At 27 inches long, it was the shortest sniper rifle in the world.

Dropping to the ground, Luka attached a telescopic sight to the weapon, waited for the squad car to cruise over the ascent opposite Tullie House Museum, and took aim.

There was a glint of sunlight on the rifle barrel. Boyd saw the flash, saw a body lying flat on the pedestrian bridge, and swerved.

A split second later, Boyd's windscreen shattered.

Luka's bullet penetrated Andrey's chest. He buckled in his seat. His head dropped to one side, and he plummeted onto Boyd's arm as the detective wrestled with the steering wheel.

Boyd felt the force of the bullet rock the car, felt Andrey's bodyweight tumble onto his arm, and then heard the wind whistle into the front compartment. He lost control. There was a deafening collision when the squad car crashed into the central barrier before lurching across the dual carriageway and colliding with the wall.

Luka was gone from the Irish Gate Bridge, gone from the scene of the crime, making for a Ford Transit van bearing the name of a gardener's company that did not exist.

Dazed, and semi-conscious, Boyd glanced at the bridge but could not see it. His eyes glazed over. He had driven underneath the pedestrian bridge which was now behind him. He twisted and saw Bannerman and Janice abandoning their cars, racing across the road into Devonshire Walk, and shouting. They were screaming, ordering, gesturing. Boyd heard shots, gunfire, and more shouting.

The darkness came. Boyd passed out. He only saw black.

A short time later, Boyd came around in the casualty department of the infirmary. Lying in a bed, he glanced to his side and saw Andrey who was being attended to by the medics on duty.

'What happened?' murmured Boyd, confused, unsure.

'It was Luka,' explained Andrey weakly. 'The political man.'

'You okay?' queried Boyd.

Drowsy, sliding into another world. Andrey replied, 'You removed me from them. They removed you from me.'

Andrey's eyes closed as a casualty officer approached Boyd and said, 'You are a lucky man, Mr Brown. Lucky to be alive. You have a head injury, concussion, and shock. You need rest. We're going to keep you here for a day or two. It will do you good and help mend your body. You've got severe bruising too, Mr Brown. All from the road accident. But don't you worry. You are in good hands. Now just relax, Mr Brown. I'm going to give you this to put you to sleep. Rest! That's all.'

'No! I need to...'

The point of a needle crushed the conversation and Boyd's eyes closed.

Somewhere in dreamland, Boyd's mind spun out of control and fell into a deep chasm called sleep.

In his private illusions, Boyd decided that when he woke, he would tell Andrey that life was just a dice that rolled and fell one side up. Dependent on where the dice stopped determined what might happen in life. Wanting to give his all, to upset the applecart, to turn a man into a traitor to the Motherland, was all Boyd wanted to do. It was his job, his life, his way. Surely, Andrey could tell him of a weakness in the ranks of the enemy so that peace might follow. Or was it all just a roll of the dice? Why couldn't the West make peace with the East? In all of Boyd's life, that's a question he had forever asked himself. The Cold War never died. It just took on another face. Why couldn't the world agree on peace in Ukraine? The Russian claim was based on history. The NATO reaction was to try and strengthen a border between East and West. Okay, it was all a mix of yes, no, agree, disagree, and squabbling over who was the most powerful. None of the countries that swore allegiance to NATO, or the Russian Federation, talked peace. They only spoke of war, of trying to outdo the other, of constantly adjusting the strategy, and then reordering the tactics that filled the cosy chat rooms and debating chambers of various politicians across the globe. People, fighters, warriors, and soldiers were just numbers in a board game that politicians played out in their privileged lives that often involved a degree of lies and deceit, corruption, of the abuse and misuse of power. No one sought peace, no one wanted harmony! Why can't we extend the hand of friendship to the enemy? Why can't...

Boyd drifted. His brain rested. A body tired of it all slept!

'Mr Brown! Mr Brown!'

A nurse shook Boyd's arm and repeated, 'Mr Brown! Are you with us today?'

Boyd opened his eyes, glimpsed the woman's uniform, glanced around, realised where he was, and replied, 'Yes! Yes, of course. Where... Where...'

'Where are you, Mr Brown?' posed the nurse. 'You're in a ward at the Cumberland Infirmary. Do you have any pain at all, anywhere at all? Please tell me if you do.'

'No,' blurted Boyd. 'Where is... Where is my friend?'

'Mr Green?' queried the nurse. 'I'm afraid Mr Green passed away through the night, Mr Brown. We tried our best, but we couldn't save him. He was too badly injured I'm afraid. He's gone. I'm sorry, Mr Brown. Was he a good friend?'

'Yes,' replied Boyd, 'He would have made a good friend.' Gradually coming to his senses, Boyd continued, 'I know he's dead, nurse. He was dead when I brought him in the car. You know what I mean? Of course, you don't, or do you? I'm confused, nurse. I want to know, is my friend dead? I mean, you know. Has he gone somewhere else with friends of mine or is he really...'

'He died. He left you this, Mr Brown.'

The nurse reached beneath the bed and produced a piece of fur. She fluffed it with her hand, and offered it to Boyd with, 'I think you need to sleep a little more, Mr Brown. You sound hopelessly confused. I'll call the consultant to you. Mr Green died an hour ago. Your colleagues were with him when he died. He was insistent in his final moments. Insistent you have this.'

The nurse handed Boyd the piece of fur.

'Ushanka!' remarked Boyd.

'Oh! Is that what you call it,' replied the nurse. 'I wondered what it was. It looks to be a warm and handy bit of kit if you don't mind me saying so. It will keep you warm.'

'Yes, it will!' voiced Boyd. 'It's not mine. It belonged to my friend. Where is he? Where is Ushanka!'

A needle plunged and Boyd fell into another slumber unaware of how lucky he had been in the crash that had written off the squad car, caused a wall to collapse, and added to the death of Andrey Petrov.

'You're more confused than ever,' thought the nurse as she withdrew the needly and quietly thought to herself, 'More confused than ever, Mr Brown, or whatever your name is. Sleep tight! I have other patients with proper names to see.'

The door closed behind the nurse when she stole out of the ward into the Casualty Department.

A trio of detectives – Anthea, Janice and Bannerman – together with Boyd's wife Meg, stood up and stepped forward.

Meg asked, 'Billy! Is he going to be alright? Is he okay? We need to know, nurse.'

'Oh yes. He'll be fine. He has a bang on the head and is somewhat confused. He'll be okay in the morning.'

A look of relief crossed the faces of Anthea, Janice, and Bannerman.

~

17

~

The Country Mansion.
Oxford.
That day.

'**Z**ero Clear Zero!' remarked Sir Julian. 'A good call from Boyd. 'Has it been actioned to satisfaction, Phillip?'

'Oh yes,' replied Sir Phillip. 'I told you Boyd and his crew were rather exceptional, and they are. Yes, Julian, the site is cleared under the protocol Zero Clear Zero.'

'I can't remember the last time that procedure was used,' ventured Julian. 'Can you?'

'Funnily enough, neither can I,' chuckled Phillip. 'I think we have to go back to the Cold War to find a match.'

'So, the final result, my friend is?'

'Nothing happened in Seven Hills.'

'That's not quite right,' smiled Julian. 'How does the media and the Russian embassy see it?'

'There was a gas explosion in a house owned and lived in by Sergey Ivanov and his wife. They lived happily in a house called Seven Hills which is situated near the Talkin Tarn Conference Centre where an international conference recently took place. Guests to the house, which had no connection whatsoever to the conference on climate change, included the Russian ambassador, the Russian cultural secretary, and staff. It was a private dinner. Anyway, forensic scientists discovered that there was a fault in the gas supply to the house. Indeed, the immediate area is now subject to reappraisal by the gas supplier.'

'Go on,' chuckled Julian.

'A gas cooker in the kitchen exploded proving that the pressure in the system had increased beyond capacity. The cooker exploded, rippled through the gas supply in the house, and killed everyone inside the building. The roof collapsed due to the force of the explosion.'

'Heartbreaking!'

'Absolutely!'

'And the aftermath?'

'None! The fire raged for many hours before it was brought under control. Locals admit seeing a pall of smoke above the building for quite some time.'

'Bullet wounds?'

'Goodness no. Zero Clear Zero! The site has been cleared of any such ambiguity.'

'So, nothing happened in Seven Hills?

'Not so you'd notice.'

'A brandy?'

'Why not?'

'Pity about Ushanka.'

'Killed by Fedora who in turn was shot dead by Detective Inspector Bannerman and Detective Sergeant Janice Burns.'

'What about Abraham and Boyd?'

The sound of liquid running smoothly from a bottle into a brandy glass followed and resulted in a pool of orange spirit giving forth the attractive odour of a celebratory drink.

There was a chink of glasses when Phillip said, 'Doing well! Both making a good recovery in their separate lives.'

A window at the rear of the Hannukah restaurant in Golders Green, London, gave way to Abraham's screwdriver. The Arab Jew slid his hand inside, fully opened the window, and then climbed into the deserted building.

Making his way to the conference facility, Abraham approached the table where the Shamash meetings had taken place. He lifted the nine-branched candelabra used in the festival of Hannukah, located a button-shaped listening device he had hidden in the base at Boyd's request, and pocketed it.

Abraham returned the menorah to its original position in the centre of the table.

Five minutes later, Abraham slid into the driver's seat of a brand-new taxi and drove away. He had a fare to collect and a button to return to an old friend when next they met.

In a private ward of the Cumberland Infirmary, Boyd entered the twilight world of neither here nor there for the final night before his release. Much improved, he dozed and fantasised, 'If only one day common sense would prevail and rather than supplying our allies with weapons of war, we sit down with the enemy at an early stage and hammer out a peace process, a methodology of mutuality in respect of peace, a procedure to develop peace and deny war. A way to forge love and understanding between us all, not hate. '

Pipedreams, whimseys, fantasies of the mind whistled through the corridors of an infirmary where people were born, where illness was rife, where care for the sick was commonplace irrespective of their age, ethnicity, or standing in life, and where people died. Power here rested in the hands of one of the oldest professions in the world.

Here, people lived and died every day. It was like the roll of a dice on the table of life. It was all to live for.

'If only,' thought Boyd. 'If only east and west could forge peace. If only...'

Boyd slept as he visualised his dream of peace.

A piece of black fur slipped from Boyd's fingers.

It fell gracefully to the floor.

It was Andrey's ushanka.

The ushanka had fallen.

~

The end..... Until the next time.

PAUL ANTHONY.

~

Paul Anthony is a brilliant writer and an outstanding gentleman who goes out of his way to help and look out for others. Paul does a wonderful job of portraying the era in which we live with its known and unknown fears. I highly recommend this intelligent and kind gentleman to all.

Jeannie Walker, *Award-winning author/songwriter and freelance writer. True Crime novelist*

A real-life Jack Bauer who is also an author! Awesome books.

Lisa Thomas *-Author*

'One of the best thriller and mystery writers in the United Kingdom today'...

Caleb Pirtle 111, *International Best-Selling Author of over 60 novels, journalist, travel writer, screenplay writer, and Founder and Editorial Director at Venture Galleries.*

'Paul Anthony is one of the best Thriller Mystery Writers of our times!'

Dennis Sheehan, *International Best-Selling Author of 'Purchased Power', former United States Marine Corps.*

This guy not only walks the talk, he writes it as well. Thrillers don't get any better than this. An excellent author whose stories reek of authenticity...

Paul Tobin, *Author, Poet and Broadcaster*

Words from a real detective...

Martin R. Jackson, *UK Novelist*

A great author & one of the nicest people in the industry!
Amber Skye, *American Novelist*

This is one tough man o' mystery.
Kate Pilarcik, *Author of suspense novels*

~

Profits from Paul Anthony's books are donated to Ovarian Cancer Action, a registered research charity supported by Paul Anthony.

Thank you.

~

Printed in Great Britain
by Amazon